1 954643 00

D1477560

FORTUNE'S DAUGHTER

Recent Titles by Mary Minton from Severn House

BREATHLESS SUMMER

DARK WATERS

THE LONG ROAD

THE STRIDENT WHISPER

FORTUNE'S DAUGHTER

Mary Minton

SEVERN
SH
HOUSE

BRN-332168

1 954643 00

This first world edition published in Great Britain 1997 by
SEVERN HOUSE PUBLISHERS LTD of
9–15 High Street, Sutton, Surrey SM1 1DF.
First published in the U.S.A. 1997 by
SEVERN HOUSE PUBLISHERS INC., of
595 Madison Avenue, New York, NY 10022.

Copyright © 1996 by Mary Minton.

All rights reserved.
The moral right of the author has been asserted.

British Library Cataloguing in Publication Data

Minton, Mary
    Fortune's daughter
    1.   Historical fiction
    I. Title
    823.9'14 [F]

    ISBN 0-7278-5215-9

All situations in this publication are fictitious and
any resemblance to living persons is purely coincidental.

Typeset by Hewer Text Composition Services,
Edinburgh, Scotland.
Printed and bound in Great Britain by
Hartnolls Ltd, Bodmin, Cornwall.

Chapter One

Mollie Paget came into the kitchen yawning. It was only half past five. But then she had got up early to let Bess the skivvy have a lie in. The poor kid wasn't well. And if the fire wasn't lit and glowing by the time Cook got up there'd be something to say.

Mollie put the candle on the bench, lit a match and put it to the gas mantle. There, that looked a little brighter. She then lit another match and put it to kindling already in the grate. Bess always laid the fire before she went to bed.

The pieces of wood had already caught fire and the sticks were soon sparking. Mollie took some pieces of coal from the bucket and laid them on the sticks. She would soon be able to fill the kettle. The milkman would be here soon and expect his cup of tea. She would have one herself. Her throat was parched. Pray heaven she wasn't going down with a cold like Bess had.

Mollie yawned again. She better go and open the back door. She took the candle with her. It wouldn't be long before Joe would be here. Bess always made sure his cup of tea was ready for him. Well, he would have to wait this morning. After all, she was the second housemaid and wasn't at his beck and call.

In another eight days she wouldn't be here. She was leaving to go and live with her aunt in London and help her to look after the shop.

Oh, Lord, was that Joe shouting?

She went into the scullery, opened the back door

and all but fell over someone sitting huddled on the step.

A blasted vagrant.

But no, it wasn't. By the light of the candle she could see it was a girl and that she looked to be about fourteen or fifteen. She had roused and looked bewildered.

Mollie said, "What do you think you're doing here?"

There was no reply. The girl wrapped her arms around herself and shivered.

"What brought you to this house?"

There was still no reply. Was the girl dumb?

"What's your name?"

"Chantelle."

So she wasn't dumb.

Try as she might, however, Mollie couldn't get another word from her. But what could she do? Cook wouldn't have her in the kitchen and the mistress hated kids.

The girl was shivering so badly now Mollie could hear her teeth chattering.

"Milko!" shouted Joe as he came up the path. "'Ow much do you want today, Bess? Oh, it's you Mollie. What's up and who's this?"

Mollie quickly explained and Joe seemed puzzled. "She looks to be upper class. Who'd leave 'er 'ere?"

Mollie noticed her clothes for the first time. She did look as if she came from the gentry.

"You'll 'ave to get the lass inside," he said. "She looks fit to drop."

Mollie nodded, "I know, but Cook won't be pleased. Oh, I'll risk it."

"Any chance of a cuppa?"

"Yes, come on in. You better bring in six pints. And you'll have to wait for the kettle boiling."

Joe grinned. "I'll wait. I want to know the end of the story."

Mollie took the girl's arm and led her inside. Once they

were in the kitchen she noticed in the light that the girl was attractive. "Sit you down by the fire," she said. "I'll put the kettle on."

Mollie filled the kettle and hung it over the now blazing fire. Joe was talking to the girl but was not getting any response.

She spoke again. "I am – not . . . Eng-glish."

Joe and Mollie looked at her, startled.

"She's a foreigner," Mollie said.

"I'll bet she's French," declared Joe. "She talks just like one of me customers who live 'alf a mile away. Only they ain't got no kids."

"But who in heaven's name would leave her at this mansion and why?"

Joe lifted his cap and scratched his head. "'Aven't a clue."

Mollie brought three mugs and they talked about the girl as they waited for the water to boil. They wondered how long she had been there and agreed they would have to let the police know.

The kettle boiled and Mollie made the tea. Then she went into the larder, brought a loaf of bread, a jar of jam and cut a slice (the butter was locked up). Then she stood for a moment looking at the girl. She was really quite beautiful.

Joe said, "Could I 'ave me tea, love? Me customers'll think I've forgotten them."

"Oh, oh, yes."

She poured it, put in milk and sugar and handed it to him. Then she filled the other two mugs and wondered how she could ask the girl if she would like a piece of jam and bread.

She put a slice on the plate and held it out to her.

The girl gave a slight, heart-warming smile and said, "Thank you."

So she knew some English.

3

She had expected the girl to gobble it up but she took a dainty piece, closed her eyes and ate it slowly.

That was her upbringing, of course.

Joe drained his mug, put it down and said he must be going. Then he added, "Tell Bess I 'ope to see 'er tomorrer. An' if you want that French bloke I'll give you 'is address in the mornin'."

Mollie wondered what Cook would say when she saw Chantelle. She could be nasty if she felt like it. She would probably say, 'Get rid of her.'

She stopped at this point. Heavens above, what was she thinking of? She would have to report her to the police first. Joe could be heard in the distance calling, 'Milko!'

Chantelle had sat down on the chair that Mollie had brought close to the fire. She was deep in thought as she nipped another piece off the bread and jam. Mollie wondered what she could be thinking. Did she expect to be accepted by the people in this house? If only she was able to talk to her.

There were footsteps on the stairs. It was Cook, who walked with purpose. Bess always crept down. Cook came into the kitchen then stopped, seeing the scene. She was a big, busty woman with a harsh voice.

"What's going on here? Where's Bess and who is this girl?"

Mollie told her quickly about Bess, who was really poorly, then she explained about finding Chantelle on the step.

"Well, you had better get her out of here. This isn't a house for waifs and strays. And how dare you feed her?"

"She's French and doesn't speak any English. I felt we must have a word with the police. She's well dressed and seems to belong to the gentry. I thought we could perhaps ask Constable Jarvis's advice."

Mollie knew she had won when she saw Cook's expression change.

4

"Yes, I suppose that's sensible. But I must admit I don't like a stranger in my kitchen. She'll have to be gone when the mistress comes down to give me the order for lunch."

"Oh, I'm sure Constable Jarvis will get all that sorted out. He's a very capable man."

Cook was not exactly beaming but she was not far from it. "When will Bess be down? We can't do without her."

Mollie crossed her fingers. "She'll probably be down in a few minutes."

"She had better be. Servants don't get wages to have a lie in of a morning. I'll have a cup of tea, but not from that pot. A fresh one."

Mollie refilled the kettle and Cook went to her office which led off the kitchen, to put on her apron and cap.

Thank goodness for that, Mollie thought, with a sigh of relief. So far, so good. She would be glad when she left to go to London, to help her Aunt Nell with the shop.

It was two years since Mollie had come into service and she had to admit that Cook had taught her all she knew about this kind of work. Not that she would miss it. Mollie wanted to expand. She was hoping when she got to London that her aunt would agree to getting a larger shop.

She still had the money her mother had left her when she died. Mollie sighed; she had never really known a proper home life. Her mother had been in and out of hospital as far back as she could remember. And always her Aunt Nell had looked after her. Mollie loved her very much.

Bess drifted into the kitchen, looking as pale as a ghost.

"You shouldn't have got up," Mollie scolded. "And now you are up, there'll be no hope of Cook letting you go back to bed."

Bess was staring at Chantelle. Mollie drew her aside and explained the position.

Cook came clumping into the kitchen wearing wooden

5

sandals and glared at Bess. "Oh, you're up then and a good job too. We've more than enough on our hands. You better start on your rounds."

Bess always lit the fires for the butler and the house-keeper, and woke the rest of the staff.

"Go on then, don't stand there looking as if it's beyond you."

Bess scuttled away.

Cook looked thoughtful. "It's just occurred to me. We could put the French girl on washing-up. Bess looks to have as much strength as a daisy. I could explain to the mistress that it's just a temporary thing. I'll have a word with Constable Jarvis when he calls this morning."

Mollie felt pleased that Chantelle would not be turned away without some enquiries having been made.

Cook took Chantelle to her office and left her there. Mollie took a chance and brought her another cup of tea and a slice of jam and bread; then after putting a finger to her lips, left hurriedly.

The staff were sat down to breakfast by a quarter to seven, which included the head butler, the under butler, the housekeeper, the top servant, second servant, the chauffeur, gardener, under gardener, and the boot boy. None of them did much talking at breakfast and when they finished they each had work to do.

Mollie knew that Constable Jarvis came about half past eight and that Cook always had his breakfast ready in the oven.

Cook always looked different when he came. It was not that she was flirtatious, but she always seemed pleased when he appeared.

She brought Chantelle from her office and told him the story the moment he arrived. Chantelle looked different without her coat and hat. She really was a beauty. She was taller than Mollie had at first thought and had finely chiselled features, blue eyes and curly brown hair.

6

Constable Jarvis tried to question her but got no response. He was a man of about forty, thickset, but not talkative.

Cook told him about the French couple that Joe had told them about and Jarvis said, "I know them. I think it might be a good idea to take her there and let them have a talk."

But when he tried to explain this to Chantelle she looked afraid and backed away.

Cook said, "It might be better to bring the Frenchman down here. God knows what's happened to her."

He agreed, and when he finished his breakfast he left with a promise to bring the Frenchman back a little later on.

Mollie was left to soothe Chantelle. "I – am – lost," she whispered. "I – I – live in Paris."

Paris? Then what on earth was she doing here? Someone must have brought her. But why had they left her here in Kettering? Mollie thought it would have been more sensible if she had been left in London. It would certainly be interesting to find out.

Bess was making an effort to clear the table. Mollie took Chantelle by the arm and got her to understand that she could help. Mollie helped too.

She poured water into the big bowl and handed Chantelle towels to do the drying. Bess put the dishes away, her feet dragging.

Cook said, "I do hope Constable Jarvis can persuade that Frenchman to come."

"He'll come out of curiosity, if nothing else," Mollie said, and she was right.

Francois Merté was indeed very curious to know what had happened and within minutes he and Chantelle were chattering away animatedly.

Cook ended up taking them to her office and she came out eventually to tell Mollie all that happened.

"It's the craziest story you've ever heard," she said. "And quite frankly I don't know whether to believe it."

According to Chantelle, she had been in hospital after an accident and found when she began to recover that she didn't know anything about it. She couldn't remember anything of her life before the accident. Only one person came to visit her and it was a woman she didn't know.

Chantelle had paused at this point, then said she had a strong feeling that the woman hadn't even known her before the accident. She went on to say that when she was well enough to leave the hospital, this woman took her to a rented flat. She told her she was not to talk; the doctor at the hospital had advised it.

Then two mornings later the woman told her they were going to visit someone. It seemed a long journey and it was dark when they arrived. She knew they were away from Paris and realised by hearing snatches of conversation that they were in England. London, probably. They travelled quite a long way further and then they were out in the country somewhere. The woman took her to the back of this house and told her to wait. She would be back in a minute. She never came back and that was why Chantelle sat on the step and fell asleep.

"So what do you make of that?" Cook asked. "A bit funny if you ask me. Anyway, the Frenchman said that he and his wife would be glad to have her until Constable Jarvis finds out if there's been any enquiries about her at the station."

For some unknown reason Mollie didn't want to lose her, but it was impossible to keep her here, so there was nothing she could do.

When Chantelle came out of Cook's office she had her hat and coat on and was much more animated. She gripped Mollie by the arms and said, "*Merci, merci.*"

Francois also came out smiling. "We shall soon have her speaking English." Then he turned to Cook and added, "I

8

very much hope that the police will find her parents. We can only have her until next Friday because we are going to a silver wedding and are staying a few days."

Mollie noticed that Constable Jarvis touched Cook on the shoulder and gave her quite a warm smile. She had never seen him smile. It changed him, and Cook.

Was marriage in the air? Mollie couldn't imagine Cook married to anyone. But there, it was none of her business. All she was concerned about at the moment was Chantelle. She wanted to know that she would be settled somewhere.

Chantelle went off happily with the Frenchman. But she did thank Mollie again, and Cook, before she left.

Poor lass, Mollie thought, she couldn't know that she would only be there for a time. She just hoped that the police would come up with something.

* * *

Bess did improve over the next few days, but her face was still paper-white. Mollie wondered how she managed to do what she did.

Every day Cook asked Constable Jarvis if any word had come in to the station about Chantelle, and every day was the same answer. "Not a thing, nor at any other station. A bit of a mystery."

The girl who was to replace Mollie came on the Thursday to find out what her duties were. Mollie liked her. She was keen to learn all she could, so Mollie was kept busy.

She had already packed her bags so all she really had to do was to pick them up and travel to London on the Saturday. But she worried about Chantelle. What would happen to her? Would she be put in the workhouse? She had no money, no change of clothes.

When Mollie discussed it with Cook, she felt the same way. But what could she do? She liked the girl, but she couldn't have her here. She could lose her own job if the mistress found out that Chantelle had been there.

On Friday Monsieur Merté brought Chantelle back and when Mollie saw tears in her eyes she knew she was not going to leave her behind. She would take Chantelle with her to her aunt.

She felt suddenly uplifted and when she told Cook of her plan, Cook looked relieved.

"That girl has great charm. She'll go far. Thanks, Mollie, for taking her with you. You've relieved my mind. But will your aunt welcome her?"

"Yes, she'll love her. She's a wonderful person."

Cook told Francois all this and he repeated it to Chantelle in French.

Chantelle's whole face lit up and she flung her arms around Mollie. "*Merci*, oh, *merci*, I – hope that I can – can—" She sought for the word she wanted and the Frenchman helped her. "Repay you!" she exclaimed joyously.

Mollie said, "I must send a telegram to my aunt and let her know I'm bringing a friend with me. I think I had better say I shall travel today, so we won't have any trouble to hide you, Chantelle. The mistress is away so she won't know that I'm leaving a day early. Oh, thank goodness that's settled."

It was not until Mollie and Chantelle were on the train to London, that Mollie realised she had been in the house for two years and that none of the staff, apart from Cook and Bess, had bothered to wave them off. She was glad to be leaving. She had worked in the house at Kettering for two years and hated it from the first day. It was about a quarter of a mile from an estate known as the Headlands. Mollie thought it would have been better to have called it the Deadlands. The house was called Beverly House. A mansion, really. It was a gloomy place, with a lot of rooms and grounds that never looked cared for. Mollie knew she would feel altogether different when she got to her aunt's house.

There was something else she had learned from the Frenchman: that Chantelle was not a child, she was seventeen.

Both Cook and Mollie had exclaimed, "Seventeen?"

"Yes, indeed," he had said. "What's more, I think she has quite a knowledge of English, but had forgotten it when she lost her memory."

That, to Mollie, made things better. Chantelle would be able to work and would, Mollie thought, be quite an asset in what she was planning. Would her dreams come true at last?

Nell had a small shop in a market in the East End of London. Mollie was hoping to persuade her to take a larger shop, but knew it would not be easy. Her aunt loved her shop . . . and her house. She lived on the premises.

Her Aunt Nell was the only one who had loved her. She always made her a cake for her birthdays – not a fancy one, just a plain sponge cake with icing on top and jam in the middle – but she had always appreciated the thought.

Chantelle was full of anticipation, and although Mollie had explained in the train about her aunt having a shop and living in the East End, this had only seemed to make her more excited. She had even stressed that they would not be living among wealthy people, but Chantelle had said, "Splen – did!" And seemed happier than ever.

When they reached London, Mollie became reckless and used some more of her money so they could both travel in a hansom cab to her aunt's shop. It was in a market. In the centre was a piece of green, then around it were market stalls of every description.

Chantelle's excitement rubbed off on Mollie.

Her aunt was waiting at the door when they arrived, and they could not have had a warmer welcome. Nell hugged

11

and kissed them both then said, "Come along in, and we'll have a nice cup of tea. Take your hats and coats off and sit down and tell me your news."

Mollie told her aunt how she had come to know about Chantelle, and Nell said, "Oh, how dreadful, Chantelle. So you don't know if you have any parents?"

"Not really. I do not feel that I have a family."

Mollie said, "That is why I brought her with me; I knew she would be happy here."

"And I am, very happy."

"Good. Now, how about some sandwiches?" asked Nell.

They talked about the shop and Mollie noticed some rolls of material in the window. She said, "That's something new, isn't it?"

Nell said, "I buy them from my brother's son. He gets it from abroad at a very low price." Mollie remembered Ritchie from when she was younger. He used to tease her on the rare occasions that they met. He was quite a handsome young man and made her laugh a lot. His mother had died giving birth to him and his father had died recently. He would probably be a lot more sober now.

Mollie was anxious to let her aunt know that she had not left Beverley House with any regrets. While they had their meal she said, "I'm glad to be out of that awful house. There was only Cook and the little skivvy Bess who talked to me. There was a handsome young butler but he treated me as if I was a bit of dirt that he had scraped off the sole of his shoe. And none of the women bothered to speak to me. Thank heavens I'm away from it all."

"You'll enjoy it here," Nell said. "Every customer is friendly."

After the meal they sat around the fire. There were handmade knitted covers on the sofa and chairs. The floor was covered with brightly coloured rugs and there was a gossamer-fine lace tablecloth, also made by her aunt.

12

Mollie, feeling it was too soon to talk to her aunt about the shop, talked about Chantelle and said she felt she would be an asset if she could get a job.

Nell said, "You could work for me. I did think that perhaps I could make some blouses with these rolls of material. They are just remnants but it's lovely stuff. Ritchie gets it from abroad. He'll be here one of these days. Oh, you know him, Mollie. He used to be here when you were young."

"Oh, yes, I remember him. But you didn't have the remnants then."

"No, because I was afraid it was stolen stuff. Now I know he's a bona fide businessman, I have some every time he comes. My customers buy the remnants and make blouses, but we could make better ones ourselves."

Mollie did not want to make blouses. She wanted a shop of her own to sell all sorts of clothes.

Chantelle said suddenly, "I can sew, I can embroider."

"You can?" Mollie said, in surprise.

"Do you think perhaps you had a shop and did some sewing and embroidery?" asked Nell.

"I can't remember . . ." She held out her hands. She had long, slender fingers and her skin was smooth, refined. "I'm sure I can sew, enbroider. I can remember making country scenes."

Just then someone came into the shop and Nell got up to attend to her customer. Chantelle, who seemed to be taken with the customers, got up to have a peep.

Mollie called out to her that it was rude to keep staring at customers. But she didn't seem to understand. Mollie told her carefully, that perhaps it was a woman who had come in for a packet of pins.

"Pins?" she repeated, frowning.

Mollie, seeing a packet of pins on the windowsill, with a lot of the pins missing, brought them to her.

Chantelle chuckled, "Oh, *je comprends*."

13

When Nell came into the kitchen again she said, "It was just a woman wanting a packet of pins." Both girls laughed and they had to explain why they thought it funny.

To this Nell replied a little dolefully, "All I seem to take nowadays is pence." Then she suddenly brightened. "No, that's not right. I sell quite a lot of these lovely materials."

Mollie saw an opportunity to discuss what she had in mind.

"I was thinking, Aunt Nell, when I saw all these lovely materials today, that if we could get a dressmaker to make some dresses, you could have quite a good trade."

Her aunt shook her head, "Not in this area. Some will buy enough to make a blouse and sew it themselves, but few people can afford a dressmaker."

Mollie took a quick breath. "Why don't you move to a bigger shop and Chantelle and I could help you?"

"No, I love my little shop. It's all I need. I love talking to my customers. They are friends. I can help them in small ways. They love the shop, it's cosy. You can do some sewing here and as I said, I can pay you a small wage. You can live here."

Being paid by her aunt was not what Mollie had in mind. She wanted to own her business, and wanted to employ assistants.

"No, I want a shop, a shop of my own. I'll find one eventually, I'm sure of it."

Her aunt then gave her a long lecture on how not to think. "Don't expect to get a shop quickly and they are not cheap. The rents are quite high and the shops get snapped up right away." Nor should she expect to make money immediately. "If you want a bigger shop you'll have to be prepared to furnish it. You need carpeting, counters, chairs, models on which to show the clothes. A hundred-and-one things. Also you will find that people will keep you waiting for your

14

money. Some won't even pay you at all. Some will think they are paying you to use their name to their customers."

Mollie was still keen. Then she said, "I do have some money to get started."

Her aunt asked her if she had something in the region of one hundred and fifty pounds and Mollie eyed her agahst.

"Oh, no, nothing like that. No."

"Then forget it. You would be wasting your time. It would be like starting in a garret. What you could be looking for is an empty market stall. Some of the people do have to give up. They perhaps have a family and don't make enough to feed them all. And don't forget, it's cold, standing at a stall all day."

"I don't want a stall, I want a shop." Mollie spoke firmly.

Nell said gently, "Look. Why don't you use my shop to begin with? We could make blouses and skirts, dresses, and all sorts of odds and ends. I could pay you and Chantelle a small wage. You could then build up, love. It's the only way."

Mollie knew she had big ideas but there was nothing wrong with that. And she had dreams. She said, "I'll think about it over the weekend."

"Good, I feel you will like my idea, love. Start small and build your way up. When I was a girl," Nell went on, "I used to make dresses, by hand, for a pittance. I wouldn't mind having another try. Perhaps make a better class of dress. We'll see."

Mollie did say that she would like to have a look at all the stalls on this side of the road.

"You can do that in the morning. I keep open. I can have a good day or a bad one, I like nice weather though, it brings the people out."

15

Chantelle was excited about this. They would start early.

* * *

The next morning they were having an early breakfast when the shop door opened and a man called, "Hello there, Aunt Nell, here's the wandering lad. Am I welcome?"

Nell ran out into the shop and the others heard peals of laughter. Both Mollie and Chantelle got up and had a look through the partly-opened door. A big, curly-haired man was swinging Nell around.

She was shouting, "Put me down, put me down!" But she was laughing.

Mollie said, "It's Ritchie, I remember him."

They both went in to the shop and Ritchie stood staring at them. "And who are these two beautiful young ladies?"

"You've met Mollie, and the other young lady is her friend, Chantelle. She's French and here on holiday." Mollie detected a proud note in her aunt's voice when she mentioned Chantelle.

Ritchie was staring with interest at Chantelle.

Then Nell said, "Mollie's interested in your rolls of material. She wants to start a shop, selling ladies clothes."

He turned to her immediately. "What a lucky man I am. I have some beautiful materials to sell, and have just acquired a warehouse for my new stock. Perhaps you would be interested in taking a look?"

Mollie said eagerly, "Oh, oh, I would, I would indeed. That is, if they are not too expensive?"

He smiled. "They're dirt cheap, but excellent quality." He took a diary from his pocket, studied it for a few moments then looked up. "Could you make it this afternoon at two o'clock?"

She was taken aback at the suddeness of the date. "I

16

– well I, as a matter of fact I shall have to find a shop first and I'm told that this is not easy. I will also need dressmakers. And money, of course."

Mollie had a feeling of being galloped up a big hill. She looked to her aunt for guidance, and Nell replied at once, "I don't see how you can refuse such an offer. Ritchie won't push you to pay back in a rush."

"Then that settles it." Ritchie turned to his aunt, "And now, Aunt Nell, how about a cup of your delicious tea? I'm parched."

"At once, sire!" She answered lightly and went into the kitchen to put the kettle on.

Ritchie said to Mollie, "You'll want some good ideas for what you want to make for your shop. You'll also need a good assistant; it might be a good thing to look into shop windows in the West End and see how the assistants act."

"Chantelle will be my assistant. She has a great deal of charm, and being French will help."

"I thought she was here for a holiday?"

This flustered Mollie. "She – she is. But she would also want to work here for a while."

"Now this won't work." Ritchie spoke firmly. "A girl must be trained to be an assistant. Assistants who work in Fortnums train for three years without pay."

"That's out of the question. I'm aiming for a small shop, not a store."

"You should aim high."

Nell came in quickly. "You started small, Ritchie, and built up your business, and it's taken you a long time. Mollie is being sensible. I'm all for building up."

"You're wrong, Nell."

"No, I'm not. An aunt once said to me when I was younger and wanted to go into business: 'Be prepared for it to take three years. The first year you pay out. The second you hold your own, and the third year you start to make a profit.' It worked for me."

"But don't forget, Aunt Nell, women didn't have businesses when you were young."

"I'm going on present-day people. It still happens. I'll go and pour your tea."

Ritchie had a huge grin on his face. "You can't win with Aunt Nell. She'll always have the last word."

"And she'll be right," Mollie said with a smile. "That's something I learned early on in my life."

Chapter Two

After Ritchie had left, both Chantelle and Mollie went to take a longer look in the window. Although the sun was bright there was a cold wind. Nell brought out their coats and hats and made them put them on, saying she didn't want them catching colds.

Mollie explained to Chantelle that her aunt had what was known as a haberdashery business and this meant that she sold things like reels of cotton; pins and safety pins; buttons; shoelaces; press fasteners; hooks and eyes; pieces of hair ribbon in pale blue, pink and white; handkerchiefs for men, women and children. Then she added, "This year she is also selling materials. It's the first time. I would like Aunt Nell to get a shop where she could sell women's blouses and perhaps skirts, but she doesn't want to leave this shop. I think that I would like a shop."

"That would be very nice," declared Chantelle. "I could perhaps help."

"I think you could. You could perhaps embroider the corners of ladies' handkerchiefs."

Chantelle smiled. "I would like that very much."

"I don't really know why my aunt doesn't sell a few better things. She would make more money. But there, I can't change her."

Her aunt came out and hustled them back into the kitchen. "It's too cold to stand about."

Mollie wanted to show Chantelle other stalls. It was all a novelty to her at the moment. She wanted her to be aware that most of what was sold now was owing to necessity.

In fact, it was difficult to get her to come out later. She was intrigued hearing her aunt talking to customers and wanted to be there to listen to what was being said.

Nell explained to her customers (a little proudly) that Chantelle lived in Paris and had come with her niece Mollie to have a little holiday.

"Blimey," said one woman, "'Oo the 'ell would want to come to this Godforsaken dump for an 'oliday. Every day I feel I wanna cut me froat."

"Oh, no," declared Nell. "It's experience."

"'Ark at 'er. Experience? Got plenty of money, I imagine."

"No," Mollie said quietly. "She hasn't any money but she can find beauty in the naptha flares on the stalls, throwing tiny waves of light around."

"Go on! Well, whatcha know? They say it takes all kinds to make a world and I'm beginnin' to believe it. 'Ave a lovely time, me duck. I better start reading me prayer book." She left, laughing and Nell smiled.

"Chantelle wouldn't do much harm if she could make a customer laugh."

"I came to the conclusion years ago that East Enders are always good for a laugh," Mollie said.

They still had their coats on and she suggested that she take Chantelle around the stalls to let her know what they all sold.

"If you're going to do that you'll want scarves on in this wind."

Nell not only brought two woollen scarves, which she wrapped around each girl, but two knitted caps as well. "They'll be a comfort," she said. "Keep the wind from your ears."

Both Molly and Chantelle smiled at Nell, and Mollie

had a nice feeling of being looked after. Something she only experienced when she was with her aunt.

So off they went, walking to the right to begin with. Although it was still early, there were quite a lot of people about. The two girls stopped at nearly every stall to see what was for sale.

The first stall sold shoes and boots. Most of the boots were for workmen, and nearly all were secondhand. Women bought them for their husbands and sons.

One girl, on her own, was buying a pair for herself.

"I've got to 'ave a pair," she said to the stallholder. "I'm tramping through mud most of the day."

She tried them on, said they would have to do and asked the man at the stall how much they were.

"You can have the pair for a tanner," he said. "They're a bargain."

She put the six pennies into his palm, then trying the laces together, she slung the boots over her shoulder and walked away.

Chantelle stared at the boots in surprise. "The man did not even wrap them up."

Molly answered, "They're easier for the girl to carry. Come along, we'll have a look at the next stall."

The next stall sold secondhand clothes for men. Two women were sorting through working trousers. "They're in good condition," called an elderly stallholder. "Shillin' a pair. Ties a penny each, some of them new."

Some of them did look new. Most of the trousers looked well worn. There were also men's underwear, most of the vests a greyish colour, and shirts, three pence each. One or two had slits in them. "A bit of thread'll draw them together," declared the stallholder.

Mollie and Chantelle moved on. The next stall was women's wear. Some of it seemed to be new. There were skirts draped over lines of thick string. All the skirts were five shillings each. Some were fingered, none were bought.

There were cotton blouses, most of them dark, too. These were a shilling each. There were also some in brighter colours. Some had gaudy patterns on them.

A girl of about eighteen was begging her mother to buy her one, saying, "We're out of mourning now, Ma."

"We gotta eat," her mother snapped back.

Mollie felt sad. A remnant of voile for six pence could have been made into a blouse. She urged Chantelle to walk on.

The next stall sold cheap jewellery. This stall had quite a few people around it, who appeared to be sorting through it. They seemed to have a little more to spend. There were necklaces of glass in red, green and blue.

One woman said to her friend, "You could take them for rubies and emeralds, couldn't you?"

"Not quite," said the friend, who went to look at rings and brooches.

Mollie was a little intrigued by the jewellery. It was a quick seller; they could perhaps make quite a good thing of it in sales. No, she must stick to her original idea. Better-class clothes. They could, of course, have a sideline. A few sidelines, in fact. She must bear that in mind.

The next stall was crockery, which Mollie was not greatly interested in, but Chantelle was enthusiastic about it. There were cups, saucers and plates, teapots, vegetable dishes, butter and jam dishes. The stall was packed with it and was doing a good trade.

Mollie could not understand why Chantelle was interested in it; everything was so cheap. Chantelle said, handling a cup, "This reminds me of something in my past. But what?"

"Chantelle, it's the cheapest crockery you can buy."

"I know, so I wonder why I remember something similar? Where could I have drank from a cup like this? And I have, I just know it. It was in connection with a river. A river, why?"

Mollie said gently, "I think you'll have to let these things come to you. Don't force them. You could have been on a picnic and were thirsty and asked, perhaps at a farmhouse, for a drink."

Chantelle shook her head. "No, there was no river. It was not the country. I do wish I could remember."

"As I said, let it come gradually."

Chantelle put the cup down and laughed. "I think you could be correct. What a lovely morning we have had, seeing all these interesting things."

"There's plenty more. Would you like to take a look?"

"Oh, yes. Yes, please."

There was only one stall which interested Mollie. This sold womens' clothes, a better class of clothes. The trouble was that very few people stopped at it. And those who did were not there long.

Mollie stopped and studied the clothes, and a youngish woman asked if she could help. "I was just looking and wondered why you don't have many people stopping to buy."

The woman sighed. "The trouble is, they're too expensive."

Mollie wanted to ask why she didn't look for a shop, but didn't want to put the idea into her head if she hadn't already thought of it,

"There are people who do seem to spend a little more money," she said. "Why not for you?"

The woman sighed, "My prices are apparently too high. And I don't want to reduce them. You have to make a certain profit if you hope to have a shop sometime."

So, she did know about a shop.

"I might have to lower the prices a little or, move to another lot of stalls."

"Well, I wish you luck," Mollie said, and taking Chantelle by the arm, led her away.

She gave a little shiver. "That wind's icy, I wonder if

we should look at the stalls on the other side after we've had our lunch?"

"I do not mind the cold, but I shall do as you wish."

At this point Mollie began to wonder if she was viewing Chantelle correctly. Was it possible that she had run away from home and come to England in a spirit of adventure? She was not known at any of the police stations in the vicinity. But then her parents wouldn't expect to enquire in England. They would presume that she was in Paris. That is, if that was where she lived.

She stopped and said, "I think we'll go back to Aunt Nell's now. I feel the cold terribly."

"I am willing," Chantelle said, smiling.

Mollie reflected that although Chantelle had been shivering the morning she nearly stumbled over her on the doorstep, she herself would have been paralysed with cold had she been sitting there all night. There was also her knowledge of English. That day she was unable to talk in English. Now she was almost perfect with it.

On the other hand, she had no luggage. Not even a handbag, and no female would leave another country without having a bag of some kind, if only to put her passport in it.

In the end Mollie gave up. She would get to know the truth somehow or other before long. And she certainly liked being with Chantelle. She was so talkative, so brightly cheerful.

The fire was blazing in her aunt's kitchen. "Come and get warm the pair of you. Here, give me your scarves and caps."

Mollie held out her hands to the blaze. "Oh, what heaven. It's freezing outside."

Chantelle chuckled. "It was a beautiful wind. I am looking forward to seeing the other line of market stalls." She recalled every stall they had looked at.

Mollie told her aunt about the stallholder who displayed womens' fashions and added, "She doesn't sell very much but would not reduce them."

"Then it's her own fault. It's senseless to display goods that no one can afford. I've put the dinner on. It's vegetable stew and a ginger pudding and custard."

"Oh, lovely," Mollie said. The talk over lunch was about stalls, with Chantelle saying that her favourite stall was the one with the jewellery, adding, "I feel that I would like to sell jewellery."

Mollie looked up with alarm. She wanted Chantelle to be interested in clothes, not jewellery. She would be an asset with her French accent. Anyway, she had no money and not even a change of clothes. There would be no choice.

Nell was interrupted by customers coming in while they were having their meal, and every time she went into the shop Chantelle would get up and go to listen to what was being said.

It began to annoy Mollie. At last she said, "It's considered to be rude in England to peer through an opening in a door to hear what is being said."

Chantelle was horrified. How dreadfully she had behaved. All she wanted to know was what was for sale in the haberdashery.

"But we won't be handling haberdashery," Mollie stressed the point. "Just women's clothes: blouses, skirts, coats eventually, and all sorts of underwear."

Chantelle's eyes went wide. "But surely you will want to sell threads, pins, needles, women's handkerchiefs? They will all add to your money."

Mollie grinned. "You have the right idea. What more can I want?" It seemed to Mollie that the girl was becoming a little more sensible.

Ritchie was back promptly at half past two. He had a wagon, and the three of them managed to sit on the front seat. This was adventure on Chantelle's part but Molly just accepted it. They passed all the stalls and Ritchie pointed out the ones that were doing the trade. "Don't let it bother you, Mollie. With the materials that I have you should do a good trade. If not," he added cheerfully. "We'll go on to something else."

Mollie did not like the word, 'We'. It was important to her that she owned the business, not shared it. She thought about mentioning it, then decided against it. These were early days and she did not want an argument now.

They left the market stalls and drove through busy streets until Mollie knew they were near the dock area by its smell. There was a faint scent of timbered warehouses, the mingled smells of the river and the oily deposit from ships and boats.

Mollie was surprised when Ritchie drew up outside quite a sizeable warehouse. She had expected it to be small. Perhaps he shared it with someone.

But no. It was Ritchie's own warehouse and stacked with rolls and rolls of materials.

"Well, there you are," he said. "You can have your pick."

Chantelle was in raptures about everything. How wonderful to have so much. Mollie could not help but be impressed. "You've done amazingly well," she said.

"Well, I've worked hard for it since I was a boy. Mind you, I've had a lot of help. I've worked with a grand lot of chaps. Have a walk around and see what you want. I'm just going to pop into my office and check some prices."

Mollie and Chantelle turned to the rolls. They were all covered with fawn calico, but on every roll was a sample of the material inside.

The two girls wandered from roll to roll, enchanted with the lovely patterns. Many of them were flimsy material, like the sarsinets of an earlier age. There were fine silks and satins and beautiful velvet; also the most delicate lacework.

Mollie wondered if lacework would be too delicate for the sort of customers she would have. No, she must cater for women who had some money to spend.

There were some fine linens too: some in light colours and some in browns, black and navy blue.

They came to calico, a stronger material to make dresses for housewives. Ritchie certainly had many varieties of materials. He had told them on the way that in a week they would all be gone.

"And then what?" Mollie asked.

"Then I go abroad again and buy some more. My next journey back will be further north."

Chantelle kept murmuring that she would like to wear a dress of such and such a material. "Look at the beautiful colours," she kept saying.

Ritchie came up to them, "Well, and have you made a choice?"

"It's difficult. I would like a roll of each!"

"When you've built up your business you will."

Mollie pulled a face. "I don't ever expect to reach that height."

"You have it in you. You'll do it." He turned to Chantelle. "And what do you fancy?"

She gave him a broad smile. "All the flimsy ones. I imagine myself in a dress with many layers and I am dancing around."

"Do you dance?"

She eyed him solemnly. "I do not know."

"Shall we try?"

Ritchie waltzed her up the stone path and back. Chantelle was glowing, but neither were breathless. Mollie felt that Ritchie had done the wrong thing. Chantelle had her arm through his.

He moved away from her, smiling. "So now we know that you do dance."

"Yes. It was wonderful. Thank you."

27

Mollie could not resist saying, "Unfortunately, there'll be no time for dancing."

"There will be, in time. Now shall we go over all the materials you like?"

He wrote each one down and when Mollie stopped he said, "You'll want more than that. Twice as many. There are warehouses where you can buy it if you run short but they, of course, will charge you twice as much."

"As I've not done this before, I shan't go mad. It's a debt that has to be paid."

"Forget it, Mollie. I won't push you for the money. You have a lot more to pay out. But remember this. You are getting a bargain buying these rolls of material."

"I know," she said, "and I do appreciate it."

They were there another half an hour, then Ritchie said he would take them to see the shop he had in mind.

Mollie began to get excited. She had been afraid to do so until she had seen the number of rolls and knew then that Ritchie was a true master of handling goods.

They left the warehouse and the docks and travelled through a number of other streets. Then they turned into a wider, busy thoroughfare full of traffic, and Mollie prayed that the shop might be on this road.

To her delight, it was.

There were dresses in one of the windows, and skirts, jackets and blouses in the window at the other side. The dresses were the kind that Mollie wanted to sell.

When they went in to the shop a tall, stately woman came forward. The next moment Ritchie was hugging her.

"Lovely to see you, Dot," he greeted her.

She scolded him, smiling. "The name is Dorothy."

"Sorry, I forgot."

Ritchie introduced Mollie and Chantelle, and the woman as Dorothy Brandford.

28

She seemed delighted that he had brought the girls. "Come into my office. My assistant is out at the moment, but she won't be long."

She pulled up chairs for them then, filling a kettle from a tap, she set it on a gas ring.

"So," she said, smiling at the two girls. "You've seen all of Ritchie's beautiful fabrics. I would never have made my way had I not known him." She turned to Mollie. "How lucky you are to have a young French lady for an assistant. And what a lovely name, Chantelle."

Chantelle gave her a beaming smile. "I shall be very happy to be an assistant."

Mrs Brandford's assistant had returned and, after being introduced to Mollie and Chantelle, she went into the shop.

Mollie learned a tremendous amount that afternoon, and was delighted when Mrs Brandford said she would be glad to help them get the new shop started.

Ritchie had told the girls on the way how Mrs Brandford had enjoyed having her shop, but her husband was opening a big restaurant in the West End and she wanted to help him, which meant giving up her work.

When she mentioned this Ritchie said, "I think you are wise. George helped you all he could, guided you, and you were very successful."

"I've had numerous enquiries about the shop but I promised you first refusal, and I'm glad I did." She said to Mollie, "You're young to be running your own business. May I suggest something?"

"Please do. I have a lot to learn."

"Well, I do think you must try to look a little older. Put your hair up. And wear a simple grey or black gown. Chantelle must do the same. At all times you must appear to be of lesser quality than your customers." She smiled, "It's not easy at first, but you soon get used to it."

Two customers came in to the shop and Mrs Brandford excused herself. She whispered before she left, "Listen to the conversation."

Mrs Brandford said in a low voice, "Good afternoon, Madam. What can I show you today?"

It was a mother and daughter and it was the daughter who needed a dress for a party. The mother had a high-pitched voice and dominated the conversation. The poor daughter had no say at all.

Mrs Brandford produced a folio of drawings of dresses and the mother eventually picked one. Mrs Brandford's assistant took the measurements and Mrs Brandford told them that the dress would be ready for the first fitting in three day's time.

The mother swept out and the daughter trailed after her, having given Mrs Brandford a helpless look.

When Mrs Brandford returned to the office Chantelle said indignantly, "What a dreadful woman, not allowing her daughter to have a say in what she wanted to wear."

"That is general. It is wherever one goes."

"I could not bear to be spoken to like that."

Mrs Brandford smiled. "Then you would be no use as an assistant, Chantelle."

Chantelle's eyes widened. "Oh, but I must. I must change my ways. I must be an assistant."

Mollie laughed. "I was in service. I'm used to that kind of manner. You just ignore it after a time."

"That's the way. Now then, shall we look around the shop and see if there's anything you would like to buy? Everything will be for sale. Clothes, fixtures, figures to carry the clothes, floor coverings, small tables, chairs . . ."

Ritchie was on his feet. "Yes, why not? Mollie will need everything that you have needed, Dorothy."

"True."

Molly marvelled that Mrs Brandford had everything priced in her mind. And everything they looked at, Mollie wanted.

She did wonder as they left if she had the courage to succeed in such a business. Would she be able to control Chantelle? They were both young for such a job. Mrs Brandford must be in her forties. And she had a beautiful speaking voice, which was important.

It also worried her that Ritchie kept talking about their business and he was not talking about Chantelle, but himself. She must make it plain to him that although she was borrowing money from him, they were not partners. She must make that clear as soon as possible.

They had not had much for tea so Ritchie pulled up outside a café. They had sandwiches and cakes and, after the meal while Mollie and Ritchie were discussing the shop, Chantelle got up to look out of the window.

Mollie took the opportunity to bring up the question of partners.

She said, "Ritchie, I want to make it clear that although you are lending me the money to get started, I want to have the whole partnership."

He replied without hesitation, "I agree. I think it's sensible." Then, after a pause he added. "But I do think that you'll have to watch Chantelle. I feel that she thinks the two of you will own the shop, although she is an assistant."

Mollie was indignant. "How could she think such a thing? Mrs Brandford was telling me that assistants in the big stores are not paid until they've served for three years. I couldn't do that, seeing that Chantelle has no parents to keep her, but she certainly will not be a partner."

"Then you must make that clear as soon as possible."

Mollie sighed. "I'm beginning to wonder if I'm doing the right thing. Am I too young? Do I talk properly?

Mrs Brandford seems to me to be so perfect for taking on such a shop."

"Of course you talk properly. You have a good voice. And I do think that you will look a little older with your hair up and in a plain dress. I think that you have everything necessary to take on this job. Chantelle is attractive and has a very fetching voice with her French accent, but she is definitely not a worker. I think she will have to be watched all the time."

Mollie felt a sudden sense of relief. It was how she felt about Chantelle and was glad that Ritchie felt the same. Could she perhaps get her another job of some kind? No, that would not be fair. She liked Chantelle. She was such a cheery person. She had brought her to London and she must look after her. That is, until such time that she got her memory back.

And with that Mollie wondered again if Chantelle was genuinely lost or whether she was just an adventurous girl who had left home and come to England. She decided to put that to the back of her mind for the time being too. She had plenty to think about.

When Chantelle came back to the table Mollie broached the subject of owning the shop.

"I'm the owner," she said. "And you are my assistant. Is that clear to you, Chantelle?"

"Y-yes. But—" She hesitated and was silent.

"What were you going to say, Chantelle?"

"Oh, it was just that as we would be working together I thought that we would be . . . well perhaps, partners."

"If two people decide to work together they share the money that it costs to buy the business."

"But if I don't take any money for being an assistant?"

Ritchie said, "Let me put this straight, Chantelle."

He explained how assistants in the large stores were not paid during the three years they served their apprenticeships. Their parents kept the girls, and he pointed out

32

that as Chantelle had no parents, Mollie would have to keep her.

"Oh," she said. "I thought we were going to work in her aunt's shop."

"Then you can work with Aunt Nell," Mollie said.

A stubborn look came over her face. "No, I want to be with you. Go where you go."

"Well, you have a choice. If you come with me, I shall pay you a small wage and provide your food." Chantelle sat in silence for some time, slumped in the chair, and Mollie had the feeling she was not going to agree.

Suddenly she sat up and smiled. "I will accept those terms."

Ritchie got up. "And on Monday we shall go to the dressmakers and see how we get on there."

Chapter Three

On the way to the dressmakers, Ritchie told Mollie and Chantelle that it was a big business, then added that men did all the cutting out. Also that some of them worked the machines. Despite this, Mollie was taken aback by the number of people working in one room.

The men who did the cutting out and the machining wore white shirts, black waistcoats and trousers. The women wore black dresses with big, white-bibbed aprons over them.

An elderly man came in. Ritchie introduced him as Mr Parkins, and introduced the girls to him.

"Come into the office," he said. "You can't hear yourself talk in the machine room."

They all sat down and Ritchie explained that Mollie was taking over Mrs Brandford's business.

He eyed Mollie then said, "You're young for that, aren't you?"

"Not too young." She spoke briskly.

Ritchie told him how many rolls of material she had bought from him and he raised his eyebrows. "As many as that? Well, seeing as you'll be taking over Mrs Brandford's business, we'll be willing to take you on, Miss . . ."

"Paget," she said.

He offered a price which had Ritchie sitting up, protesting, "No, we want the same price that Mrs Brandford was paid."

Mr Parkin shook his head. "I can't do it."

Mollie decided it was time to show that she was not too young for the business. She got up and said briskly, "I understand your position, Mr Parkin. We have plenty of addresses to go to and one who did seem keen to take us on. Thank you for your time."

Ritchie was on his feet by then, and so was Chantelle.

Mr Parkin coughed. "Well, er, perhaps I have been a little hasty, but as you understand, our prices are very low."

"I can understand that I may not be able to do the trade right away that you had from Mrs Brandford, but she would also have struggled at first. But not to worry, Mr Parkin. We'll manage."

They were all at the door when he called them back.

"Just a minute, you're right. I'll take you on. If, however, your trade does not increase in two months, well . . ."

"It will," Mollie said firmly. "I know my limits."

They shook hands and when they were out of the building, Ritchie burst out laughing.

"I take my hat off to you, Mollie. You were perfect. Couldn't have given better answers myself. I should take you abroad with me."

"Haven't the time," she said with a smile. "I'm glad I've made my mark."

"You certainly did. Wait until I tell your Aunt Nell about this!"

"I have a devil of a lot more to learn, but thank heavens Mrs Brandford has offered to help me all she can."

"You'll do all right. I know it."

Ritchie was full of how Mollie had behaved at the factory and Nell said, "Well, good for you, Mollie. I wish you all the luck." She turned to Chantelle. "You are quiet this morning, which is a little unusual."

"I think I am just realising how much there is to be done."

"Good. See you keep on thinking that way."

Mollie thought there was another reason why Chantelle was so quiet. Ritchie had told them on the way home that he would be leaving the next day to go abroad.

When she asked if he had sold all his rolls of material he had said, "I have. It will all go this afternoon. I have a reliable man who will deal with it."

Ritchie mentioned to her aunt that he would be leaving for abroad the next day.

Nell looked up. "So soon? When will you be back?"

He shrugged. "Could be a week, could be a month."

"A month?" Chantelle exclaimed, tears in her eyes. "It's a long time."

"It depends what kinds of material are available. I want twice as much this time."

Chantelle blurted out, "Can I come with you?"

Ritchie stared at her. "Of course you can't."

"I love you, Ritchie, I can't do without you."

"You'll have to and you'll have to stop this loving business." There was anger in his voice. "I thought you were settling down and were looking forward to working with Mollie. I think it might be a good idea if she finishes with you. You're no good, Chantelle."

She burst into tears. "No, please, I will work, I will work hard. I promise. Honestly."

Mollie suddenly felt sorry for her.

"Look, Chantelle," Ritchie spoke quietly. "You don't know how lucky you've been. If Mollie had not taken you under her wing and brought you here, you could be in a home for lost children. Yes, you are still a child. You must start to grow up. Mollie is allowing you to work as her assistant; take the job and make up your mind to help her all you can. You say you love me. That is a child's attitude. No grown-up girl would tell a man she loved him. I have all the girls I want in different countries. Think of that and forget me."

Mollie felt her heart miss a beat when he mentioned this.

Thank goodness she had put him from her mind. It would be easier now.

Chantelle wiped her eyes and told Ritchie she would work hard in the shop.

He patted her hand. "Good."

Mollie was glad they were friends again and hoped that Chantelle would accept it.

Ritchie left shortly afterwards and promised to see them in the morning before he left.

Mollie asked him to come early as she wanted to go to the shop to get to know more about the business.

He grinned. "A typical owner, laying down the law."

"I pray I'm a typical owner. If I'm not, I'm sunk."

"You won't be sunk. You'll be on the crest of a wave before long. See you all in the morning. Early!" He left, laughing.

Chantelle was standing, shoulders drooping, looking utterly miserable.

Mollie said, "For heaven's sake cheer up. I'm the one who should be worrying."

"I'm sorry. It's just that I love him so."

"Well, it won't get you anywhere. Snap out of this mood or I will have to get rid of you. I mean it."

Chantelle made an effort and by the evening was laughing with Mollie and Nell.

The next morning Ritchie was there about an hour after breakfast. Nell offered him a cup of tea but he said, "No, I have a call to make before I leave. I must say goodbye now. I'll try and be back in a couple of weeks. I got another big order last night for rolls."

Mollie said, "Can you give Chantelle and I a lift to Mrs Brandford's?"

"Yes, if you get your hats and coats on now."

"We have them here. Give us a couple of minutes."

They were on the seat of the van in less than two minutes.

And they talked all the way about the shop, with Mollie saying she wanted to get to know as much as she could from Mrs Brandford.

Ritchie said, "Get her to show you her visitor's book; you'll learn a lot from her remarks in it. Also, ask her if she will show you the dress she had made then took to pieces, to see how it was made. Mrs Brandford stopped at nothing to get to know as much as possible."

"Then I shall be the same," Mollie said.

Chantelle had her say, too. She wanted to see all the designs of dresses in the books. She wanted to know how to measure the dresses for the people who wanted to buy.

"That's the sort of thing that's needed," Ritchie said. "Keep that up and the shop will be a success."

Ritchie dropped them off at Mrs Brandford's and left immediately. Mollie guessed he was pushed for time.

Mrs Brandford greeted Mollie with hands outstretched. "I'm so glad you've come. I've got a few things out that I wanted you to see." One was a book with the names of the customers, and another was the dress that Ritchie had mentioned. She told Mrs Brandford about them and she laughed. "He was always curious to know these things. That's why he's so successful, of course."

Chantelle was managing to smile and she asked if she could see a book of dress designs.

"Of course." The assistant brought the portfolio and the two of them sat down to study it.

Mollie said to Mrs Brandford, "I had hoped that your assistant might have stayed for a while so that we could get into the swing of things."

"So did she after she'd met you. She might still be able to stay for a while, as the person she's to replace wants to stay at her place for a few more weeks. We'll know in another few days. I'll let you know."

"Thanks, it would be nice. Not only for me, but Chantelle as well."

"Well now, let me tell you about my customers." She brought the book over and opened it. "Not many of them are pleasant. The trouble is they're not wealthy but want to appear so." She listed the unpleasant ones. Then she said, "The nice ones do have money and are not in the habit of flaunting it. One of my nicest customers is Mrs Macy-Meldrum." Mrs Brandford turned some pages. "She's an elderly lady and an absolute darling. She has a huge family and lots of granddaughters. She's always buying them something. And none of them are greedy. They all love her and insist they don't want anything expensive. If only I had a few more like her. She was so grieved that I'm leaving, but I've told her about you and she will be coming in to meet you on Friday."

"Oh, how nice, thank you so much."

Mrs Brandford brought out a box with the dress she had taken to pieces. "It's a beautiful dress. My husband thought I was mad taking it apart but I felt I had to know what made it so beautiful, and sometime, in the future, I shall have another one made."

She lifted the pieces out, saying it took twelve yards of material to make and as many yards of braid.

Mollie gave a small gasp when she saw it. The material was flimsy and the top part a delicate shade of green. Underlining this was a rose pink. The shading was really exquisite.

Mrs Brandford laid them out. The tops of the sleeves were puffed and the back of the skirt was full and rouched up. There was braiding on the front in a deep rose. It had the effect of a jacket with a nipped-in waist above a curved, shaped peplum.

"There are some lovely dresses in the book, but this will always be my favourite. I think it is the rose pink under the delicate green."

"I agree with you, Mrs Brandford. Someday I hope that I can wear a shaded dress."

Mrs Brandford smiled. "I'm quite sure of that. Now then, shall we go over the skirts and jackets and the blouses again?"

Mollie was pleased with the skirts and jackets, but she was not too pleased with the blouses. She asked if they sold well, and Mrs Brandford hesitated.

"To be honest, I'm not too pleased with the sale of them and I don't know why. The material is attractive."

"I feel there's something missing at the neck. Some of them perhaps need a frilled collar or a collar that could be looped? Or a sailor collar?"

"Do you know, I think you're right!" she said excitedly. "Yes, you are right. Why didn't I see this? I'll sketch some." She sat down at the desk and before long had six blouses on a page, just as Mollie had imagined.

"You are splendid at sketching," Mollie said. "I wish I was as good."

Mrs Brandford's eyes were twinkling. "Practice makes perfect. Here." She pushed a piece of paper across to her. "Have a go. I'll make a cup of tea."

They were like children. Molly scribbling, discarding, scribbling again and getting a blouse that would go with a panelled skirt. And Mrs Brandford scribbling in-between cutting cake and making the tea.

"That's lovely," she said, looking at Mollie's blouse and skirt. "We could make some. I have a machine."

"I've never used a machine."

"Now's the time to start. I'll teach you."

"No. I must concentrate on my customers," Molly spoke firmly.

"You're right of course. I get easily carried away."

"But you made a success of your business."

"Yes, I did. But if I had concentrated more, I could

41

have done better. We all have our little idiosyncrasies. I'll pour the girls some tea."

Mrs Brandford went to the door of the office, then beckoned to Mollie. When Mollie came to the door she saw the two girls not only pouring over books, but both sketching.

Mollie whispered, "Well! I've never seen Chantelle with a pencil in her hand before."

"Perhaps she has a flare for it. We'll get them in here and later we'll walk out and take a peep."

But two customers coming in put an end to their jollity. It was a man and a woman. Mrs Brandford went in to the shop and the two girls left what they were doing and came in to the office.

"Good morning, Mrs Brandford," the woman said. She was quietly spoken. "I need a new dress for a theatre evening. Not too flashy, but smart. What can you recommend?"

Mrs Brandford went to get the design books and turned to the pages of dresses for the theatre.

"Would you care to take a look at these, Mrs Welton?"

Mrs Welton said to her husband, "Do take a seat, Hector."

He took a seat behind her and Mollie noticed he was watching the girls in the office. Chantelle, happening to look up from her sketching, saw him smile at her and she returned the smile.

Oh, heavens! Mollie told Chantelle she must not smile at the man but Anne, blushing, said that Mrs Brandford had never stopped her from smiling at the men, and added that the men liked to be smiled at by assistants.

Mollie then murmured, "Oh, goodness," and left it at that. Perhaps she would broach the subject later. In fact, she must, with Chantelle being friendly with everyone.

It didn't take the woman very long to choose what she wanted. She went through the swatches of satin pieces that

Mrs Brandford showed her and choose a royal blue satin. The style she chose was quite plain.

Anne was called in to take measurements and Mollie saw that Chantelle took a great deal of notice.

When the couple left, Mrs Brandford came in and said that that had been a simple order. Then she added, "Not that Mrs Welton ever makes a fuss over any dress she orders. I did wonder whether I should have introduced you to her, but then I thought that perhaps you might want to wait a little longer."

"I'm glad you did. I feel I need some breathing space."

Chantelle went out to Anne and they looked at the work they had drawn. Mrs Brandford went out, picked up their sketches and brought then in to Mollie.

"There you are. Not bad for youngsters, are they? That is Anne's drawing and that is Chantelle's."

Mollie was astonished at Chantelle's designs. She was gifted. She called her in. She looked a little sheepish. "I have never done any sketching before."

"I would say you had. These are excellent drawings."

She beamed at Mollie, "Oh, I am so glad you like them. I wish that Ritchie could see them, then he would know that I am not so helpless as he thought."

Mollie wished that she would leave Ritchie out of it.

"You must practice at Aunt Nell's."

"Yes, I will do that. You are pleased, Mollie, aren't you?"

"Yes, I am. Very pleased. Go and do some more. Do some blouses."

Chantelle went out to Anne and the two girls settled to their drawings.

Mrs Brandford said to Mollie. "Strange that you never knew she could draw."

"Drawing never came in to my life and I must remember

that Chantelle has been involved in a road accident and lost her memory."

"Oh, I didn't know that."

Mollie told Mrs Brandford how she came to know Chantelle and she said, "Well, how intriguing. So you don't really know what the girl is capable of?"

"No, I don't."

"You could perhaps lose her."

"I could, but I hope not. I paid for her train fare to London and my aunt and I have kept her. She's sensible in many ways and not so sensible in others. I have a feeling that she wants to stay with me. I'll encourage her with her drawing, of course."

"Anne seems to have taken to her."

"Yes, I was pleased about that."

"I hope that I can get started in the business with both of them at hand."

"I think you will. Anne is a good worker. And if she does stay for a while, she'll keep Chantelle in line."

"I hope so."

Chantelle was excited about her drawings and took them home with her that night to show Nell.

Nell was impressed with them, and asked if she couldn't remember doing drawings. Chantelle, looking vague, shook her head. "No, I cannot ever remember doing any drawings."

"Well, don't let it go to your head, child," said Nell. "You would have to practice for a very long time to become a designer."

"Could I become a designer?" There was excitement in Chantelle's voice.

"Not for several years, my love," Nell said. "Do the designs, but don't think of them as important in your life."

Mollie knew that her aunt was trying to get Chantelle to stay with her, and was grateful. At the same time she knew it would be wrong to keep the girl with her if she could make a more lucrative living on her own. She would let it go on as it was for the time being.

Chantelle was tired that night and went to bed early. Mollie brought up the question of the drawing and found it was right that Chantelle would have to be apprenticed to earn a living eventually at designing.

"And then I don't know whether she would get anywhere," Nell said. "You learn bits here and there, but I do know that men are preferred for jobs like that. There are men who want to be artists and don't ever make it. Ritchie has a brother like that. He went to America full of himself and never became an artist. So that's how it is. I only hope that Chantelle will stay with you for some time and gets some sense into her. Heaven knows if we will ever discover who her family are."

Mollie hesitated a moment then said, "I would like to talk to you about that, Aunt Nell. I've often wondered if Chantelle is a girl who left home seeking adventure. Or, if she is genuine."

Nell nodded slowly. "Strange, but I've wondered the same at times. If she is not genuine she'd make a very good actress."

"Yes, she would. But I couldn't help thinking today that if she was able to draw as she has done, she would have done it before now."

"I don't think so. She would have wanted to show it off."

"Yes, that's true. On the other hand, who would bring a girl all the way from France, leave her at the back of a house and disappear? Why? Not unless Chantelle is mixed up with the people in the house where I used to work."

"But surely anyone wanting to leave a girl at a house would have taken her there in daylight, rang the bell and told whoever came to the door that she was leaving Chantelle to live with her aunt, or uncle?"

It was Mollie who nodded her head this time. "I've thought exactly the same. I do know, however, that my mistress hated children."

"So, she wouldn't have her there and that is why the person left her, so she would have to take her in."

"No, it doesn't seem right somehow. If Chantelle's parents had died, she wouldn't accept that she would be left at the back of the house. There has to be another answer."

"And the only one," said Nell, "is that Chantelle ran away for adventure. She's a good actress."

"Time will tell. At the moment we're guessing. Something will give us the answer. She's a girl that people can't help liking, I like her."

"So do I," Nell said. "But I would feel I would want to kill if she'd been playing a lie. I can't stand liars."

Mollie laughed. "I don't really know how I would feel if she had been playing a part. She gets away with a lot. Gets fed and taken to places. Openly says she's in love with Ritchie."

"And he was pretty mad at that. He doesn't want women in his life."

Mollie looked up quickly. "Oh, why?"

"Because he was madly in love with a girl who let him down and went off with another man. As far as I know he hasn't been in love with another girl since."

"The way he was talking yesterday, he had a girl in every country he went to."

"All talk, Mollie. I'm sure of it. If there had been anyone else he would have had photographs of them. But never ask him."

"As if I would."

"I thought you might, seeing that you are in love with him."

"I thought I was, Aunt Nell, but I soon put him from my mind. I can't start loving a man and running a business."

"Plenty do," Nell replied.

"I discovered, I'm not in that line."

"Take my advice," she said softly. "Don't wait too long."

Mollie lay in bed thinking about that during the night. It was not that she thought she had a chance with Ritchie. He had enough charm to get other girls if he wanted them, but she felt he was like herself in that business came first. It would have to with her. She wanted to build it up, make the business larger in time. Not that she expected to have a store as they had in the West End. But she would see that her business was twice its size. All it needed was dedication. Yes, dedication. She would do it. Work her fingers to the bone, but she would win in the end. With or without Chantelle.

Chapter Four

On Friday Mollie met Mrs Macy-Meldrum, a small, gentle person with snow-white hair.

She clasped Mollie's hand. "How nice to meet you, Miss Paget. I was grieved at losing Mrs Brandford but she assures me that I shall be very pleased to be dealing with you."

"It was nice of her to say so. She speaks very highly of you, ma'am. I do hope I can give you want you need."

"I'm sure you will. I want a dress for one of my granddaughters. It's to be a surprise. She has tawny hair." She laughed softly. "If I'm honest, it's ginger. What colour do you think would suit her."

Mollie said, "How about a delicate green in a silk material with a pattern of pale lavender flowers?"

"It sounds rather nice." She called to Mrs Brandford. "What do you think of Miss Paget's suggestion for a dress for Diedre?"

"I think the colour combination is excellent." She turned to Mollie. "But how about the dress you were talking about yesterday. The one with the underlining of pale lavender?"

Mollie opened her mouth to say she couldn't use Mrs Brandford's design, but Mrs Brandford gave a small shake of her head. "I think that would be perfect for Diedre. She has lovely green eyes."

"Yes, of course," Mrs Macy-Meldrum enthused. "It would be just right. I shall bring her in tomorrow."

They talked about clothes for a while then the old lady said to Mollie, "It's quite refreshing to have an owner so young." Then she added quickly to Mrs Brandford, "And that is no slight on you, Mrs Brandford. You are a delightful owner. I wish that you could share the shop."

"So do I," Mollie said.

"Well, I will be here another two weeks to help her to get used to it."

"Good. And now I must go. I'll bring Diedre tomorrow."

When she had gone Mollie said, "Oh, Mrs Brandford, your lovely dress. I ought not to have agreed."

"I thought about it and from now on I'll be dealing with things to cook. I couldn't have made a better suggestion to one of my nicest customers. And believe me, she'll get new people for you. I know she will."

"Thank you, thank you very much indeed. The two colours would shade very well."

Mrs Brandford kept finding things to give Mollie. "I have a big, down cushion," she said, "on an easy chair in my office. Afternoons are sometimes quiet and I like to sit in the chair and close my eyes. It's so relaxing. You will appreciate it."

"Oh, I couldn't. You must take it with you when you leave."

She laughed. "There will be no chance of sitting down in my husband's restaurant. He's a very energetic person. I want you to have it, please. It would give me pleasure."

Mollie felt forced to accept it.

The next thing she offered was a pin-cushion that fastened around the wrist. "You'll find it very useful if a dress should need a small alteration."

Then there was a silver teapot and crockery she pressed her to take and again, she stressed that her husband had a mass of such things.

Mrs Brandford then said she wanted to make a blouse. One with a frill at the neck. "I just have to try it. I have a small machine in one of the rooms upstairs."

Mollie said in surprise. "I didn't know there were rooms upstairs."

"Yes, they should be cleared out. There's all sorts of rubbish in them. You know how it is."

Mollie suddenly wondered if she and Chantelle would be able to live in them. When she asked, Mrs Brandford said, "Yes, I would say you could. There are fireplaces in them, but wouldn't you want to go home to your aunt every night?"

"I should really. I feel a little guilty as I came originally to help her with the shop. But now, having a business, it would be costly to travel every day on the horse omnibus."

"I'll take you up to have a look at the rooms. They may not be to your liking." She called to Anne to let her know if a customer should come in and they climbed the narrow staircase.

There were three rooms, all larger than Mollie had expected, and all of them packed with boxes and packages.

"They'll take some clearing out but it can be done. We can set the girls to start clearing them."

Mollie had the feeling another small world was opening for her. These rooms would be ideal. All they would need at first would be a bed each, a small table, and chairs. She wondered how Chantelle would react to living above the shop.

Chantelle was not at all pleased about the rooms. She liked living with Aunt Nell at the little shop. It was cosy.

Mollie explained carefully about the expense of travelling but Chantelle was awkward about it. Wouldn't they be able to pay for the travelling when they had the business going?

She was right, of course, and it would cost money to keep a fire going in the rooms upstairs. Then she thought she would not see Ritchie very often when he came home from abroad because, with room to spare, if they left her aunt's shop, he would stay there.

In the end she gave in, but Mrs Brandford did say they would start clearing the rooms anyway; they might be glad eventually to come and live there.

It was agreed that they would come on the Sunday and see what they could take out. Mrs Brandford said she would bring her nephew to help them. He was a sturdy young man who enjoyed hard work.

When Mollie told her aunt about the rooms Nell said, "It seems sensible to live there if you can. But, surely you would need one room at least to put things in from the shop?"

"Yes, I suppose so, but we'll see what's there when we go on Sunday."

Chantelle was very loving towards Nell and kept saying she wanted to stay at the little shop. "I feel at home here, it's so cosy."

Mollie began to wonder if Chantelle had run away and was missing her own home. And at the same time thought that the only home she herself had known was with her Aunt Nell.

Perhaps it would be just as well to live with her aunt.

Mollie enjoyed the evenings when the shop was closed and the three of them sat toasting themselves in front of a blazing fire and talked about all sorts of things. Nell asked about Mrs Brandford and said she seemed to be a very generous person.

"Oh, she is," Mollie enthused. "She always says that you must be generous too. I'm sure she would come here to see you. Shall I ask her?"

"It would have to be a Sunday evening because you'll

not have very much free time when you have the business under way."

"No, but I'm looking forward to it." She told her about the customers she had met and explained that they were not all 'stuck up' people. Some were quite friendly.

"Does Mrs Brandford perhaps exaggerate?"

Mollie shook her head. "No, no. I think it's just that I've been lucky to meet the decent ones. The first customer I saw was anything but nice. But I'm not going to start worrying. I was with some unpleasant people when I was in service. I simply got used to them."

"I'm glad you're out of that house."

Chantelle laughed. "And that is where you met me. Thank goodness."

Mollie ruffled her hair. "Yes, and I wish we knew your history."

Chantelle became serious. "I wonder if I ever will."

Nell said quietly, "I would like to know too."

The moment passed as Nell started to tell them about a customer who was going to get married again after having been widowed for ten years and bringing up eight children.

"*Eight?*" Chantelle exclaimed. "How did she manage to look after them and what is this new husband like?"

"She's a strong woman. She took in washing and the older children helped with the ironing. The husband is a farm labourer. He's never been married and seems a very caring man. I think they'll get on all right together."

"I wish I could get married," Chantelle said, a sadness in her voice.

"Just listen to her," Nell teased. "She's barely more than a child and already wants to get married. Enjoy your youth, girl. There's plenty of time for marriage."

"I wonder when Ritchie will be home?" she said, still wistful.

Mollie jumped up. "I think it's time we had a cup of tea."

* * *

By the weekend Mollie had met quite a lot of Mrs Brandford's customers and most of them said they would keep on at the shop. Only two had said they would go elsewhere and Mrs Brandford said she'd be well rid of them. They were nasty; sarcastic.

As Mollie and Chantelle were leaving, Mrs Brandford said, "So, we'll see you in the morning at ten. My nephew will hire a horse and cart so we should get quite a lot of stuff moved out from upstairs."

All Chantelle was interested in was the nephew. She said she hoped he was nice, like Ritchie.

Bob Taylor, a friend of Nell's, offered to run them to the shop the next morning and bring them back, if they knew what time they would be leaving. Mollie thought Mrs Brandford would want to be home about one o'clock.

"Then I'll be there for you."

* * *

When they arrived at the shop on the Sunday morning, Mrs Brandford's nephew was stacking boxes on the cart.

"Good morning," he called.

Mrs Brandford introduced him as Clifford; a tall, slender young man with dark hair and dark eyes. His manner was gentle. Chantelle kept giving him shy glances and he, in turn, eyed her. Would they be drawn to one another? Mollie hoped so. It would keep her from longing for Ritchie all the time.

Not long after they arrived Anne came to help, and Mollie quickly saw why by the way she looked at Clifford.

She only hoped there would not be any jealousy between the two girls.

They all got on quite well together however, and Clifford didn't seem to give one girl more attention than the other. Once or twice she heard them all laughing. It was free and easy laughter, there was nothing forced about it.

At eleven o'clock Mrs Brandford had them all stop for coffee and it was a really pleasant break. They had already emptied one room and she remarked how attractive it was. Mollie agreed, and kept it in mind – one room would have to be kept to stock things for the shop.

They also unearthed some pieces of clothing which had been packed away and forgotten, including a very attractive blouse in cream silk with the kind of collar Mrs Brandford had been going to make.

"Well, would you believe it!" she exclaimed. "This one has been handmade. Tiny little stitches. How well it's survived all this time. I wonder if we can sell it?"

"There's no harm in trying," Mollie said. "You should get quite a good price for it."

"It's yours, not mine. You found it."

A friendly argument took place and in the end they tossed for it, and Mollie won. Mrs Brandford laughed, "Why don't you keep it for yourself? Wear it on a Sunday."

"I might at that," Mollie said, "if we have company coming."

She was thinking of Ritchie as she spoke, and decided she would make herself a gored skirt to go with it.

Before they left Mollie made up her mind that if she did use the rooms, the second-largest would be the living-room, the smaller one a bedroom, and the largest would be kept for all the stock from the shop. But perhaps that would be for the future . . .

* * *

The following week was very busy and Mrs Brandford let Mollie deal with the customers, keeping careful watch in the background. Mollie was nervous at first, but once she had made several sales, she became more sure of herself.

"You've done extremely well," Mrs Brandford exclaimed. "Much better than I did at first. I think you were born to the job. I'm glad it's worked out so well as I shall be leaving you soon."

"Oh, not yet," Mollie pleaded. "Could you manage another week, I'd be so grateful?"

"Well, one more week won't hurt," she smiled. "Actually, I'm loath to go."

Clifford came to see the girls one lunchtime and Mrs Brandford let them go into the office. "But don't make this a habit," she said.

"I won't. I just felt I had to see them. I would like to take them to the theatre one evening."

"I don't think Mollie would very pleased about that – or Anne's mother. You're all too young. Someone would have to accompany the three of you."

"You could do it, Aunt Dorothy."

"I don't know, I'll have to ask Mollie."

Both girls were pleading to go and Mollie, not wanting to be a spoilsport, said she would agree as long as Mrs Brandford was with them. Mollie was amazed that both girls got on so well together and that there seemed to be no jealousy between them for Clifford's favours.

The trip was arranged for the following Saturday evening; Mrs Brandford saying she would close the shop at six, which she had done a few times in the past. No one had objected to it, as long as she gave them notice. She also said that Chantelle could stay at her house for the night. Anne only lived a street away.

Mrs Brandford tried to persuade Mollie to come, but she said no, she would go to her aunt's house. She smiled. "I think she enjoys hearing all about the people I meet."

Both girls were beside themselves with excitement and Mrs Brandford said there would no theatre if they didn't calm themselves. They subsided at once.

Chantelle wanted to know what was on at the theatre and Mrs Brandford told them it was *The Mikado*, it was showing at The Savoy in the Strand, and she would hire a cab.

Mollie had given Chantelle two of her own dresses when she came to the shop with her, but knew she would have to have something special to wear for the theatre. She was wondering if there would be time to make one when Mrs Brandford offered her a dress.

"Don't be offended," she said. The dress was a deep cream, the only trimming a pale blue sash with a bow at the back and long trailing ends.

Chantelle was in raptures about it.

* * *

When the evening came, Anne wore a turquoise dress with frills at the hem of the skirt. Chantelle thought it nice, but liked her own dress better.

Mrs Brandford had lent Chantelle a black velvet cape and Mollie thought how elegant she looked in it. She really was a most attractive girl. Her eyes sparkled and Mollie thought too that Clifford eyed her a little more than he did Anne, but then she could be wrong.

Her aunt's friend, Bob Taylor, came to pick her up and Mollie found herself wishing that she was going with them. But she showed none of this when she waved them away.

Bob nudged her, "Ay, it's nice to be young, i'nt it," making Mollie feel about forty.

Then she laughed, "One of these days I'll have myself a trip to the theatre."

The old man shook his head. "Never been meself. Nor the missus. Never could afford it. But we're 'appy enough and that's all that matters."

"Yes," Mollie said quietly, "that's important." She thought about Ritchie and wondered when he might be home again.

When she arrived at her aunt's, Nell said, "Well, I expect they'll all be sitting in splendour now. Pity I won't hear about it until tomorrow evening. I'll make a cup of tea and we'll sit down by the fire and have our usual natter."

They sat roasting themselves over the blaze and Nell gave a sigh. "Do you know, Mollie, I'm glad you didn't move into those rooms at Mrs Brandford's. I'd miss you both. You tell me about your day and I find things to tell you. I never went to the theatre when I was young."

"Were there theatres in those days?"

"Oh, indeed there were; pantomimes, too. I don't think my mother ever saw a pantomime either, but she knew all the stories: Cinderella, Jack and the Beanstalk – there were a lot more, but Cinderella was always the favourite. I loved Prince Charming!"

Mollie laughed. "I remember when you read them all to me. I loved Prince Charming, too. We had to depend on dreams in those days."

"Yes, we did. My husband was no 'Prince Charming'. But he made a good husband. There was never any question of being in love."

Mollie looked up. "I didn't know that."

"My father told me he had asked for my hand, and I accepted. I couldn't do anything else. I might never have got another chance."

"Did you—" Mollie hesitated, then went on, "did you ever fall in love with another man?"

"Yes, yes I did. I fell in love with the Squire's son. And he was, well, fond of me. But he was told he would be marrying the daughter of a wealthy family. He wasn't in love with her. Never was, but they had six children." Nell slapped her knees. "How about another cup of tea?"

It was the first time her aunt had talked about

her life, but Mollie sensed she wanted to change the subject.

After that Nell talked about Mrs Brandford and her husband, starting a big restaurant in the West End, adding, "I don't suppose they'll want for anything."

"But what kind of a life is that? Mrs Brandford enjoyed having her own shop. Deep down she's really sad to be leaving. She never had any children and that's why I think she's so fond of Anne and Chantelle. And she's fond of you, Mollie. I can tell. I feel that she would like nothing better than to stay at the shop with the three of you."

"I wish she could. I dread her going."

"You'll manage, Mollie. You're just made for a job like this." Nell stifled a yawn. "I feel ready for my bed."

"You go. I'll be following you soon. I've got a feeling I should be waiting for someone, and it's Chantelle, of course. It'll be strange going to work on my own."

Nell smiled. "Well, I'll hear the whole story tomorrow evening. Can't wait. You'll remember to turn the gas out?"

"I won't forget."

Mollie sat for a while going over various things. She was glad now she had not taken the rooms over the shop. She hadn't realised how her aunt looked forward to having them both at home.

Where was Ritchie now? It would have been nice if he had come home while Chantelle was out. But it could be another few weeks before he arrived.

Mollie washed up the cups, lit a candle, turned out the gas and went upstairs to bed.

A nightmare woke her, but she could not have told anyone what it was about. She lay awake for a long time, and when she did fall asleep, it was only into a fitful rest.

* * *

She was downstairs about ten minutes before her aunt. Nell said, "You were restless last night, weren't you?"

"Yes, I had a nightmare, but it was a mixed-up thing; I couldn't think what it was. I was at the docks, and I remember the river. I was possibly thinking about Ritchie."

"I didn't sleep very well myself, but I didn't have nightmares thank goodness."

They were having breakfast when there was a knock on the shop door.

Nell got up. "Who on earth can it be? The people know I don't open until eight o'clock."

Mollie said, "Could it be Ritchie?"

"No, he wouldn't come at this time in the morning."

Mollie heard a man's voice, then she heard her aunt say, "Oh, my God!"

Mollie jumped up and went into the shop. The man was a constable and her aunt's face, paper-white.

Mollie's heart began to pound. "What is it, what's wrong?"

Her aunt whispered, "The shop ... it's been burnt down."

"Mrs Brandford's shop?"

"Yes," her aunt said, "and Anne is missing. Her bed hasn't been slept in."

Mollie felt as though her legs wouldn't hold her. "Could Anne have been – in the fire?"

"No," the policeman said. "No one was found in the shop. Mrs Brandford said to tell you that—" he looked at a piece of paper, "that Chantelle and Clifford are all right. It's just Anne who's missing. She said she thought you would want to come."

"Yes, I'll come at once."

Nell said, "I'll come with you. I'll put a notice on the door."

Without another word they put on their hats and coats and got into the police van.

Mollie felt she was unable to think straight.

The shop burned down.

Ritchie had paid the rent for three months and had also paid for all the goods in the shop.

Mollie decided she must put that to the back of her mind for the time being. She must think of Anne, and what could have happened . . .

Chapter Five

When they arrived at the shop, a lot of people were standing around. Then Mrs Brandford, Chantelle and Clifford came out of the shop next door. Mrs Brandford began to cry. She put her arms around Mollie.

"Oh, my love. I don't know how this happened. No one knows."

Chantelle, looking like a ghost, came up and kissed her, then Clifford, his face drained of colour, said, "If only I hadn't suggested going to the theatre."

"It's not your fault," Mollie said, her own eyes full of tears.

The policeman approached them. "Would you like to go inside, Miss Paget?"

There were two firemen on the premises trying to sort things out.

Mollie stood staring at the terrible aftermath. There was not one whole garment anywhere. The smell of burning was overpowering.

One of the firemen called out, "I wouldn't come in any further, Miss. Materials are still smouldering."

Mollie was aware that everything on the floor seemed to be covered with water. The policeman said, "If you come out now, Miss, perhaps the people next door will let us go into their back room. I want to make some more notes."

The woman in charge of the next shop was talking to the others and agreed at once that they should go into her office. She brought more chairs in, then left. The policeman brought out his notebook.

"Now, let's see if we can shed some light on this subject. I have asked Mrs Brandford if she can account for the fire. She says that she was not aware of anyone smoking in the shop that day." He turned to Mollie. "Can you account for it, Miss Paget?"

She frowned, trying to think, then said that she also was not aware of anyone smoking that day.

He asked if petrol was used for cleaning materials, and again Mollie said, no.

He then asked if Miss Anne Colledge could have had a grudge against anyone in the shop, and there was a concerted, "No".

Mollie stated quickly and firmly, "She was a delightful girl who got on with everyone."

The police officer asked Mrs Brandford, apparently for the second time, what exactly had happened after they came out of the theatre.

She told him they had got a cab and taken Anne home. They met her mother, who said she saw Anne into her bedroom, but this morning when she went to call her, the bed had not been slept in.

He asked numerous questions to all present, including Aunt Nell, wanting to know if she knew Anne Colledge. Nell said, "No, but of course Chantelle had talked about her," and added how close the girls seemed to be.

Mollie realised he was trying to find out if there had been any jealousy at all in the girls' friendship with Clifford. Nell had answered firmly, "No, definitely not."

Mollie, at times, could see no reason for some of the questions, but accepted there must be a point to it all.

When at last he closed his book, the policeman said, "Well, that's all for now. I may want to see you all again."

After he had gone, Mrs Brandford asked Mollie if she

would like to come home with her. Mollie thanked her for the invitation, but refused, explaining her aunt had left the shop to come with her and she must go back with her and Chantelle.

Mrs Brandford nodded, "How silly of me, I'm not thinking straight at the moment."

Mollie, feeling her distress said, "I could come and see you tomorrow, if that would be all right?"

"Oh, I would be so grateful if you could, Mollie. I'll send a cab for you."

"No, I'll see to that. I don't know yet what time I'll be able to get away."

Mrs Brandford put her arms around her crying, "Oh, Mollie, I'm so terribly sorry this has happened."

"I know. We'll talk about it tomorrow."

Clifford insisted on ordering a cab for them though, and Mollie was forced to give in.

As soon as they got back Nell talked about making a meal.

"I'm not hungry," she said, "and I doubt whether either of you will be, but we must eat something."

Both Mollie and Chantelle said that a few sandwiches would be enough.

They talked very little while they ate, but once the fire was built up, Nell said to Mollie, "I don't know what you will do about the shop. You didn't have time to insure it."

"I know. Ritchie paid two months' rent in advance and then there was the payment for all the things in the shop."

Chantelle said, "Mrs Brandford must give you all the money back."

"She has a right to keep it. I have receipts for everything."

"All the same—"

Nell said, "I imagine that that was why she invited you

to her home. She's a very nice person and I'm sure she wouldn't want you to lose out on the deal. She would have the shop insured."

"I'm sure she would, but then she would want the money. And then there's Ritchie to be paid. Oh, heavens, what a mess!"

"It certainly is," Nell said. "If only we could find out who started the fire."

Chantelle said, "Let's talk about something more cheerful. I haven't told you yet about the show last night."

She was bright and smiling.

Mollie was angry. "This is not the time to talk about it. I have a lot on my mind."

"I thought it would help you. I'm sorry."

There was a hurt look in Chantelle's eyes.

"Oh, Lord, I'm sorry. I'll take it all back."

"Don't," Nell said quietly. "It's not the time. Perhaps later in the week, but not now. There's a terrible sadness about the situation. Not only the fact that Anne is missing but the fact that money is involved all round."

A customer came in and Chantelle begged to go and serve.

"All right," Nell said, "but they're all used to me serving."

Chantelle darted into the shop, but seconds later she was back, saying, "It's you she wants to talk to, Aunt Nell."

She looked so disheartened that Mollie said quietly, "The people will have to get to know you, Chantelle. They often come in just to ask Nell's advice. Some of them seem to think of her as a fairy godmother."

"A fairy godmother?" Chantelle exclaimed. "I wish I had one."

Mollie felt anger rising in her again. "I think you should be thankful with what you have. Where would you be now if I hadn't brought you here or Aunt Nell had refused to have you? Don't forget you've been fed and clothed. I know they were only two dresses of mine, but then you had a dress from Mrs Brandford and a trip to a theatre. Be thankful for those at least!"

"Yes, yes, I'm sorry. I wasn't thinking."

"No, that's your trouble."

Nell, returning, said quietly, "Now let's forget it. It's been a dreadful time. It makes us all nervy. I think instead of discussing *The Mikado* we should all be trying to find a reason for the fire and why Anne disappeared. There has to be one."

Chantelle said in a sulky voice, "I don't know any reason."

"Does she have any more boyfriends?"

"I've already been asked that by the policeman and I told him no."

"Well, think again. When you were asked the question you were keyed up."

"I do not know, I tell you."

"The two of you talked a lot. What did you talk about?"

"Just little things."

"What sort of things?"

Mollie could see that Chantelle was getting agitated.

"Small, everyday things."

"Such as?"

"Her family. They have money. She did not like working at—"

She stopped and Nell said softly, "At the shop?"

"Yes, no. I do not know. Look what you are making me do. I am saying things I ought not to."

"You are saying the right things, Chantelle. Anne didn't like working at the shop so she decided to set fire to it?"

"No, no!" She burst into tears.

"You must tell us the truth." Nell spoke sternly.

"That is all I know."

"She did have another boyfriend?"

67

Chantelle looked up. "How did you know that? Oh, look what you have made me say. You are putting words into my mouth."

"Who is this young man?"

"I have no idea. She never told me his name."

"But she wanted to run away with him?"

"I am tired, worn out, I want to go and lie down and, I do not want to be questioned any more."

"The police must be told of this."

"No. I shall deny it." A stubborn look had come about her mouth.

Mollie said, "Do you realise that I will be losing money? Ritchie's money? I am owing that, all because Anne wanted to set the shop on fire."

"She didn't set it on fire. And I shall stick to that."

Nell, grim-faced, said, "Then you will leave here and never come back."

"No, no, I could not bear it. I love you both very much. You are all I have. Please, please, do not send me away! I am so very tired. May I please go and lie down?"

"Yes," Nell said, "but when you come down you must agree to tell the police what you know."

"I will think about it."

"Very well."

She left and went upstairs.

Mollie and her aunt exchanged glances. Nell said, "Well, and what do you think of all that?"

"I don't believe it."

"Why?"

"Chantelle is an actress. I watched her gestures and knew she was making it all up."

"Do you think then that she set the shop on fire?"

"No, she wouldn't have the courage. She was jealous because she thought that Clifford liked Anne better than her."

"But she did run away."

"As far as we know."

"What are we going to do?"

"I don't know. The trouble is I'm fond of Chantelle, I can't help it."

When Chantelle did come down she said she was willing to tell the police what she knew.

* * *

As it turned out the next morning, however, there was no need to tell the police.

There was a piece in the Stop Press news in the paper which said, 'MAN ARRESTED FOR SETTING FIRE TO SHOP'.

Underneath it said this man had strenuously denied the charges, but three men going to work said they had seen him entering the shop in the early hours of the morning.

Then a neighbour came in and said that this same man had been arrested before for trying to set fire to a shop.

Nell and Mollie were in the shop when this was being told by their neighbour. Then Mollie became aware of Chantelle standing in the doorway.

Chantelle turned and went back into the kitchen and when Mollie and Nell went in she said quietly, "So I won't have to tell the police what I know after all."

"No," Mollie said, "but neither Nell nor I are happy about this. They should be told that Anne must have paid the man to set the fire going."

Chantelle made no reply but Mollie guessed there would be some uncomfortable days to follow.

At eleven o'clock Mollie went to the first crossroad to catch an omnibus to the shop. From there she would she would get a cab to Mrs Brandford's.

She caught comments from passengers about the fire. "The shops on either side could have caught fire . . ."

"The whole street could have been alight . . ."

"Why should a man want to set the dress shop alight . . .?"

Mollie had no wish to see the derelict-looking shop again and got off the omnibus at the taxi rank and got in a cab.

Mrs Brandford was at the door as soon as the cab arrived.

"Oh, I'm so glad you managed to come," she greeted Mollie. "Did you see the piece in the paper this morning about the fire? What made that man set fire to the shop? It's a puzzle."

They went into the living room and Molly thought how beautifully furnished it was. A maid brought in coffee. After Mrs Brandford had poured it, she offered plates of cakes and biscuits to Mollie. Mollie took a piece of fruit cake then told her what a neighbour of her aunt's had told them about the man having been arrested for setting fire to another shop before.

"Isn't that terrible? Why should he have chosen our shop? Why not the china shop or the shoe shop on the other side?"

Mollie had to laugh. "It's typical, isn't it? None of us wants our place disturbed."

Mrs Brandford laughed too, then quickly sobered.

"Do you think, Mollie, that someone had paid him to do it? Anne, perhaps? I can't think why. But then someone must have wanted us out of the way. Anne always seemed very settled. She never once complained. She was a charming girl."

"Why has she disappeared?" Mollie asked. "Did she have a boyfriend that we don't know about? They might have run away to Gretna Green to get married."

"I doubt it. On the other hand they could have done. Young people are very secretive. I was, when I was young. But there, what we must discuss now is the money problem.

70

I do have the shop insured and will get some money back, but I want you to have your money back too."

Mollie had not wanted Mrs Brandford to know that Ritchie was paying for everything and she would be paying him back when things got underway. Now she knew she must explain.

When she told her the position Mrs Brandford was aghast.

"But where are you going to get the money from to pay him?"

"I'm going to work for it. I worked it all out in bed last night. Using some of the material my aunt has in the shop, I shall make blouses. She does have a machine. I'll keep the prices reasonable. There are people in the market who do deal with people who have a little more money to spend. If I sell some blouses I can give my aunt money for the material and can start paying Ritchie. He told me over and over again that he wasn't in a hurry for the money."

"Oh, dear, this is awful." Suddenly she brightened. "I know what I can do. Some of the furniture will go to the house in the West End. But, I have one or two antiques I intended to sell. I'll sell them right away and use the money to buy you material from your friend. That would be a help, wouldn't it?"

"I couldn't take it."

Mrs Brandford smiled. "When I was a child my nanny was always telling me that there wasn't such a word as 'couldn't'. I agree with her."

They argued over this but Mrs Brandford was adamant and in the end Mollie had to give in, saying, "Well, when I get some money I shall give it back to you."

Mrs Brandford tried to persuade Mollie to stay for lunch but she said she must get back – she smiled, "I have work to do."

"But you will come again?"

"Yes, I promise."

*   *   *

71

Mollie found a difference when she got back. Her aunt and Chantelle were laughing together.

Nell held up a lady's white handkerchief. A pattern had been embroidered in the corner. "We've been working. What do you think of this? Chantelle did it."

"It's beautiful."

"And how about this? I've just started, I'll soon finish it."

It was a blouse cut from one of the rolls, partly-stitched on the machine.

"It's lovely." She flung her arms around her aunt then gave Chantelle a hug. "We'll soon get the money back if we all work. I can believe it."

They talked all through the meal. Mollie told them about Mrs Brandford selling some of her antiques so she could give her some money, Nell about the sewing machine she had dragged out and about cutting out the blouse and started stiching it, then Chantelle thinking about embroidering the plain white handkerchiefs and trying to sell them.

Nell said, "Anyone listening to us would think we had had a small fortune coming in."

Mollie said happily, "It's as though we have."

* * *

They were all up earlier than normal the next morning and started working right after breakfast.

Mollie sorted through the rolls, choosing what she thought were the right materials. Chantelle had drawn patterns in the corners of the handkerchiefs and was soon busy doing the embroidery and Nell had cut out the blouses.

Nell decided if Mollie would stitch up the blouses she would make the buttonholes. She added that she used to be a dab hand at buttonholes when she was

72

younger, and Mollie declared she was a dab hand now.

They worked the whole day but stopped after the evening meal to discuss where the finished blouses would go in the window.

"Right in the centre," Mollie declared. They had finished five and they could hardly believe it. Chantelle had embroidered ten handkerchiefs and said that her fingers were nearly dropping off. Nell teased her, saying she wouldn't have any fingers left by the end of the following week, and went to lock the shop door.

The next moment she gave a yell and shouted, "Ritchie!"

Chantelle rushed into the shop but Mollie went in slowly, knowing what she had to face.

Ritchie had swung both Nell and Chantelle around, then said, "And here is the boss of them all!"

He began to swing Mollie around too but then his smile died. "What's the matter?"

"Bad news I'm afraid, Ritchie. The shop was burned down."

"What!" He ran his fingers through his hair. He turned to Nell. "I'm parched. I could do with a cup of tea."

They all went into the kitchen.

"What happened exactly?"

"Just as I said. It was burned down. Nothing could be saved."

Chantelle said quickly. "A man did it. He had been arrested before for burning other shops."

"Good God! A madman." Ritchie took off his jacket and sank into a chair. "Well, I'll be damned. And everything lost, you said?" He addressed Mollie.

"It was all a shambles." She explained about Mrs Brandford, Clifford, Anne and Chantelle going to the theatre. "It happened during the night."

Nell then told him about Anne disappearing.

73

"What the hell was going on?" Ritchie demanded. "Was the whole thing set up?"

Mollie sighed. "We just don't know."

"Well, I'll tell you this, if it's the last thing I do, I'll get to know. I'll go to the police station tomorrow."

Mollie, seeing Chantelle go pale said, "They were most thorough about the whole thing."

"Not thorough enough. I invested money in this."

Mollie told him quickly about how Mrs Brandford was going to sell some antiques and give her the money back. "She's being very generous. I didn't have time to insure anything."

"I'm not blaming you, Mollie. I want to know who got this man to set the shop alight. Obviously someone who held a grudge against Mrs Brandford."

"No one had. She's definite about that."

"I don't care what anyone said. I'm sure that he was put up to it."

Mollie, noticing Chantelle getting more and more distressed said, "Why don't you go and see Mrs Brandford in the morning? I'll go with you."

"I might at that, but I'll also go and see the police."

Chantelle asked in a low voice if she could go to bed and Nell said, "Yes, of course," and added to Ritchie, "She's taken this badly."

"Good night, love," he said. "Try not to worry about it. I'll get it sorted out."

Mollie prayed he never would.

To try and distract him from the burnt-out shop for a while, she asked him how his journey had been.

"Splendid – couldn't have been better. But this has just about knocked the stuffing out of me."

"It had us in its clutches last night. We decided this morning to make some blouses. Nell cut them out and I stitched them, and Chantelle has been doing some embroidery on the corners of ladies' handkerchiefs. It was good for us."

"That won't get you much money."

"No, but it does keep us occupied – which is important."

She was getting to the end of her tether.

Ritchie sighed. "All right, we'll both go and see Mrs Brandford tomorrow."

* * *

The visit turned out better than Mollie had expected. Ritchie not only took to Mrs Brandford at once, but was fascinated by the house and how well-furnished it was. He wanted to know which pieces of antique furniture she intended selling and when he saw them and found out what price she would be asking for them, he said at once that he would be interested in buying them.

She smiled. "To sell again?"

"No! I want them for my own house."

"Then they're yours."

"No, I can't accept that. I must pay something."

"I don't want anything. You either take them or leave them."

He grinned. "How could I refuse?"

There was a chest, a wall cupboard and a big chair, all beautifully carved.

He ran his fingers over the chest and said to Mollie, "Aren't they truly lovely?"

"They certainly are."

Mollie had not known that Ritchie had a house of his own. Had he a wife? She felt a sudden pang that he could be married. She would ask him later.

They came away from Mrs Brandford's with Ritchie saying that getting the pieces of furniture made up for losing the shop.

"Not to me, it didn't," she said shortly. "I finally felt I was on my way up in the world."

"We'll get another shop. Don't worry."

"I'll build up a another business myself."

"Don't be silly. It could take you months to get started."

"I expect that. It took you a long time to build up your business." She paused. "By the way, are you married?"

He laughed. "What gave you that idea?"

"You, buying the furniture."

"No, I'm not married. But I do have a house. It's partly furnished."

"Why didn't you mention it?"

"Should I have done?"

"No – not really."

Mollie began to think that she had worked with some strange people. There was Ritchie to start with, then Anne, who had no liking for her work. What about Clifford? He had not really said much about the burnt-out shop. There was Chantelle who was strange too. Would she ever know the truth about her?

Her aunt seemed to be the only sensible one. They would work together. But even as she thought it she knew that Chantelle would have to be involved. And could she do without Ritchie? He had the rolls of fabric.

Oh, to the devil with everyone else. If she was to get anywhere, she would have to use all these strange people. She would be successful . . . one day.

Chapter Six

When they got back to Nell's shop, Ritchie was all talk about the furniture he had bought.

Chantelle, who had looked down in the mouth, asked him if he been to the police station and he said, no, what was the use. He had got his money back in the furniture that Mrs Brandford had given him. He was satisfied.

Mollie said, now she thought about it, she was the only one who had suffered.

"What do you mean by suffered?" he asked. "You've had some experience in a shop and it hasn't cost you anything. I'll bet you know a great deal more now than you knew when you started. You've not only met Mrs Brandford's customers but were popular with the majority of them. Surely that's worth something?"

Although Mollie felt annoyed she had to agree with him. She had not only talked to customers but had learned how to design dresses.

Should she accept his offer of more rolls of material and try to build up a business again? She felt she needed to have another shop. Ritchie got up, saying he must go, he had some people to see.

Chantelle said she thought she would start embroidering some handkerchiefs and Aunt Nell said she must just pop in to see a neighbour who was ill.

"I'll be back about six o'clock," Ritchie said, "and you can decide what you want to do, Mollie. We'll need to find another shop."

There was that 'we' again. She disliked to be beholden to Ritchie to get started once more.

He and Nell went out, leaving Mollie to keep an eye on the shop. Chantelle was sorting out the handkerchiefs and Mollie sat down to do a little more thinking. She would like to make blouses without having to borrow from Ritchie. She could use the material that her aunt had and let her have some extra money. On the other hand, doing it this way would mean very little money for herself. Far better to have a dressmaker turning out the blouses and her aunt would get some profit too. She needed to be paid. She was keeping Chantelle and herself. Chantelle would expect to have a little too. She was doing the handkerchiefs.

Oh, to the devil. She would start making a few blouses and see how it went. If it didn't work out she would have to lower herself and take Ritchie's offer of help.

Mollie had cut out a blouse and had started to stitch it when Nell returned.

"My goodness, it's cold," she said, throwing off her shawl. "If you wait a few moments I'll cut out the blouses and you can get on with the stitching."

Mollie was about to retort that she had been waiting for Nell to return to cut out the blouses then clamped her mouth shut. Complaining would only start a row. Things were bad enough as it was. Chantelle was not in a good mood. She was working in silence, head bowed. Mollie forced herself to ask her aunt about her neighbour.

"I thought she was a little better today. She's not a moaner. She had made an effort to get up. I would hate to be tied to my bed. As long as I can do some work."

Mollie suddenly felt mean.

When Ritchie returned just after six o'clock he was in a jaunty mood. "I've had another good order. I'll soon have to open a bigger warehouse. I did have a look around the shops but couldn't find one to let. Not to worry, there'll probably be one next time I'm home."

This was also said in jauntily and Mollie answered, "I'll just go on making blouses. We'll get some money. As long as we have enough for food. I don't want it to worry you."

"Who said it won't worry me? Of course it does. The difference is that I don't show it, you do."

"Strange," she said calmly. "I thought that I was treating the problem lightly."

"Look, I'll give you some rolls of material."

"No, I'm buying it from Aunt Nell and Chantelle is doing some embroidery. We're doing alright. I'm not grumbling. I think actually it will be a good thing to start from the bottom and build up."

Nell put in, "It's hard work, but at the same time, worthwhile."

Ritchie waved a hand. "Well, as long as you all feel it's worthwhile, what more can you want?"

He picked up the morning paper and began to read. This was something that Ritchie had never done before. He had always talked to them and they had always enjoyed his chatter.

Mollie began to stitch up a blouse and found that her hands were trembling, feeling that she was at fault. She forced her self to say, "Ritchie, I hope I haven't spoiled your chatter. Nell always enjoys it and so do I. And I'm sure that Chantelle does too."

"I do," Chantelle said eagerly. "I love to listen to Ritchie. He has such an exciting life."

Ritchie put down the paper and gave them a broad grin. "I've always plenty to talk about for those who want to listen. Now then, what shall I tell you?"

Nell said, "What part of the North are you going to?"

"I'm starting at Newcastle-on-Tyne and going to the mills around that part. There are lot of men out of work and I get the benefit. They have to sell the material cheaply."

"That's sad," Nell said. "I want something to make me laugh."

"Oh, I'll soon fix that. When I was up there the last time I was crossing a field and I saw a girl standing at a gate. She was a bonny lass. She waved to me and I waved back and she opened the gate and began to run. I did think it was a bit cheeky, but then I found there was another man running too. They ran ran into one another's arms and I felt a big fool."

They all laughed and Ritchie went on telling them several other funny things. Then he began to tell them about sleeping in a house that was supposed to have a ghost.

"I was very cocky and said I would sleep in the house, I didn't believe in ghosts. A few men came with me and were laughing when I left them and went into the house. I saw that the front and back doors were locked and bars put across them. I also made sure that each window could not be opened, then I went upstairs. I locked both doors in the bedroom and put the handles of chairs underneath the locks. I must have been sitting over an hour when I began to feel sleepy. Then suddenly I sat up, wide awake as I thought I could hear someone coming up the stairs.

Was there another way into the house? From the cellar perhaps? I got up, smiling to myself and thinking that at least the 'ghost' would not be able to get into the room with a chair propped under the handle. Footsteps came firmly along the landing and I could have laughed aloud. Come on, cleversides, I said to myself. Come in if you can and I'll believe in ghosts. There were lights flashing on the ceiling and I guessed that the men were having a bit of fun outside with torchlights. The next moment I was standing, tense with shock, as a big tall man came through the closed door, passed me and went through the opposite wall."

"What did you do?" whispered Chantelle.

"I ran to the door, flung the chair aside and unlocked

the door, then I ran along the landing and all but fell down all the stairs. I moved the bar from the front door, fell down the terrace steps, picked myself up and kept on running."

"Where were your friends?" Mollie asked.

"They had disappeared. They had got a shock too. When I found them they were shaking like me. They had seen the man go through the closed door."

"And do you believe in ghosts now?" Mollie asked.

"I certainly do."

"What was the story of this one?"

"He was a nobleman who had found his wife dead and he had been determined to find the person who had killed her. Apparently he had killed a man, but he was the wrong one and the nobleman has haunted the house ever since he died. It was on the Northumberland moors. I never went back."

Nell said, "I asked for something to make us laugh, but I must say I've never heard that story before."

Once Ritchie was encouraged to continue with his stories there was not much work done that night.

*　*　*

He left early the next morning, promising that he would be back again in another two weeks.

Nell said, as he left, "And don't go looking for ghosts."

"I certainly won't. Be sure you carry on with your sewing."

They made a lazy start but got into the mood before lunch and were delighted when they sold two blouses. Then in the afternoon Chantelle sold two handkerchiefs at twopence each, for birthday presents. She was proud to be helping the funds.

By the end of the week they had sold seven blouses and nine handkerchiefs.

Although all were thrilled they realised that very little money had come in. There was also a little controversy. Nell wanted to pay Mollie a small wage, but Mollie refused. It was her business and she insisted that she would pay Nell for the material and Nell refused to budge, with Mollie pointing out that she would not be a businesswoman if Nell paid her. Eventually Nell gave in, saying that Mollie was right. She was satisfied with selling the material.

So Nell was going to pay Ritchie for the material and would get a small payment from Mollie for doing the sewing. Mollie was also to make a small payment to Chantelle for doing the handkerchiefs but both Mollie and Chantelle would pay Nell for their keep.

It was the right way, but Mollie felt that her profits were very small. Still, she was in business and she was pleased with that. It was a start.

* * *

At the end of the fortnight when Ritchie was due back Mollie had made up her mind to accept a shop if he could find one. The constant all day sewing was getting her down. She needed to be a shop owner and sell the goods, not make them. Chantelle wanted to be an assistant. Her fingers were all pricked. Nell, however, was willing to go on making the blouses.

When Ritchie arrived he said he had looked all over but there were no empty shops. He added that he would keep on looking. Mollie was bitterly disappointed. Especially as she had made up her mind that she wanted to sell, not make things. Ritchie even took her with him when going to the warehouse to see if he could find a shop that might be coming vacant. But there wasn't a single one.

She was staggered when they went into the warehouse to see the huge addition to the rolls. "And they will soon be moving out," Ritchie said. Mollie asked where he would put the rolls if he got any further orders. "There will be more. I shall take another warehouse."

Mollie liked the feeling of the river. The constant movement, the barges, the small boats, the smell of oil. She felt at that moment that she would like to live her life on the river. When she mentioned this to Ritchie he pulled a face. "It's a lonely life. You stay on land. A shop will come up soon. Be patient."

"It's all right saying, be patient. I don't mind making one or two blouses, but I find it dreary work doing it week in and week out."

"I do the same thing week in, week out but you have to throw off such a mood. It doesn't do a bit of good."

"But you meet people. They're your friends."

He laughed heartily. "Friends? That's because you don't meet them. Some are friends, but some call you all sorts of things. I never lose my temper with them because I know what trouble I had when I first started. You must learn to be patient, Mollie. You have to take into account that for two years you were working in a house, doing the same thing day in and day out. I bet you didn't even think it was boring."

"I – suppose I accepted it. On the other hand I did have it in mind that I would eventually go and live with Aunt Nell. I have had a taste of freedom. Once I had the shop all I could think of was building it up. And then came the blow. The burning of the shop. That still rankles with me."

"Put it from your mind."

Mollie sighed. "I'll try. I really will. And I'll hope that one day another shop will crop up."

"It will. And if not in this district, another one."

Ritchie was a busy man and they saw very little of him this time. Chantelle grumbled about it, said she thought he had another girlfriend and she didn't like it one bit.

Nell told her gently she was not to think of Ritchie as her boyfriend. She was too young. She had a lot of growing

83

up to do. She often mentioned Clifford and wondered why he didn't even get in touch with her. Again Nell said to forget him. He lived in another world.

* * *

And so they plodded on, Nell cutting out blouses, Mollie doing the stitching and Chantelle embroidering the corners of the handkerchiefs.

Then, one day, while Nell was clearing out a cupboard she found a piece of canvas. "This isn't much use," she said. "I may as well throw it away."

"No, wait." Chantelle held out her hand for it. "I used to do these as pictures, when I was younger. Yes," she added, with some enthusiasm, "I used to draw a scene on them. Someone else worked with me, but I cannot think who it was."

"A sister, perhaps?" Mollie suggested.

Chantelle shook her head slowly. "No, it was not a sister. But I do know that I drew a picture on it and then I stitched it . . . with wools! Yes, I remember now. I had a nanny. Oh, how lovely to remember."

Both Mollie and Nell shared her excitement. Nell said, "There are wools here. All different colours. I can't remember using them."

She pulled out a mixture of wools. Chantelle took them from her. "I once made a screen. It took me a long time. Do you think I should try and make another?" Both Mollie and Nell encouraged her, saying it might help her to remember how she came to be there. They offered to help her to sort out the wool. Nell found her some crayons and Chantelle began to draw on a piece of paper. Before long there was a horse at a fence and also a man and a girl in riding habits. The drawing was rough but Chantelle had certainly been used to drawing. She filled in the scene with trees and foliage.

"I shall make a screen." she declared, her eyes shining.

It took her hours to get it right but then she was ready to use the wools. It was slow work but gradually the screen began to come alive. They all realised it would take weeks to get it completed, but then she should get a decent price for it.

Ritchie arrived the night it was finished and Chantelle's eyes shone when he praised it.

"It's wonderful. Do you want me to try and sell it for you?" he asked.

"Oh, yes, please. How much do you think I shall get for it?"

"I have no idea. But I'll find out. You're a clever girl, Chantelle."

He gave her a hug, but when she threw her arms around him he disentangled himself and said, "No love stuff."

Although she seemed disappointed at first, Chantelle told Mollie and Nell later that she knew he was in love with her. It then took Mollie and Nell half an hour to try and convince her that Ritchie had other women and he had hugged her as he would a child. She said she understood, but both knew by the look in her eyes that she still thought she was right and they were wrong. Mollie decided that when she had the opportunity to have a word with Ritchie she would ask him not to give Chantelle hugs.

When he came the next time and she told him this, he said, "The trouble is I think of her as a child."

"Well, you'll have to get that across to her. She refused to believe Aunt Nell and me."

He raised his shoulders. "But how? I take her arms away, tell her no more of the love stuff, but she obviously ignores that."

"Have you any photographs of the young women you know?"

"No," he grinned. "But I can get some."

When he came back that evening he laid a packet on the table. "Take a look at those."

There were seven or eight photographs of some very attractive young ladies. He grinned. "They're all actresses. I borrowed them from a friend."

"Will Chantelle know that?"

"I doubt it. She's only been to the theatre once. I'll bring these out later."

When he showed them to her, after they had had a meal, she became sulky.

"It is not fair. You let me think that you loved me."

"It's what you thought. I hug a lot of people. I hug Aunt Nell and and Mollie, but they don't think that I love them. No, that's wrong. I love them in a way, just as I love you in the same way but I don't want to marry them, nor do I want to marry you. Can you understand that?"

"No, you are just saying it."

"Oh, Lord! Look." He banged the table in exasperation. "If you don't stop thinking in this way, I shall stop coming here."

There were protests from Nell and Mollie.

Mollie said, "Don't you realise that you are being babyish, Chantelle? You sound like a three-year-old who says, 'Daddy loves me more than any of you'."

Colour came to Chantelle's cheeks. "I will not say it any more."

"Well, thank goodness for that," Ritchie declared. "I'll still give you all a hug and a swing around when I arrive and pray that no more will be said on the subject."

Although Chantelle said she would not say it any more Mollie knew, by the adoring look in her eyes when she looked at Ritchie, that she would go on loving him for ever more.

He did not visit them so often this time and he put it down to business. "It's flourishing, but I've had to work for it."

One of Nell's customers told her she had seen her nephew the night before with a young lady. They were going into a restaurant. "An expensive one," she added.

Both Mollie and Chantelle were in the kitchen and had heard it. Chantelle, who was doing a corner of a handkerchief, looked up quickly, then lowered her gaze again.

Mollie tried not to feel hurt and knew that if only she had a shop it would not have affected her so much. She was living such a dreary life. The same thing day after day with no variety. Even her aunt's customers never changed. If only she could get a shop. Should she take time off to go searching? Ritchie had not been able to get one but how far had he looked? He talked about the days flying by with his own business deals. Wasn't she being a bit too trusting? She snapped off the thread. Yes, she would definitely go around, asking other shopholders if they knew of anyone likely to be leaving a business.

She felt brighter and worked more quickly. She told her aunt what she had planned after Chantelle had gone to bed that night. Nell was not so enthusiastic.

"Ritchie is very reliable. You can depend on him. He pulls one thing in with another. While he's dealing with a man buying materials he'll say, casually, 'Do you know of a shop that might be let soon?'"

"How do you know that he would say such a thing?"

"Because his customers told me once. He used to bring them here at one time."

"Was that when he was first starting?"

"No, one man was here just before you and Chantelle arrived."

"Why didn't you tell me?"

"I didn't think it right that you should know all about his business."

"That surprises me. I feel I'm close enough to him to know all his business."

"But why should you, Mollie? I've always felt that a man is the boss. He has a right to do what he thinks best."

"But surely, if he's handling the business of a woman, she should have some rights too."

"I'm sorry, my love, but I don't agree with that. In my small world I think that Ritchie should handle all the business and all the money and pay you a wage."

Mollie felt quite staggered. "So I would be just a servant?"

She nodded. "Yes, I suppose so."

"You do know that there are many women who handle a business nowadays and are very successful?"

"Yes. It's just that I don't hold with it."

"But *you* are a businesswoman."

"I would rather not be."

"Then why didn't you marry again?"

She smiled. "No one asked me."

"Oh, Aunt Nell. I just don't know what to say. I want to be a businesswoman and I will be, some day. I want to get started as soon as possible. That's why I want to have a day off tomorrow to see if I can find a shop. I may not be successful but at least I can try."

"I'm not stopping you. You do realise that you might be wasting a full day when you could be making a little money?"

"I'll sacrifice what I would have earned and add it to your money the following day. Would that satisfy you?"

To Mollie's surprise her aunt said, "Yes, fine."

She had never thought of her as a money grabber. Well, perhaps she should be, too.

*   *   *

Mollie left early the next morning. Chantelle had wanted to go with her, but Mollie wanted to be on her own. She caught the horse omnibus and got off at the stop past her former shop. It was still in a derelict state.

She went into every shop along the road, but had no luck. When she went into the third shop in the next section, and asked her question, a middle-aged man with a quiet manner who introduced himself as Mr Ferris, said, "As a matter of fact, I was thinking of renting my shop."

It was a jewellers. He and his wife had managed it but she was unwell and was unable to work any more.

"Oh, I'm sorry. Actually, I was looking for a shop suitable for ladies' wear."

A faint smile touched his lips. "A jeweller's shop gives a very good reward. Is it for yourself?"

Mollie had borrowed her aunt's squirrel coat and knew it made her look older.

"Yes, it is."

"There's one shop in this section which sells ladies' wear and another one in the next section. You would have some opposition. Why not sell jewellery? Mind you, although the shop is for rent I would like the person who takes it to take all the jewellery too. It sells quickly and makes a good turnover. You would soon get your money back. May I ask if you were planning to run it on your own, Miss—?"

"Paget. No, a businessman will be involved."

Her heart was pounding. Was this a lucky chance? She had not thought of selling jewellery, but it would be a start.

"Have a look around, Miss Paget."

He took her over everything, necklaces, rings, watches, brooches, scarf pins. Mollie stood, uncertain. Dare she take the chance? Would Ritchie be willing to put the money into it? She could at least ask. She took the plunge.

"This businessman would have to see the stock, but he may not be able to come until tomorrow, or even the next day. If he isn't interested I'll let you know right away."

"I'll hold it for you." He smiled suddenly. "It's strange but it was only this morning that I decided I wanted to give up the business and be with my wife. If you had asked yesterday I would have said no."

She smiled too. "Then I'm glad that I decided this morning I would look around for a shop. Was it fate?"

"Oh, definitely."

She left a few minutes later, her heart soaring to the heavens.

It was when she was on the omnibus going back to the shop that she began to worry. She would need to have a male assistant in the shop. And then what about Chantelle? She had been very interested by the jewellery on the market stall and said she would like to sell it. There would be more male customers than females. It wouldn't do at all to have Chantelle working with her.

Then, of course there was her aunt who would lose out in making up the blouses. No, she was wrong. She would probably not be making them at all if Ritchie was agreeable to her taking the jewellers.

As it turned out her aunt was not only all in favour of Mollie having the jeweller's shop but insisted that Chantelle should help.

"Think what an asset she would be. Your customers, as you say, will be mostly men. She would revel in it."

"But I wouldn't," Mollie said grimly. "I would be the one who would have to keep her on the straight and narrow. Anway, I'll have to wait and see what Ritchie has to say about it."

"Oh, he'll be all for it. He'll get his money back more quickly. By the way, you'll have to have a man helping in the shop and I know just the man. Mr Redgrave used to run a jewellery business until his wife died. He retired but regretted it later. He's a very nice person. Warm, caring and does have a great deal of knowledge about the business. I'll write to him this evening and I feel sure he'll say yes."

"It all depends on Ritchie. For heaven's sake, don't say anything to Chantelle until we have talked to him. You know what she is. Always wanting to be with him."

Mollie stitched the blouses that Nell had cut out and the afternoon dragged. What if Ritchie did not come until late? Would he accept that she had a chance with a different kind of shop. She was not as sure as her aunt that he would get his money back more quickly. There would be Mr Redgrave to pay, if he was willing to take the job.

Ritchie arrived at six o'clock, ready for his meal and Mollie knew it would be ages before they could get rid of Chantelle so they could talk. She usually went to bed at about ten o'clock. She was genuinely tired by then. But would Ritchie stay so late? The last two nights he had left around nine o'clock.

She decided to write him a short note. She put on it, "Must talk to you this evening, without Chantelle. Can you arrange it?" and slipped it to him when Chantelle was making a pot of tea.

He answered it, saying, "I'll think of something."

As it happened it was Nell who solved the problem. About eight o'clock she asked Chantelle if she would take a piece of cake to a neighbour. "My feet are killing me this evening."

Chantelle got up right away. "Yes, I like your friend, Mrs Ewart. She once lived in France."

When she had gone Nell said, "Now we must get to this business of the shop right away. Chantelle won't be long."

Mollie told Ritchie what she had done and to her surprise he said, "Good, I know Mr Ferris. I also know that it will hurt him to leave the shop, but then he and his wife are very close. Yes, we'll go tomorrow and have a talk with him."

Mollie, overjoyed that he liked the idea, talked about Chantelle and like Nell, Ritchie thought she would be an asset. Mollie made no attempt to explain that she would be the one to suffer.

Nell then told him about Mr Redgrave and again Ritchie was all for it. The whole thing was settled before Chantelle returned, full of Mrs Ewart's talk of France.

Mollie thought that Chantelle had changed a little since Ritchie had had the talk with her. Perhaps she was eager to show that she was not trying to cling to him.

Ritchie had arranged that he would take Mollie out with him the next morning, saying casually that he had a glimmer that he had found a shop for her and, praise be, Chantelle did not ask to go with them.

Chapter Seven

The next morning when Mollie and Ritchie arrived at the jewellers Mollie had a feeling that the fact of the two men knowing one another would help to settle the deal.

They laughed and talked about their earlier days, but when it got down to business Ritchie asked numerous questions and refused to pay the price that Mr Ferris had asked for the jewellery.

Mr Ferris said quietly, "I have only one thing to say, Ritchie. I buy the best I can. I have an excellent clientele. They like what I buy. You, of course, can buy a cheaper brand if you wish and risk losing the custom."

Ritchie grinned. "I knew I would never get the better of you, Frederick, but I had to try. I know that Miss Paget is keen to have the shop and I shall say yes. But there is one thing. Your customers are used to you and your wife and I know of a man, Mr Redgrave, who retired from his jewellery business. I think he might be willing to come and help. Do you know him?"

"Indeed I do. He regretted retiring. I would advise you to ask him. He's a gentleman of the first water. I'm sure that Mr Redgrave and Miss Paget would work well together."

"Splendid. I'll settle up with you now. I want Miss Paget to be the new owner."

Mollie's hand was shaking as she signed the form that Mr Ferris had made out.

Before they left Mr Ferris made tea for them and, in

between customers coming in, they had a long talk about jewellery.

During the first break Ritchie asked Mollie, smiling, if she was satisfied. "Oh, definitely. Thanks, Ritchie, I'm very much in your debt. I only hope I do well. It's the last thing I thought of doing and I only hope that it will work out."

"You can't fail if we can get Mr Redgrave to come and help out. Your aunt knows him. He had a wonderful business. I never understood why he retired so early."

"Was he married?"

"Yes, his wife died a few years back. I think she was a very jealous woman. She didn't like her husband to be in business. She was sure that he had women after him."

"How awful."

"Yes. I only hope he'll accept working with you." He gave her a cheeky grin. "And our Chantelle, of course."

"That worries me. You'll have to make her understand that she's not to make eyes at any of the men who come in."

He flung out his hands. "She's a born flirt. What can I do?"

"I think your talk did her some good. She didn't beg to come with us this morning. Anyway, I'll keep my fingers crossed."

Whenever Mr Ferris came back from a customer he added a little more to their knowledge, told them what the person had bought and why. "You will get to know a customer's tastes. If a woman wants to buy a watch for her husband she will want a masculine-looking one. But quite often the husband, if he had had the chance would have bought a much more delicate-looking one. Not all customers are the same, of course. These things you will learn in time."

* * *

94

It had been a most fulfilling morning and Mollie hardly stopped talking as Ritchie drove her back home. Ritchie managed to say that he knew that the project would be successful. "Mr Ferris is a most reliable man and if you can get Mr Redgrave to work with you, you're made."

Mollie couldn't wait to tell her aunt the news and when Nell said, "Well, and did you succeed?" Mollie laughed.

"Yes, we did. Not in ladies' wear, but in jewellery!"

Chantelle, who had been in the kitchen, came flying into the shop. "Jewellery? Oh, I cannot believe it! How wonderful. Do you remember how I wanted to be in jewellery when we were looking round the market?" She paused and when she spoke again all the excitement had gone.

"But you will not need me, will you?"

Ritchie said, "I think we will need you, Chantelle."

She stared at him. "Are you sure?"

"But there is to be no making up to men. No throwing them saucy glances. Is that understood?"

"Oh, yes, yes. I will be so good. Thank you, thank you."

She flung her arms about Nell. "Did you hear that, Aunt Nell? I will be working with beautiful jewellery."

"Remember, Chantelle, you will only be there as long as you do as you're told."

"I will be perfect. I promise." She turned to Mollie. "What will I have to do?"

"I don't know, Chantelle, until we get started. At the moment I feel shattered, but," she added, with a brief smile, "I'm sure we've done the right thing."

Nell had the meal ready and when they sat down Ritchie asked her about Mr Redgrave. She seemed to know more about him than Mr Ferris, praised him to high heaven and became dreamy about him. "A wonderful person, he knows so much about jewellery, especially diamonds. You must get him to talk about them. He had a terrible job with his wife. A nasty woman, wanted him always at her side. I shall call on him today. It will be lovely to see him again."

Mollie began to wonder if her aunt had once been in love with him.

After the meal Ritchie said he must go to the docks. He had quite a lot of work to do. Mollie found herself wishing that Ritchie could have worked with them. But, of course, it would have interfered with his usual work, work that had obviously made him a lot of money.

That evening Nell went to see if Mr Redgrave was at home. He was and said he would call later that evening.

Ritchie was back when he arrived.

Mollie liked Mr Redgrave at first sight. He was a tall, slenderly-built man with grey hair and a charming and gentlemanly air. He bowed over her hand when he was introduced to her and said he was pleased to meet her.

Ritchie had persuaded Chantelle to go upstairs when he came but promised her faithfully she would be introduced before he left. He explained that he did not want Mr Redgrave to get the idea that he would have to deal with two ladies in the business. She went, with a good grace.

Nell had part of a bottle of wine and poured some for the men. Mollie liked the way he spoke to her aunt, treating her as if she was someone special. Nell blossomed, talking of how they had known each other for a number of years, and said she hoped he would come back into the business.

He smiled. "I find it very tempting."

He asked numerous questions and wanted to know if Ritchie had been in the business before. Ritchie explained that he was in a different line and talked about it at length, then went on and told him how the shop that Mollie had rented had been burned down.

Mr Redgrave was shocked. He had read about it. Ritchie

96

explained how Mollie, quite by chance, had asked Mr Ferris if he knew of a shop in the vicinity that might be available to rent and how Mr Ferris had decided only that morning to leave the business.

"How amazing," Mr Redgrave said. "I think it's a question of fate." Then he added to Mollie, "I shall be very pleased to work with you, Miss Paget."

When a wage had been settled Mollie knew that they had to face telling him about Chantelle. She let Ritchie tell the story of how Mollie had become involved and Mr Redgrave was full of praise for Mollie, who had been so generous as to bring the girl to her aunt. He smiled at Nell. "You deserve praise too."

Colour came to Nell's cheeks and Mollie felt sure that her aunt must have been in love with him at one time and could still be in love with him.

Ritchie called to Chantelle to come down, and she behaved so shyly that Mollie felt Mr Redgrave might accept her in the business. She prayed that she would not suddenly change and be all excited.

But no, she thanked him and she promised that she would never be in his way.

He smiled and was gentle with her, saying, "I feel sure there will there will be plenty of small jobs to keep you busy, Miss Chantelle."

Mollie let out a small sigh of relief.

After Mr Redgrave had gone, Ritchie gave a small sigh too.

"There's one thing I must say; I don't think we could have got a better man for the job."

Nell, who was looking a little dreamy, agreed.

Mollie could not help thinking how strange life was. The last thing she would ever have thought of handling was jewellery. Pray heaven it would be a paying project.

*   *   *

All the next week Ritchie spent a part of every day with Mollie at the shop. Mr Ferris helped them both to cope with the stock. He was delighted for them that Mr Redgrave had agreed to come and work for them.

"A charming man. You must get him sometime to talk about diamonds. He has a wealth of knowledge. He lived abroad for a few years to learn about the big diamonds. I do have some small diamonds in rings and brooches, but of course they are nothing to compare with the Koh-i-Noor, the biggest diamond in the world. While I think about it I shall show you a diamond in the rough."

He brought out what appeared to be a rough stone. "They are nothing," he said, "until they are cut and polished. Many have flaws in them and when they are cut they split in the wrong places. The natives dug for them and if any of them were caught stealing they were killed at once."

Mollie gave a little shiver. "How awful."

"It did keep stealing down. I will, however, leave it to Mr Redgrave to explain all about them. Now, shall we talk about watches? I must introduce you to the two men who do all our repairs."

Mollie was fascinated with everything. She knew that Chantelle was itching to get into the shop too, but never asked to go with them. She stayed with Nell and embroidered her handkerchiefs while Nell cut out blouses and stitched them up.

At night Mollie would stitch blouses too and the majority of them were selling. Some days Nell had very little chance to do any stitching and was talking of giving some to a woman who had a large family and was looking for work.

"I feel sorry for her," Nell said. "Her husband's never sober and she has all these children to feed. He knocks her about and she never says anything, knowing if he hit her any more than he did she would be ill and not able to look after the wee ones."

Chantelle said, "Why do the children not get together and knock their papa around?"

Mollie said, "Just take care that you don't get knocked about."

Nell laughed. "I'm a lot stronger than I look. I bet I could tackle two drunken men and put them on the ground."

"Don't try it," Mollie begged.

But Nell did try it, simply because the husband tore up a blouse that his wife had finished.

"I was just so mad," she said. "All that work wasted. I stormed into the house and tackled him. I know I have a bump on my face but he has two black eyes and a nose pushed out of joint. Do you know he was actually cringing on the floor?" and she was laughing about it. "He's not the first man I've bashed about and he won't be the last."

Ritchie said, "Well, don't try any more tricks like that."

"I'll do it again if he ever tears another blouse. And I'll tell you this. The older boys say that they will tackle their father if he should hit their mother again."

"Good."

There was no need to tackle the husband. He still drank, but in moderation, and so far had not attempted to strike his wife again. Nell was praised by all her women customers and she was satisfied.

Then came the day when Mollie and Chantelle were to move into the shop. Ritchie took the whole day off. Mr Ferris stayed to help and Mr Redgrave came too.

It was an eye-opener to Mollie. Customers kept coming in to wish Mr Ferris well. Some women brought flowers and some had made cakes. Nearly every man who came brought a bottle of wine. Mollie was quite moved by it. So was Mr Ferris.

* * *

The Monday that Mollie took over the shop was quiet. Chantelle did not come in that day. Ritchie had said to leave it for a few days.

He called during the afternoon and when he asked how business was Mollie said, "It's terrible. A few people, very few have been in but no one has bought anything."

Mr Redgrave said, "I explained to Miss Paget that this does happen. It happened to me when I took over a business. People have to get used to the idea that the previous owner has left. It will start to get busy in a few days' time."

Ritchie looked thoughtful for a moment then said, "Can I make a suggestion? I think it would be a good idea if you let your customers think that you and Mollie are related in some way. She could be your niece. That is, of course, if you are both willing to accept it."

Mollie said that she wouldn't mind and Mr Redgrave smiled. "I would feel honoured."

"Good, then that's settled. Far better to be related than having them wondering if Mollie is an assistant or a lady friend."

They all laughed at this and if there had been any tension it was now gone.

Ritchie said, "I've been told, Mr Redgrave, that you have a knowledge of diamonds. I would be very interested in hearing about them and I know that Mollie would be too."

Mollie nodded. "I would indeed and, by the way, you will have to call me Mollie from now on."

He swept her a bow. "I shall not forget."

And so, in pleasant mood, Mr Redgrave began to tell them how he learned about diamonds.

"It started when I was a young man and visited an aunt and uncle who had been living for several months in India. My uncle had a government post out there."

"I was very adventurous at that time in my life and

discovered that diamonds had been found out there. I learned that in the past, natives had worked searching for diamonds. They were paid a pittance, they were really no more than slaves and if any man stole a diamond, no matter how small, he was killed at once."

"How awful," Mollie said quietly.

"It was the only way that they could stop the thieving. Diamonds are beautiful when they are cut and shaped but they are just like a piece of rough stone before they are cut and polished. I'll bring you a piece tomorrow to study.

"Some really beautiful diamonds have been found and cut. They are probably the hardest substance in nature. My uncle told me how in 1866 a visitor to a South African farm saw an unusual-looking piece of stone lying on the floor. He asked the farmer if he could buy it and was told it was only a child's toy picked up in a field and he could have it if he wished. The man took the stone to a mineralogist and was told that it was worth a considerable price."

Mollie said, "I hope the father of the child had a share of the money."

Ritchie laughed. "Trust a woman to make such a remark."

Mr Redgrave smiled. "I feel sure that my wife asked the same question." He paused then went on.

"The discovery in the same region of a stone which later became famous as the Star of South Africa caused a diamond rush as hectic as a gold rush. And there were many rushes to follow and many large diamonds were found.

"Some Indian diamonds are so exceptionally large that they have obtained almost world renown. Queen Victoria, who was Empress of India, was presented with the Koh-i-Noor, The Mountain of Light. It weighed over a hundred carats. 150 carats are equivalent to one ounce."

"That surely must be the largest diamond there is," declared Mollie.

"At the moment, yes," said Mr Redgrave. "But I am sure there will be larger ones." He then went on to speak about cutting and polishing and there was a note of reverence in his voice. "The flaws have to be avoided, otherwise the stones are useless. Diamond dust and oil have to be used, they are the only strong materials that will do it. I've seen many a stone wasted. Diamonds have naturally aquired their own mythology, some of the stories of the Koh-i-Noor being reminiscent of the Arabian Nights. Quite a few stones have disappeared mysteriously, to reappear, no less mysteriously, in the gem market some years later cut to a small size.

"The disappearance of one famous diamond necklace, in which Marie Antoinette was said to be involved, is indeed notorious as a historical mystery which has yet to be solved."

The bell above the shop door tinkled and the three of them stared at one another. Mollie said, "You go, Mr Redgrave. I'm afraid I haven't enough knowledge yet to serve."

Ritchie and Mollie sat silent, listening to Mr Redgrave and the customer talking. After about five minutes the bell tinkled again and a moment later Mr Redgrave returned to the back room.

"No luck yet," he said, surprisingly cheerful. "Just another customer wanting to know who is taking over. He was quite pleasant. Said his wife wanted to know. I explained that my niece and I would be running the shop and he seemed quite satisfied. Don't worry. By the weekend we should be busy. Now, where was I? Oh, yes, I think we must study a few gemstones."

"I looked at some of them with Mr Ferris," Mollie said, "but I don't think I took any of it in. Now I definitely will."

"Well now, like the diamond, rubies and sapphires were

first known in the east where they are still obtained from deposits, being picked out from the gravel by hand, or by other simple methods." Mr Redgrave gave a small sigh. "See how small diamonds in a ring or brooch sparkle. But look into the heart of a diamond and you will see a glory that you have never seen before. I think I shall stop there. Tomorrow we shall look at all the jewellery and study the gemstones. They are lovely to study."

Ritchie said, "Well, Mr Redgrave, you have already opened my eyes. I'm grateful for this talk."

"So am I," Mollie said. "It's been a wonderful day. I've never owned any jewellery. Now I almost feel I could talk to customers about it. And after a few more days learning about gems, I shall be an expert."

"Good, I'm glad. You will need to know, Miss Pa—" he smiled, "Mollie, about the workings of a watch and the repairing of a necklace catch, a bracelet catch, a brooch that has perhaps come apart, but all in good time. I think it's unwise to try and take it all in at once."

"Perhaps we could bring Chantelle tomorrow when I am learning about gems. Ritchie, will you be able to come tomorrow?"

"I shouldn't, but I'll make time. I must know all these things too."

Mr Redgrave suggested they shut the shop at seven o'clock. "I think it's too soon to stay open later. Customers will get to know our closing time. Some of the big stores don't close until nine o'clock and assistants have to clear everything away after that. We can always alter if we think we must. How do you both feel about this?"

Both Ritchie and Mollie agreed.

Mr Redgrave took Mollie home that evening, even though she insisted it was not necessary. He spoke to her Aunt Nell and Chantelle but would not stay.

When he had gone Nell and Chantelle demanded to know how things had gone. Had they had a lot of customers? Mollie told them no, but after she had explained all Mr Redgrave had told Ritchie and herself, Nell said, "A sensible man."

Chantelle started to grumble. Why had she not been there? She had to know about all these things.

Nell said sternly, "That's enough, Chantelle. Another grumble from you and you will never go to the shop."

To Mollie's surprise, Chantelle grinned. "I forgot for the moment. I shall never complain again." And she then began to tell Mollie how much she and Aunt Nell had done in the sewing line.

"I embroidered six handkerchiefs and started to embroider another screen panel. And Aunt Nell made three blouses and sold them all. Is not that splendid?"

"Oh, wonderful," Mollie enthused. "Three and sold them? That's very good indeed. I feel quite envious. But now I'm home a little earlier than I expected, I can do some sewing this evening."

Her aunt wouldn't hear of it. Once the shop started to get busy she would be worn out by seven o'clock. "Forget it, Mollie. I'll manage on my own. I've done so for many years."

Mollie left it for the time being. She would see how things went.

Chapter Eight

Chantelle did not go to the shop that day, as Nell thought it would be unwise to have two women in the shop who were learning the trade. Chantelle did not press to go and afterwards Mollie was glad she had stayed with her aunt.

It was a totally different day to the one before. There were customers who came in early, all of them buying something. Mollie went into the shop but stayed in the background, feeling she had not sufficient knowledge to take part.

Mr Redgrave introduced her to each customer, "This is my niece, Miss Paget, who is learning the trade. Soon, she will be able to serve."

Some of the men eyed her with interest. Two of them said with a smile that they would be pleased to be served by her when she was qualified. She returned their smiles and thanked them.

Ritchie came about ten o'clock and there was a lull.

"I think we should take time to study some of the gemstones," Mr Redgrave said. He brought a tray of brooches and one of rings and put them on a table in the back room.

"Now, which shall we study first? Perhaps the rings." He picked out a ring set with a ruby.

"This is a gemstone that—" He paused then added, "Oh, yes, I must tell you first about women who will come in and ask to speak to you, Mollie. They will want to know which gemstones have healing qualities."

Mollie frowned. "Healing qualities? In what way?"

"That is what I must explain. When my wife and I were in business together, she was constantly being asked about this. In most cases the women would ask what she thought were the best gemstones to use and ask her if she agreed they had a healing power."

"This, of course, goes back a long way. Kings in ancient India were advised to collect the very best gems to protect themselves from harm. Early works, written in Sanskrit, were dated 400 B.C. They made elaborate observations on the origin and power of stones to counteract the negative powers of the planets. Medical practices of many ancient cultures included wearing talismans and amulets around the neck."

"And did they work?" Ritchie asked.

Mr Redgrave shook his head. "That I don't know. But I do know that my wife believed they healed. In most cases they had healed when a doctor had failed to cure his patient of an illness."

"Well! That's good to know, isn't it?" declared Mollie. "Were any particular stones used?"

"Ruby, topaz, quartz, turquoise, diamonds. Oh, there was one, amber. It's not a crystalised form, nor can it be qualified as a stone. Actually, amber is petrified tree sap that is millions of years old. It's a beautiful golden colour that can be made into stunning jewellery worn for beauty as well as for grounding and stabilising effects."

The doorbell rang again. Ritchie got up. "I must go. Pity, I was enjoying hearing about the gemstones. I'll see you tomorrow."

Mollie went into the shop with Mr Redgrave and, as usual, stood in the background. It was a woman this time. After Mr Redgrave had introduced Mollie she said, looking a little shy, "Actually, it's the lady I would like to talk to."

106

Mollie felt her heart flutter. Surely she was not going to ask her about the healing quality of gemstones?

But that was exactly her intention and Mollie felt suddenly calm. Mr Redgrave suggested that Mollie take the lady into the back room and drew out a cushioned chair for her. Then he left.

"Now, ma'am. Is it for yourself that you wish to know about the healing powers of gemstones?"

"Yes, it is. I haven't felt well for a long time and the doctor doesn't seem to know what to do. I haven't much strength. I tire quickly."

"Perhaps a tonic would help?"

"No." She spoke firmly. "This shop cured a friend of mine. I'm sure it can cure me if I have the right gemstones."

"Then I shall go through them and see which will be best for you."

Mollie gathered her wits together and told the woman most of what Mr Redgrave had told Ritchie and herself earlier.

The woman's eyes looked already brighter. "That sounds wonderful, absolutely splendid. What would you recommend for me?"

This was where Mollie knew she would have to be careful.

"I suggest you choose something yourself, ma'am." She added, "Most of the women do."

"Well now, money is no object. I fancy a necklace. A single-stranded one. One that is fairly close to the neck. I could have a few diamonds, some rubies, some turquoises. Oh, yes, and some quartzes."

Mollie got up. Her legs felt weak. "I shall explain to Mr Redgrave."

When she told him he looked solemn for a moment then suddenly he smiled. "Your first customer, it can only be good."

"I hope so."

He came into the shop with Mollie and told the customer he would have the necklace ready in a week's time. (It was the first Mollie knew of Mr Redgrave making necklaces.)

Mrs Dawson was such a changed person that Mollie wondered if faith worked wonders. Just faith? After thinking this over Mollie was not sure she was right. Mr Redgrave had said that many women had been cured after a doctor had been unable to cure any of them of their illnesses. Well, this was something she would have to find out. When Mrs Dawson had left, Mollie put this to Mr Redgrave.

"I wish I knew, Mollie. I don't think it was just faith with the people that I knew who were cured. They were unhappy people. Nor did the stones do any good for about two weeks. And even then it was still slow."

"I'm glad to hear that. I hope that this is a slow progress. I would hate to have her come in the next day and say the necklace was working."

"I don't think she will. Anyway, we can only hope. After all, we don't want the shop to progress by this means."

"No, definitely not."

They had quite a number of customers and every one who came in bought something. At one point Mr Redgrave gave Mollie a broad smile.

"I'm so glad they like us."

"So am I. It's given me a lot of confidence."

When Mollie got back to her aunt's that evening and told Nell and Chantelle all that had happened, Nell said that she had known of women being cured by wearing gemstones but Chantelle dismissed it.

"It's imagination. How could gemstones cure an illness?"

"I don't know, Chantelle. I shall have to wait and see."

"Well, we had a very good day. I embroidered five handkerchiefs and Aunt Nell made two blouses and sold them."

"Why that's spendid. Congratulations."

"It was good." Nell was modest about it but Mollie knew she was pleased.

"And I have made up my mind that I will not go to the jewellery shop," Chantelle said. "I know you do not want me there. I shall stay with Aunt Nell and help her."

Mollie, realising that Chantelle was in one of her moods, was determined not to encourage her. "I think that's sensible. There's not enough for more than two people to do."

"You and Mr Redgrave seem to find plenty to do."

"Not really. I would like to see Nell have some blouses to sell. On Sunday I shall stitch some up."

"That won't be necessary," Nell said. "You'll get busier as time goes on and you'll need to rest on Sundays."

"Well, we'll see, shall we?"

Chantelle went into a sulk and, picking up a piece of canvas, began to embroider it in silence. Nell winked at Mollie and began talking about the people who had been in the shop. Chantelle, realising that they were taking no notice of her, laid down her embroidery and said she was going to bed.

"Good night," said Nell and Mollie repeated it.

Chantelle stormed out without a word.

Nell smiled. "She's been as good as gold all day and then gets herself into a tantrum as soon as you come in."

"It's a pity, but really there isn't enough work for three people and especially for someone like Chantelle, who would have very little to do."

"She'll get over it and possibly settle down here with me. She does like this shop, she's always interested in what people want to buy, and I've let her serve some of the customers. I think what bothers her is that Ritchie has gone to your shop and stayed a while but was in here only a few minutes before he called on you this morning."

"It's only natural. He's paying the rent and has paid for all the stock. He'll want to know whether it's selling. I only wish that it was my business."

"Of course it is. Ritchie won't be after money from you until you can afford to pay."

"That bothers me, Nell. I want to be the owner. It's a dream of mine."

"Well, stop dreaming and think how lucky you are to have someone like Ritchie to pay for it."

Mollie sighed. "I know. But I can't stop the way I feel."

"Try thinking of Chantelle, who has no family, no money and is depending on us for her keep."

"Yes, I should, but I can't get it out of mind that she's a spirited girl who left Paris, thinking she would get a job and be fine. She's found it very different to what she imagined."

"I no longer think in that way. I feel sure there's a mystery about her and she has no idea what it is. She was talking today while we worked together and I felt really sorry for her. Don't be too hard on her, Mollie. You've fallen on your feet. First with the ladies' clothes shop and then this one. And you couldn't have a better man to help you than Mr Redgrave."

"I know. I should be grateful. I try to be," she gave a wry smile, "but somehow I still go on wishing it was my very own business."

"For heaven's sake, girl. It will be yours someday. Don't be greedy."

"Oh, dear," Mollie said. "That's a dreadful word. I hate it."

"Well, hate it enough to forget it."

"Look, Aunt Nell, I meant it when I said I would stitch some blouses on Sunday."

"I think we'll just let things take their course and hope that Chantelle will be in a better mood in the morning."

* * *

She was. She came down early all smiles and seemed anxious to be getting on with more embroidery. She even walked with Mollie to the crossroads to get the omnibus and waved to her when it left.

A strange girl, Mollie thought. But then Chantelle probably thought that she, Mollie, was strange!

Mollie began to think of the jewellery shop and to wonder if she could learn some more about the gemstones that day.

Mr Redgrave was there before her and after he had greeted her asked about her Aunt Nell.

"She's had a very hard life," he said. "I admire her courage in starting the shop and she's never aimed too high."

Mollie felt the colour come into her cheeks. Did he think that she was aiming too high? There were women in jewellers' shops. She had seen them. All a little older than herself. She was lucky to have Mr Redgrave. Very lucky indeed. No wonder her aunt had given her a little lecture the night before. But then, no two people were alike. She had worked hard at being a housemaid. Surely no one could deny her the right to have a business of her own. Oh, to the devil, she was not going to worry about it.

* * *

The following day they were busier still and all of the customers were pleasant to Mollie, women as well as men. She shared with Mr Redgrave in helping one or two of the women choose a gift for their husbands. Two of the women chose what Mollie had suggested.

111

One was buying a watch, the other a pair of gold cufflinks. Mollie had chosen a thinner watch, seeing that the husband did not have much strength, explaining that some of the watches were really heavy to keep handling.

"Now that is sensible," the woman said. "And he is a man who seems to like looking at a watch innumerable times. There's a clock in the room, but no, he wanted a watch that he could look at."

Mr Redgrave said, smiling, "I bow to my niece's choice."

"And that is sensible too," declared the woman. "It's not often that you find a man giving in to a woman!" To Mollie she said, "Thank you, my dear."

The other woman wanted a pair of cufflinks for her husband's birthday. "He's a big man and likes to show off a little." She smiled and Mollie thought she saw a look of mischief in her eyes. "He likes the ladies, does my husband, and I'm glad they like him."

Mr Redgrave brought out a tray of gold cufflinks, all deeply traced with patterns. The woman examined one or two, then she spoke to Mollie. "What do you think, Miss Paget?"

"Well . . . might I suggest something a little more noticeable?" She brought out a tray of cufflinks which were studded with a single ruby, a diamond and a turquoise. Mollie picked out a pair with sizeable turquoises.

"How about these? You could also buy him a tiepin to match, if you wished."

Mollie brought out a tray of tiepins.

The woman laughed and her eyes had a look of merriment in them. "Oh, he would love these. But can I afford both? Oh, well, I'll take them."

To Mr Redgrave she added, "You have a very wise niece, Mr Redgrave. You will be worth a fortune before long."

He opened his mouth to say something and Mollie,

guessing what it would be, said, "My uncle has a rare gift. I learn from him."

"Good."

She went out smiling, with two wrapped small boxes.

Mollie said, "Now . . . Uncle. Don't ever tell anyone that I own the shop. You are the expert—" She paused. "Oh, I can see it all now. The cufflinks were not what you normally would have chosen. What you did was to give me a chance to please the customer."

He gave her a broad smile. "Well, I had to get you started."

"Thank you," she said softly, knowing that she could never go wrong with a man who could act so generously.

Ritchie arrived just after twelve, saying, "I didn't know whether I was going to get away today." He looked around him. "Chantelle not here?"

"No, she wanted to stay and help Aunt Nell by doing her embroidery."

"Well, Aunt Nell will be pleased about that."

"She was, and I shall try in the future to help make some blouses on a Sunday."

"You'll need a rest on a Sunday, Mollie. Don't, for heaven's sake, overdo it."

"No, I won't." He sat staring at Mollie and she asked him what was wrong.

"It's Chantelle. It seemed to me that she couldn't wait to get here."

"It was probably that Aunt Nell and I told her that there wouldn't be much that she could do here. We didn't want to ruin the shop by having two assistants who didn't know anything about the work."

"Y–es. I suppose you did the right thing. The trouble is, of course, she's so touchy."

"Then she'll have to be touchy. We can't keep bowing to her and giving in all the time."

"Have you upset her?"

"Ritchie, she was smiling when she came down for breakfast this morning. She walked with me to the crossroads and waved me off when I got on the omnibus."

"Oh, then that's all right. I didn't want her upset. I can't help but feel sorry for her. As you know, she has no one belonging to her."

"I see you've been talking to Aunt Nell," Mollie said drily.

"No, I haven't. I do have a mind of my own."

Fortunately a customer came in and Mr Redgrave left them together.

Mollie said, "Sorry about that. But I do think that Chantelle will be better with Aunt Nell for the time being."

"You're probably right." He got up. "I think I'll go and have a word with them."

He left her, called something to Mr Redgrave and left.

Mollie was fuming. Damn Chantelle! It looked as if she was likely to upset her life.

A few minutes later she had calmed down. No, she was the one who was likely to upset her own life. It was stupid to blame Chantelle for the trouble. Chantelle had been most amenable this morning. Now Ritchie was upset. She had only herself to blame because she wanted a be a shop owner.

Well, that was something she was not going to change, not even if Ritchie was in love with Chantelle. If he was there was nothing she could do about it.

All the same there was a hurt feeling inside her. Blame yourself, she kept thinking, blame yourself. You're lucky that you will always have your aunt to love you.

At that moment two customers came in within five minutes of each other, and Mollie went out to see if she could help.

Ritchie did not come back that day and she wondered

if he would stay away for a while. He would, of course, be soon going abroad again.

When she got home that evening Nell and Chantelle were sitting over the the fire in the kitchen, chatting.

Aunt Nell said, "I'll make a cup of tea. Supper will be ready soon."

Mollie took off her coat and hung it up. "Well, and how has the day gone?"

"Very good," Nell said. "Chantelle embroidered another six handkerchiefs and sold three."

Before Mollie could reply, Chantelle said with a beaming smile, "And Aunt Nell made three blouses and sold two."

"I can't believe it!" Mollie laughed. "I'll be wishing I was back in ladies' wear again."

Chantelle seemed to close up. "I don't want to be back in that line again."

"I was only teasing."

"I don't like to talk about it."

Mollie decided to change the subect. She said brightly, "Did Ritchie call?"

Her aunt answered. "Yes, he did. He stayed quite a while. He was saying he would be going away again on Saturday. We'll miss him. He's always so cheerful."

At least he had not been talking about her, Mollie thought.

"But then," Chantelle said, "he has a right to be cheerful, with all the rolls of materials he sells and having a shop selling jewellery. He was saying how well the shop was doing."

Nell corrected her. "The jewellers does not belong to Ritchie. It's Mollie's shop."

"Not yet, it isn't. Not until she's paid her debt."

Chantelle was being nasty again. Mollie clenched her fists.

"I hope he hasn't spread that around."

"No he hasn't, Mollie," her aunt said sharply. She turned to Chantelle. "And I hope you haven't told anyone this?"

"Everybody knows it."

"Who is everybody?"

"Well, a lot of people. Customers who come in to the shop."

"None of my customers know any of this from me. Have you told them?"

Chantelle lowered her head. "No."

"Then who are these people? There aren't any, are there?"

"No." It was no more than a whisper.

Nell got to her feet. "Well, there's only one way to settle this. You'll have to go, Chantelle. I won't have lies told about Mollie. She's worked hard all her life. She's working hard now and you, just out of jealousy, tell lies about her. It can't be anything else."

"I won't any more, I promise."

"You've promised before and you haven't kept those promises. Well, I'm telling you now, Chantelle, and I will not tell you again, if you lie once more, or go into the sulks, you're out. I've had a hard life too and I see no reason why I should keep you on here to make our lives a misery."

Tears welled up in Chantelle's eyes and ran down her cheeks.

"What's more, tears don't soften me," Nell declared. "I've had Mollie here in my house and she's never, ever lied to me or troubled me in any way. And I don't see why we should suffer you, who are not in any way related to us."

Chantelle dried her eyes. "It won't happen any more and I mean it. I won't ever again tell lies or say nasty things or sulk. If I do, I shall leave at once."

116

"Good. Now, shall we have some supper?"

Mollie thought, good old Aunt Nell. Pray that Chantelle keeps her word, because she knew that Nell meant every word she said.

Chapter Nine

Although the evening before had been a bit of a trial, Chantelle was quite bright the next morning.

Nell was up earlier than both the girls and already had two blouses cut out ready to stitch. "I thought I would have a good start. I want to be prepared in case there's a rush."

For a few seconds Mollie had a yearning to be back in ladies' wear. Then she thought how lucky she was to be in jewellery. There were more goods sold in a day than in a ladies' wear shop. In her kind of shop anyway. In a store it was different.

Chantelle insisted on cooking the breakfast, something she had never done before. But when Mollie was ready to walk to the omnibus, Chantelle did not ask to walk with her. Mollie was glad. She had no wish to make idle talk.

Mr Redgrave was again at the shop before her. It would probably stay like that because he came in a cab. There was no omnibus that would get her there before him.

As soon as Mollie had taken off her hat and coat she dusted all the shelves, including the trays of jewellery.

She studied the stones as she worked. Mr Redgrave came in saying, "They are lovely, aren't they?"

"Did your wife like them?"

"Most of them, not all."

"Oh, why was that?"

"She had worn bracelets, rings, necklaces and brooches

at different times and she said she found that certain stones always brought bad luck."

"Which stones were they?"

"I'm afraid I won't tell you that."

"Why?"

"Because you would perhaps avoid them."

"I wouldn't. I'm not superstitious."

"Nearly every person I know says they are not superstitious but, if they were wearing certain stones and every time they had worn them some trouble had occurred, they would blame the stones for the trouble."

"I'm sure I wouldn't blame them."

He laughed softly. "I'm not going to take the risk."

Mollie became more and more serious about wearing stones. She just had to know. Unfortunately, she didn't have enough money to buy one. Then one day she found a box of mixed stones in a box under one of the shelves. When she asked Mr Redgrave why they were there he said they were all slightly flawed and added that one of these days she should send them back to the men who cut and shaped them.

She asked if it was the stones that had flaws in them that were the ones which brought the bad luck.

"Not at all. Perfect stones are involved."

"Do you know of any other people who have this feeling of bad luck?"

"Oh, indeed yes. I should imagine it's something that's gone on for centuries. There is a story of a king who had a stone taken from his crown because it was bad luck. His three children had died, with no known illness and then his two brothers died. One of the brothers had told the King to take this particular stone from his crown to stop the deaths. He did so and no one else died for many years."

Mollie smiled and asked if he would tell her what the stone was, and he said, "It was never known."

Whether it was or not she had no idea.

Once she asked a customer if she was satisfied with a stone she had brought recently. It was an aquamarine.

"Oh yes, indeed," the woman said. "It's a lucky stone. So many lovely things have happened since I bought it. Both my daughters have become engaged. My son's wife has given birth to triplets and they are all so strong and very good babies. And also my husband has been promoted to a very good job in his firm. I would not part with it. Look how it shines." She held out her hand. "Isn't it just beautiful? I have no regrets. I tell all my friends to buy an aquamarine."

Mollie gave up – at least for the time being.

She missed seeing Ritchie. He had gone away this time without coming to say goodbye. She tried not to feel hurt, but the thought was with her every day that he could at least have left a note for her.

Then, what hurt her more than ever was that one evening when she went home Chantelle was joyful. She had received a letter from Ritchie.

"It's the first letter I've ever had in my life!"

"The first one you know about," Nell said quietly.

"Of course."

"So what does he have to say?" Mollie tried to speak casually. "Where is he this time?"

"Holland. He's enjoying it. He should be back in a week's time."

"Good."

Chantelle held the letter to her, her eyes shining. "I shall put it under my pillow tonight."

Nell said wryly, "It's not a love letter, Chantelle, it's just a few lines telling us where he is."

"I would put any letter I get under my pillow," she said quietly and, picking up her sampler, she did some stitches, then looked up. "Please don't begrudge me," she said, glancing from Nell to Mollie. "It really is special to me because a friend bothered to write me a few lines."

Mollie felt how mean she had been. She must mend her ways with Chantelle. The girl was right. Ritchie must have known how a few lines would please Chantelle.

* * *

When Mollie went to the shop the next day she took a small ruby out of the 'flawed' box and after wrapping it in a piece of cloth she put it into the pocket of her dress to see what would happen.

Nothing, bad or good, happened.

On the Saturday morning she replaced the piece of ruby for a piece of aquamarine.

To her pleasure Ritchie came in breezily during the morning and stayed talking, telling Mollie and Mr Redgrave how well he had done in Holland.

Mollie could not help smiling. The aquamarine was doing its work. "So you have some more customers," she said. "Where are you going to put all your rolls of materials?"

He grinned. "I've rented yet another warehouse on the docks."

"You are doing well. May your good luck continue."

Mr Redgrave was in the shop attending to a customer and Ritchie said, "I think that you're doing very well in this business. It'll be a success, I feel it. More so than the other shop you had. Do you enjoy being in the jewellery trade?"

"Yes, I do. There are so many beautiful items. I still have a lot to learn, of course, whereas I didn't feel that way in the other trade. I felt when I moved in that I knew everything."

"I still wonder at times who burned the shop down," Ritchie said. "I know that bloke was arrested for it but I think that someone put him up to it."

"So do I. I'm sure it was Anne. Why should she have vanished? There was no reason to do so. I think it was done out of jealousy. She thought that Chantelle was after Clifford. I haven't set eyes on him since the theatre night."

"Nor do you want to. I wouldn't be surprised if someone told me he was involved with Anne."

"I don't think he would have had the courage."

"Don't be too sure. I always thought there was something strange about him."

Mr Redgrave came into the back room. "Well, we've had a good start this morning. We've sold two expensive watches, a diamond brooch, a necklace and an engagement ring."

Ritchie smiled. "Keep it up. I must be going. I'm going to Aunt Nell's this evening, Mollie. If I can catch you in time I'll pick you up."

"Oh, splendid, it will be a nice change. Those horse omnibuses are so slow."

With a cheery wave, Ritchie was gone.

Mr Redgrave said, "I could take you home some evenings, Mollie. I do have a carriage."

"Oh, no, I wouldn't think about it."

"I couldn't take you every night, I have meetings, but there are evenings when I could take you. And I would like to see your aunt. My wife and I and Nell were very good friends at one time. It was when we both got shops that we separated. We were tied to our shops. It was such a pity. She has a hard life."

"Yes, she has, but she loves her shop and her customers. She would be delighted to see you again, I know."

"Then I'll do that. Oh, another customer."

It was a very busy day and Mollie felt she was getting on quite well with the customers. The aquamarine was working.

When closing time came she was ready for Ritchie to

pick her up. But he didn't call and in the end she had to run to catch the omnibus.

She was breathless when she sat down and found herself thinking of the aquamarine. Not so good as she had imagined.

When she opened the door she heard talking and laughter. Someone must have called on her aunt.

When she went to open the kitchen door it opened and her aunt said, "Oh, it's you, Mollie. Ritchie is here. He thought he would be too late to pick you up."

Mollie was fuming but was determined not to show it.

"Oh, there you are, Mollie," he greeted her, getting up. "I was just too late to catch you."

"Well, I did wait for you and then in the end had to run all the way to catch the omnibus. But never mind, no harm done."

Mollie took off her hat and coat and Chantelle said, "Ritchie, you didn't finish telling us the story."

"No, I didn't, did I?"

Mollie was too angry to listen. Nell said, "The meal is nearly ready, but Ritchie says he has to be going. He was only waiting to see you."

Mollie made no answer but began to set the table.

Ritchie got up and came over to her. "I haven't upset you, have I, Mollie?"

"No, of course not." She turned to her aunt. "Oh, Aunt Nell, while I think of it, Mr Redgrave will bring me home tomorrow night. He wants to see you again. He said that you and his wife and he were good friends at one time."

Colour came to Nell's cheeks and she began to tidy her hair as though he was coming at any minute.

"It will be nice to see him. It's been such a long time."

Ritchie repeated that he must be going and Nell said, "Oh, sorry, Ritchie. I'm neglecting you. It was nice to see you. Look after yourself."

"I will, see you sometime." He waved a hand and was away.

Chantelle said, "I don't think that either of you were very nice to him. He came especially to see us, yes and Mollie too, and although he said he must be going, Mollie starts to tell you about this Mr Redgrave."

Mollie said, "I mentioned it then because I thought I might forget to tell Aunt Nell later. And because you think that the sun shines out of Ritchie doesn't mean that we do. He's a good friend, that's all."

Chantelle looked angry. "Yes and—"

"That's all," Nell said. "Subject is closed."

Molly went over the evening when she was in bed. Was Ritchie unconsciously in love with Chantelle? He could be. He obviously had not made any attempt to call for her. It was the way he had handled it that annoyed her so.

Then she thought, but why should she be so upset? He had a life to lead. Even if he had been in love with her she had no wish to be married. All she wanted was to be in charge of a shop. Her own shop.

It was the letter of course that had irritated her. He had never once sent her a letter when he had gone abroad. There was nothing to stop him sending her one too. After all, they were in business together. Perhaps it was just because he felt sorry for Chantelle. She had no family. Well, she would not think any more about it.

The next morning Mollie was quiet and when Mr Redgrave asked if anything was wrong she said, "No. No, it was just that I was thinking about the woman who swore that wearing an aquamarine had brought her luck."

"The stones do mean a lot to many women."

Mollie gave a little laugh. "Well, I tried it but—"

"Nothing good happened, is that it?"

"Well, I tried a small ruby, one of the flawed ones and nothing good or bad happened. Then I thought I would

125

try an aqamarine. At first I thought it was working well, then everything went wrong, so I gave up."

"Now then, everyone has a different stone. It depends on their birth date. What is your birth date?"

Mollie gave him a quick grin. "I don't think I'll tell you."

He smiled. "Right, I think we should have a talk about the stones. Many people buy them without knowing that the stone they have bought may not be for them. For thousands of years people have depended on the stones to cure them from illnesses. And they still wear them. Men as well as women.

"This is something you should know because you will be able to tell customers what the right stone is for them."

Molly looked at Mr Redgrave with some curiosity. "Do you believe in them?"

He seemed hesitant for a moment then said, "I'm not quite sure. My wife had great faith in her stone, but she died. On the other hand, people can't live for ever."

There was pain in his voice and she said quietly, "I'll learn about the stones sometime for the sake of the business."

He straightened his shoulders. "No, Molly, I think we'll start right now. I've been very lax with you. I should have thought about it before now. Quite a lot of female customers want to know about the different stones and how they will benefit by wearing one. We'll go into the back room and discuss it, while we have the chance."

Mr Redgrave pulled out a chair for Mollie while he took a book from a shelf and sat down opposite to her.

He began, "There are a number of ways of dealing with the stones, and most of them start with Aries, which is March, and finish the twelve months at the end of February in the following year." He paused. "Actually, there are a number of different lists and I found one that I like better than all the others. It starts at the beginning of January, goes on with the dates until the twenty first then starts

126

the second half from the eighteenth and ends at the last day in the month. The first one on my list is the ruby."

He opened the book.

" 'This stone takes its name from a Latin word meaning its red colour. The gem has for thousands of years throughout the Orient been esteemed for its marvellous beauty and the precious gifts it confers upon the wearer. Its attribute is contentment.

'Rubies vary in hue from a delicate pale pink to the deepest of reds. Like certain other gems of rich colour the ruby is believed to grow paler when illness or other misfortunes occur.

'Worn on the brow the gem was said to give insight and mental power. When applied to the heart, its influence was a very stimulating one.

" 'Ruby' people have strong marriages, very few ever part.' " He looked up and smiled, "I don't think that anyone can fault that. To have contentment is a wonderful thing.

"Now I must say that these lists vary a great deal as there are dozens and dozens of stones. You may find some in my list that are not on the lists that other people have.

"For the second half of January we go on to rock crystal."

He looked to his book again.

" 'Rock crystal is a colourless, transparent variety of quartz. It's the stone from which crystal gazers' globes are fashioned. Of great repute in the Orient, rock crystal is used for magic purposes in the forms of charms and talismans.' "

Mr Redgrave paused once more. "You may not believe this but when I was abroad and in my teens I had my fortune told by a crystal gazer. My goodness, how true it was. Although then, when I came out of the tent, I laughed myself silly at all he told me. But so far, everything he told has come true." He suddenly looked very solemn.

"He even told me the day and the year that my wife would die."

Mollie gave a little shiver. "How terrible."

"Yes. Well now, we must move on."

"'The medicinal use of this mineral goes back to early times. A small quantity of powdered rock crystal would be sprinkled over the body and the person would not only sleep soundly but any small pain would have disappeared by the next morning.'"

Mollie smiled. "One of these half months is going to make me happy."

"Oh now, there can be snags. Some of these stones may do nothing for the wearer, in spite of them being that person's birth stone. So you may have to experiment. But I must say now that there have not been many failures. There are dozens and dozens of stones to try for success."

"Good. I hope I find that my birth stone will be successful."

Mr Redgrave's eyes twinkled. "Are you still going to keep your birth date from me?"

Mollie chuckled. "Yes, until it comes up."

"Well, we'll finish the rock crystal first. 'These people are musical. And most of them are very good. Quite a lot get to the top of their profession. A musical man will very often marry a musical women. They get on well, seldom quarrel. Or, if they do, it's soon over.' You're not bored, are you?"

"Not at all. I find it quite fascinating."

The shop door bell rang and Mr Redgrave spread his hands.

"A customer at last. I'll go out but you'd better follow in case it's a lady wanting to buy an article to try her luck."

The customer was a tall, attractive young man, well-dressed. He said to Mr Redgrave, "I want to buy a present for my mother."

He spoke beautifully too.

Mollie kept in the background but he must have been aware of the movement and turned. He lifted his hat and smiled. "Perhaps you can help me too. I want to buy a present for my mother's birthday. It's tomorrow."

Mr Redgrave said, "This is my niece, Miss Paget. She's learning about jewellery and I'm sure that together we'll find something suitable."

Mollie said calmly, "Have you any idea what you think your mother might like? A brooch, a ring, a watch?"

His smile widened. "My mother is a very difficult woman. She doesn't wear jewellery but today when I asked her what she would like she said, 'Get what you like, but not chocolates.'" He spread his hands. "So?"

Mollie said, "Why not take a brooch and see how she likes it? If she's against it, we'll take it back and refund the money. That's right, Uncle, is it not?"

"Oh, yes. Yes, of course."

"Well, that is fair. It's very kind of you. I shall look at brooches, but I shall let you choose one, Miss Paget."

Mollie brought out a tray with some beautiful brooches, some of them studded with tiny stones. There were several of birds. Mollie took one of these and held it out. The bird was white and the tail was made of tiny stones shading from pale blue to a deeper blue then to dark green.

He took it from her. "This looks attractive. But would Mama wear it? Still, she left it to me. I'll take this one."

Mollie said they had other trays of brooches but he said no, he really liked that one. And, if his mother was not interested then he had sisters and dozens of cousins who all liked pretty things.

Lucky man, Mollie thought. A big family.

She found a box, and wrapped the brooch while the young man paid for it.

"Thank you so much," he said. "You've been most kind."

"It's been a pleasure," she replied.

"You shall see me again."

He raised his hat to both of them and left.

"Well, that was a very nice sale," Mr Redgrave said. He gave Mollie a broad smile. "I think you have that selling quality. He didn't know me, but I know him – at least I know his father. He has a big business in the West End. I wonder what brought his son to these parts?"

"I've noticed that quite a few people with money come into the shop."

"Mr Grainger is a millionaire."

"Oh." Mollie's eyes were wide. "As rich as that? Goodness, we could do with a few more millionaires."

Mr Redgrave said solemnly, "Rich men are not usually big spenders. We shall have to wait and see if Mr Grainger's son will come again." Then he added, "Now then, do we go on with the months of the year?"

"I certainly find it interesting."

"We've finished with January so we'll move to the first half of February, which begins with the amethyst. 'Begin with a few amethysts. First rub your hands together, then place your hands above the stones. Hold them for a few minutes. If you don't feel a coolness then the stone is not for you.

'It's a form of quartz with a beautiful violet or purple hue. In earlier times, the amethyst was believed to have a calming and soothing influence. When its wearer became ill the stone changed colour. When brought near poisoned food it lost all its brightness.

'An amethyst wrapped in silk and bound tightly to the temples is reputed to be a remedy for a nervous headache.

'Amethyst people are kindly folk, they always try to help others in trouble. They make good, sensible parents.'" He paused. "Should we go on to the second part of February, which deals with the opal?"

"I would like to."

"Good." Mr Redgrave was back to the book.

" 'The opal brings miraculous order to a wealth of patterns and colours. It's the stone of hope and justice. Upstart and tyrannical monarchs, exloiting the miseries of their subjects, were once terrified of this gem. Alexander the Great proudly wore an opal in his girdle. Queen Elizabeth I, though she collected opals, was afraid to wear one. Queen Victoria had more opals than any other monarch and gave one to each of her daughters on their wedding days, but seldom wore one herself.

'It needed faith to wear an opal and those who did have faith found that they had a happy and colorful life. They were very healthy people and had healthy children.' "

Mollie's face flushed. She got up. "I think that someone has come into the shop."

Mr Redgrave got up. "Are you sure?"

He hurried out but was soon back. "A pity, you were mistaken. I hope we are going to have some customers soon."

As he finished speaking the door bell pealed. "Oh, thank goodness!" He flashed a smile at Mollie. "You'd better follow in case it's a few millionaires."

"That will be the day!"

It was quite a busy day. Nothing really expensive was sold but the amount added up.

Mr Redgrave said solemnly, "Well, you know, I would be satisfied if we could keep on having days like this, and I'm sure you will feel the same."

"I do, definitely."

"It'll soon be time to go to your Aunt Nell's. I'm looking forward to it. It's such a long time since I've seen her."

Promptly at seven they went out to the carriage. It was bitterly cold and when Mollie was settled in her seat Mr Redgrave wrapped a tartan shawl around her.

She thought how nice it was to have a man look after her. Ritchie would never think of such a thing.

When the carriage started Mr Redgrave said, "Would you mind, Mollie, if I asked you one or two questions about your aunt?"

"No, of course not. Ask anything you wish."

"It's a long time since we met. Is she still the dear, friendly person she was when I knew her? Some people when they get older become tetchy."

Mollie laughed, "There's nothing tetchy about Nell. She does look frail at times but she's quite strong. She enjoys her shop and her customers. She's always helping someone and often I think gives them a little money."

"Dear Nell," he said softly. "We were such good friends when we were younger. Oh, please," he went on quickly, "don't get me wrong. There was no affair, or anything like that. We were really just good friends."

"I understand," Mollie said softly.

She wondered if he had been in love with her aunt. He looked a little bit dreamy.

Her Aunt Nell was there waiting for them when the carriage arrived and looked so different that Mollie marvelled at the change in her.

She had never known her aunt wear anything else but a plain black dress after her husband died. Also, her hair was always drawn severely back and pinned in a bun.

Now, although she still wore a black dress, it was trimmed with a beautiful white lace collar. And her hair had been curled and fastened on top of her head, with curling strands framing her face.

She came forward, colour in her cheeks, a definite look of love in her eyes. She held out her hands.

"How wonderful to see you again, Philip."

He gripped her hands and said softly, "You haven't changed a bit, Nell."

"Come into the kitchen," she said. "I've made a bit of a dinner."

He began to protest but she put a finger to his lips. "It's beef and Yorkshire pudding. Give me your hat and coat and I'll hang them up."

When they entered the kitchen, Chantelle was waiting, looking very shy. Mr Redgrave gave her a slight bow.

"How are you, Miss Chantelle?" he asked. "It's good to see you again."

"I am pleased to see you," she answered demurely.

Nell motioned them to the table. "Shall we all sit down? The meal is ready."

Mollie simply could not get used to the change in her aunt. It was easy to picture what she had been like when she was young. She wanted to help Nell serve the meal but everything was ready in the kitchen stove. Mr Redgrave and Nell talked about when they were young and for once Chantelle did not have anything to say.

They talked about the picnics they used to have, a time that Mollie had no memory of, but it was all so simple and sweet that she wished she had taken part in them.

Mr Redgrave talked about their walks over heather-clad fells and said how wonderful it was that they could stand and enjoy the singing of the birds.

Mollie just had to know if they were both married then and Nell said solemnly, "No, we were just friends. Six months later we were both engaged to different people. A year after I married, Tom was lost at sea. That was a dreadful time."

There was silence for a moment, then her aunt sat up.

"Do any of you want more meat or Yorkshire pudding? Don't forget there's trifle to follow."

Mr Redgrave replied smiling, "The meal was most enjoyable but I also enjoy trifle."

Nell allowed Mollie to serve it.

Chapter Ten

Chantelle had little to say that evening but after Mr Redgrave had left she said what a lovely man he was, then added she was going to bed.

"What has happened?" Nell asked as she took pins from her hair and let it fall over her shoulders. "Has she fallen in love with Philip?"

"It's possible, anything is possible with Chantelle. The question is, however, have you fallen in love with him?"

Nell sighed, "I've been in love with him since I was eighteen. He wasn't in love with me then. He met Elizabeth two years later. Then I met Tom and the rest you know.

"After Tom had drowned Philip told me that his wife had said she was not in love with him. She had married him because her parents told her it was time she was married. She was then twenty-three and he was twenty-five." She paused. "Apparently she was a good wife and agreed to go with him into the jewellery business. It was so sad, because eventually she became ill and died. I think she had cancer."

"Were you in the shop then?"

"Yes, I took it after Tom had died. As you know I kept having you come to stay with me when your mother had to go into hospital. You were like my own child. Philip and I didn't meet any more. He never, ever hinted that he was in love with me."

"Would you marry him if he asked you?"

"I don't know, Mollie. I really don't know. We're not young any longer."

"You looked lovely today."

"Chantelle did my hair for me. What a strange girl she is. She swears she's in love with Ritchie and also swears that he's in love with her. What do you think?"

Mollie drew herself up. "All I want is a shop that belongs to me. I'm – fond of Ritchie and I would be hurt if he did fall in love with Chantelle, because she would never bring any happiness into his life. Today was the only time that she hasn't made eyes at a man when she's been in contact with one. I can't understand why she didn't fuss over Philip."

"Perhaps she guessed he was in love with me."

"I really don't think it would have stopped her making a fuss over him. She knew that Ritchie liked me, but that didn't make any difference to her."

"I'm a lot older than you, my love. Perhaps she wanted me to have some special happiness. I don't know. I'll just let things take their course. I always have done. I'm sleepy now and ready for bed."

Mollie lay awake a long time going over everything but eventually drifted into sleep.

* * *

When she went downstairs the next morning Nell was busy cutting out a blouse and Chantelle was cooking the breakfast. They both greeted her cheerfully. Nell and Chantelle talked about meals when they sat down. No mention was made at all of the previous night. So . . . what did it mean? She probably would never know. Then she wondered if Mr Redgrave would want to talk about it. Well, she would just have to wait and see.

Although he greeted her cheerfully when she arrived at the shop, he spent the first twenty minutes studying a ledger. Was he not going to talk about the meeting either?

They had a customer and after the man had been dealt with he said, smiling, "Well, I thought it was

136

a very good evening last night. What did you think, Mollie?"

"I found it very – interesting."

"Nell hasn't changed. I was glad. Did she say anything this morning?"

"No, not a thing." Then, seeing a disappointed look in his eyes, she said, "I think it was something she wanted to keep to herself. She would, no doubt, want to think it over. I know she enjoyed the evening. It went very well." Mollie smiled. "I feel she probably sensed that there was something between the two of you and didn't want to spoil it."

Mr Redgrave was bright again. "Do you feel you would like to get on with the stones of March?"

"Yes, I would, but after I've done all the dusting."

With the dusting finished they both went into the back room. Mr Redgrave brought his book from the shelf and turned to the right page, then sat down.

"Now the first half of March begins with the sapphire, and I'll get started.

'It's related to the ruby – a fact that not many people know. This remarkable stone comes in a whole range of colours, but the best-known and loved is the dark blue variety. In healing terms it is excellent against fevers and illnesses of all kinds.

'The cornflower sapphire and other vibrant hues are reputed to lengthen life and keep their wearers looking young. It also nourishes the central nervous system. The pink-violet sapphire encourages selfless love.

'There are many sapphire wearers, but quite a few think only of themselves. The dark blue sapphire would help this type of person to think before they act.'"

Mr Redgrave closed the book. "That's the sapphire done. I think now that we shall stop and have a cup of tea. And hope for customers. Is that all right with you, Mollie?"

She smiled. "Yes, of course, but I must admit I enjoy hearing about the birthstones."

While Mollie drank her tea Mr Redgrave talked again about the evening before and Mollie had a feeling that he sure that Nell was ready to marry him.

She spoke to him gently. "Are you not expecting too much, Mr Redgrave? You haven't seen Nell for a very long time, and when you do you expect her to fall into your arms right away."

He looked a little sheepish. "Oh, dear, was it so obvious? It was with all this waiting. I never thought of myself as someone who rushed into things. I must alter my tactics."

Mollie was silent for a few moments, then she said, "I'll try and pin Nell down tomorrow. I can't promise any progress but she will probably want to talk about it too. Some more tea?"

"No, not for me, thanks."

Before the cups were washed some more customers came in and before they could get to the back room again, who should come in but Mr Grainger and two young ladies. They appeared to be between fourteen and sixteen. They were both attractive and well-dressed.

Mr Grainger smiled and swept off his hat. He greeted Mr Redgrave, then bowed slightly to Mollie. "Good morning, Miss Paget. I was telling my two sisters about meeting you and how kind you had been in helping me to choose something for Mama's birthday present and they insisted I bring them to meet you. They want a present for a friend."

"It was a pleasure," she said. "Did your mother like the brooch."

"We don't know, do we, girls?" He laughed his lovely laugh and his sisters chuckled.

"Mama did say thanks but that was all."

His sisters became helpless with laughter, then suddenly stopped, apologised and the elder one said, "We are so sorry for our behaviour but our Mama is never quite sure whether she likes a present or not. We think she liked it. The brooch was pinned to her nightdress this morning."

Their brother said, "Now tell Miss Paget why we are here this morning."

The elder girl straightened her shoulders and said, "We have come to buy a friend a birthday present and Nicholas thought you would advise us."

So his name was Nicholas. Mollie liked it.

"I would be very pleased to help you. Have you anything in mind?"

"Yes, we know she would very much like a watch. Not a big one. Something small and pretty. Not too expensive."

Mr Redgrave brought chairs for all of them to sit at a table where customers could make a choice. Then he stood aside, smiling a little as Mollie brought a tray of watches from one of the big cases and put it on the table. She lifted out two watches. The first one was silver, quite small, with tiny forget-me-nots woven in and out of the numbers.

The younger sister said, "Oh, isn't that one pretty?"

The older sister picked up a gold one, cut in an octave shape, which had Roman numerals.

Mr Grainger chose a slightly larger gold watch with nothing fancy about it at all. "I like this one," he said.

"But it's not pretty," declared the younger girl. "Marian loves pretty things."

"Marian," said her sister, "is a clumsy girl, who is forever falling over. This watch would be utterly useless in a few weeks' time."

"We have many more watches to show you," Mollie said. She lifted another tray of watches out and the girls studied them, picked some out and put them back, both saying they were not really sure what they wanted. Mr Grainger turned to Mollie. "Would you make a choice, Miss Paget, please?"

Mollie knew she must not offend any of them.

"Well now," she began, and paused a few seconds before going on, "I take it that you want to buy your friend something she will be really pleased with."

"Oh, yes," the two girls said and the gaze of all three went to went to the watches they had chosen. The younger sister picked up the one which was her choice, her sister picked up hers and Mr Grainger smiled.

"I think we all know what you mean, Miss Paget. Our friend Marian likes pretty things. If she falls down and breaks the watch there's nothing can be done about it. For a time however she'll have enjoyed her present. You are a very sensible young lady, Miss Paget. We shall have the watch and we shall come again for further presents."

Mollie was delighted with the response but she said modestly, "Thank you, sir. My uncle and I will be pleased to serve you."

She put the watch in a small fancy box and wrapped it while Mr Redgrave received payment for it.

Before they left Mr Grainger said, "It will not be long before we shall be seeing you again. So many birthdays to deal with." The girls smiled and dipped curtseys and they were gone.

Mr Redgrave had a broad smile on his face.

"It looks as if we have fallen on our feet, as the saying goes. If they come to buy gifts regularly—"

"That is, *if* they do," Mollie replied, somewhat drily. "Some people are all talk."

Mr Redgrave rubbed his finger under his chin. "I don't think that applies to Mr Grainger. One senses people over the years. We shall see them again. I know it."

"Good. I hope you are right. It will raise our sales if they come fairly regularly."

Mollie could hardly wait to get home that night to tell her Aunt Nell. She was not quite sure how Chantelle would take it. Would it make her determined to serve in the shop? Determined or not, she would be barred.

Whether people had seen the visit of the Graingers Mollie was not sure, but they did have quite a lot of customers in and not one left without buying something.

There was no time for further talk that day of the stones. Mollie had to travel by the horse-drawn omnibus that evening and she practically ran to her aunt's once she was off the bus.

She was into the kitchen before her aunt had time to get into the shop. Then she stopped. Her aunt was on her feet but sitting before a blazing fire were Ritchie and Chantelle.

A bitterness soured Mollie's tongue. Ritchie got to his feet. "Hello, Mollie. I knew you were due home so thought I would stop and see you as I was passing through."

He was lying. He had glanced at Chantelle with a loving look. And she was brazenly staring at him with a look of conquest in her eyes.

"Give me your hat and coat, Mollie," her aunt said, "and I'll hang them up. You look frozen, go and sit by the fire. How has the day gone?"

Mollie pulled herself together. "Oh, splendid. Mr Grainger was in with two of his sisters to buy a birthday present for a friend and he's promised to buy more presents."

"A good show," Ritchie said, all his attention was on Mollie. "How much did he spend?"

She told him. Chantelle listened but never said a word. Mollie described their clothes and talked about all of the customers who had come in that afternoon. She was excited and began to wonder if she had wronged

141

Ritchie and Chantelle. She could have done. Anger always exaggerated things.

Ritchie said, "I felt right from the start that this shop was going to do well. How could it fail with Mr Redgrave in it?"

"As I see it," Nell said, "it was Mollie who sold Mr Grainger a brooch for his mother the first time and today she sold the watch. Mr Redgrave had nothing to do with it."

"Thank you," Mollie said. "I'm glad someone recognised my strength."

Ritchie laughed, "Oh, come on, don't be peeved because I praised Mr Redgrave. He is a good businessman."

"Yes, I know. But even he had the decency to praise me for what I had done and told me I had the gift of salemanship."

"And so you have, my love," Ritchie said softly.

Chantelle sat up straight. "Don't forget, Mollie, that you would not be in the shop at all if it was not for Ritchie who . . ."

"Let's forget it," Ritchie said quietly. "I do appreciate the fact that Mollie is cut out for such a job and I'm grateful, very grateful. Now, I must go. I'll call and see you in the morning, Mollie. I'll give you a lift to the shop. I have to be up very early in the morning. I won't let you down, I promise. Good night all."

There was a silence after he had gone, then Nell said, "The meal will be ready. Let's have it."

They sat at the table eating, without saying a word. Then Mollie spoke. "This seems to be becoming a habit. We must stop going on in this way."

"I'm to blame." There was misery in Chantelle's voice. "I shall try very hard not to say all the wrong things."

Nell told them that she was as much to blame and Mollie said, "Let us all forget it. Tell me how you've got on today?"

142

The pettiness had gone as Nell told them that she had made and sold three blouses and that Chantelle had made five handkerchiefs again and sold all five.

"Oh, that's splendid," Mollie said. "You'll be needing a bigger shop soon."

"Never!" Nell declared laughing. "I'm attached to this old shop and shall probably end my days here."

They were friends again, and as always Chantelle went to bed before Nell and Mollie were ready.

When they were alone, Nell shook her head slowly. "Why is it that Chantelle always gets my back up?"

"She does mine and always will do. I keep wondering if she is in love with Ritchie and if Ritchie is in love with her."

"I don't think that Ritchie is in love with Chantelle. And, in fact, I would say he's in love with you."

"I don't think so."

Nell said, "Has Philip mentioned me today?"

"Yes he has, several times. Can you give him any hope?"

A dreaminess had come into Nell's eyes. She had her plain black dress on again, but she had kept her hair up and tendrils of hair at the sides made her look much younger.

"I have thought a lot about him today. I would like to be married to him – but not yet."

"Why not?"

"I'll have to give up the shop, and of course I have my customers to think about. Also, there's Chantelle. I won't have her living with Philip and myself and I know that you don't want her in the shop. It wouldn't work."

"I know, but I'm responsible for her. I brought her here with me. I shall have to think of something if you and Philip get married."

"Well, I can tell you now it will be another year before we do marry."

143

"A year? That's a long time. I don't think that Mr Redgrave will be pleased about that."

"He will, if he really wants me." Nell spoke softly.

Mollie thought, well she's known him long enough. She must be sure that he'll wait.

* * *

The next morning Mollie was up earlier than usual. She washed and had had a quick breakfast when Ritchie arrived. She asked him if he wanted anything to eat and he said no, that he thought it would be a chance for the two of them to talk as he was passing this way.

"You don't usually come this way," she said as she got into the van.

"No, I – er – have some new customers in the vicinity."

He was always joyful when he had some new customers but not this time. In fact, last night in the gaslight he had looked very tired.

"Are these new customers worthwhile?" she asked. "You don't seem very pleased about them."

"Of course I am. The more the merrier." He was quite glum.

Should she change the subject? She decided it might be wiser to ask him if Chantelle had ever mentioned wanting to work into the jewellery shop.

"She has once or twice but I never felt she was really keen about it. She seems happy enough working with Nell. By the way, is Nell in love with Mr Redgrave? Does she want to marry him?"

"Y-yes. But she wants to wait a year."

He turned his head to look at her. "Whatever for? It's not as if they're youngsters."

"I know, but Nell is thinking about her customers. She loves the shop and her customers. They tell her all their troubles."

144

"She's a fool." He sounded bitter, which was unusual for Ritchie. There was something wrong with him. Had he fallen in love with Chantelle and did not want to mention it? She took the plunge.

"Ritchie, are you in love with Chantelle?"

He was silent for a moment and Mollie's heartbeat quickened.

"I think so," he said at last, "but I know I would be a fool to tell her so. She always wants to cling to me. But it seems she falls in love with every young man she meets. Not that she does meet many men nowadays."

Mollie was aware of a pain deep inside her. She had herself to blame. She had not wanted a man in her life. She wanted to have her own business. She said, "But why do you keep going to Aunt Nell's so often? Chantelle will think you go just to see her."

"I do. That's the problem. Oh, God, what a mess I'm in."

Mollie pulled herself together. "You will have to make up your mind. Either stay away from her or tell her you love her."

"But I don't know!"

"That's rubbish. You either want her and will want her always or you don't want her enough to marry her."

"I tell you, I just don't know." He spoke quietly this time.

"There's something else bothering you, isn't there?" Mollie spoke quietly too.

Ritchie made no reply for a while then he said, "Yes, but there's nothing you can do to help."

"Try me."

"No. Leave it at that, will you?"

"We are friends."

"Friends will be no help."

"Look, I—"

"Please. I don't want to talk about it any more."

Nothing else was said until they arrived at the shop and then Ritchie said, "It's not an insurmountable thing. I'll be going away tomorrow. I'll be back in about a fortnight." He helped her out of the van. "I'll come and see you then, hope all goes well for you. Bye." He gave her a quick kiss on the cheek, then he was gone.

Mollie stood watching the van disappearing, then she walked to the shop door and unlocked it. What on earth could be the matter? Was he short of money? No, not when he was able to fill three warehouses with rolls of material. He was away again tomorrow, no doubt to buy more.

Surely he could have told her what was wrong?

She made a cup of tea and sat down to drink it. It was so unlike Ritchie to be in such a mood. Her heart began to thump as something occurred to her suddenly. Had Ritchie made love to Chantelle and gotten her pregnant? That would be enough to make him bitter. On the other hand he was a man of the world and would not put himself in such a position. If only he had told her what was wrong.

The shop door opened and Mr Redgrave called, "Mollie—"

She jumped up. "Yes, Mr Redgrave, I'm here."

She came out of the back room and forced a smile. "I didn't expect you so soon. Ritchie brought me, he was leaving early. There's tea in the pot. Shall I pour you a cup?"

"I would welcome one. Thanks." He took off his hat and coat and hung them up. "It's a nasty morning, a misty fog."

Mollie had not noticed. He came over to the table, sat down and took a drink of the tea. "That's very welcome. I wonder what sort of day it will be today? I wonder if Mr Grainger will come with some of his youngsters?"

"I doubt it. We can't expect him every day."

"No, I suppose not."

They chatted about small things for a few moments then he asked Mollie quietly if her aunt had said anything about him.

Glad to get forget her problems, Mollie said brightly, "Indeed she did. She said she would marry you."

"No! I can't believe it."

"But not for a year."

"That's not important," he said smiling. "And it's all thanks to you, Mollie. I'm absolutely delighted. I know how your aunt loves her shop and her customers. There are just so many people she's helped over the years. Some people have talked to me about her, not knowing that I've loved her for such a long time."

Mollie was puzzled to know why he had waited so long to ask her aunt. But then, that was their business.

She kept trying to put Ritchie out of her mind but it was impossible. Perhaps someone had not paid him for the rolls of material. No, Ritchie would not let anyone have the goods if they had not paid. He was very strict about that. It was a mystery.

Mr Redgrave said, "It's not a very nice morning. Not many people will be out early. Shall we move on to the next gemstone? We were ready to do the second part of March."

"Yes, I wouldn't mind at all."

Mr Redgrave went to get his book.

When he sat down, he said, "This gem is the bloodstone and if I remember rightly the description of it is quite short."

He opened the book and turned a page and began.

"'The bloodstone is a very dark green and is speckled with red. This gem is noted for courage. It is used for cameos, seals and signets.

'It is said that on the hill of Calvary that some of the blood of Christ fell on some green jasper that lay beneath the Cross and tinged it with red.'"

147

Mollie gave a shiver. "Oh, I don't like this one."

"It's short, it will soon be over."

"'The bloodstone contains iron impurities that work with the blood stream against light-headedness.'"

He looked up. "It does a lot of good. Its corrective properties enable it to break down deep-rooted diseases. It is also said that it has magic properties.'"

He looked at the page again. "'No one was ever known to drown if they wore the stone. And it was also said that no young people died of an illness if the stone was rubbed across their foreheads.

'Those who used this stone were sunny-natured. And if they wanted anything special they would work hard to get it.'"

Mr Redgrave grinned. "I do know a lot of people, men and women, who wear the bloodstone."

"Don't you know any more about their lives?"

"No. I don't want to know."

At that moment the door bell pinged.

It was not a madly busy day, but they were kept going for most of the day. When they both left the shop that evening, Mr Redgrave said, "Well, we shall see what tomorrow brings."

Mollie had two things on her mind. Mr Grainger and Ritchie. Ritchie was a worry and she hoped she would soon get to know what was wrong with him.

Chapter Eleven

For two days trade was steady, too steady to enable Mr Redgrave and Mollie to do any more birthstones. The following morning, however, Mollie had just finished dusting when there was a noise in the doorway that sounded as if a crowd were holding a party.

The next moment a man's voice said sternly, "Quiet, or you will all go back home." There was complete silence.

Mollie smiled to herself. It was Mr Grainger and a number of young people. He opened the door and gave them a broad smile.

"Good morning, Miss Paget, and good morning to you, Mr Redgrave. I've brought some of my family to buy a present."

He came in and about six or seven young people followed him in. They looked as if they were walking on tiptoe.

"I've told them that in this shop they are given the right kind of present to buy. Am I right or wrong?"

Mollie glanced at Mr Redgrave and he gave her a nod.

"My uncle and I will do our best to find you the right present, Mr Grainger."

Mr Redgrave then said, "And what can we get for your family this morning, Mr Grainger?"

Mr Grainger turned to the young people. "Give your pieces of paper to Miss Paget."

She took them all and read them quickly. There were some with 'ring' written on them, others with 'watch', 'brooch' and 'necklace'. She smiled from one to the other. "Now then, who is this present for?"

A small boy of about eight piped up. "It's for our sister, Elizabeth. She likes expensive things."

"So why not put all your money together and buy her something expensive?"

There were protests at this. They all wanted to buy her something different. Even the older ones.

"The trouble is," said Mollie, "that it will be difficult to give your sister something expensive."

"I'm her cousin," said a girl of about twelve or more.

Mollie smiled. "I shall remember."

"And I am a friend of Elizabeth's," declared a young lady.

"I shall remember that too."

Then she had a sudden brainwave. She said, "If you all want to give the lady something different it will not be the expensive item she would wish for, would it? When is her birthday?"

A chorus of voices said, "The eighth of February."

"Then the ruby is the fortunate stone for that date."

"What do you mean by the fortunate stone?" one of the children asked.

"That would be her birthstone and would be lucky for her to wear. It deals with one's health and has done so for thousands of years."

This created a feeling of excitement. Could Miss Paget tell them more about this birthstone?

Mollie said that Mr Redgrave was a master at it. Perhaps he would tell them.

Mr Redgrave, smiling, said they had better come into the back room as it would take some time, and they must sit down.

When they were all seated, he began . . . and kept them enthralled for some fifteen minutes. Then he said, "That, of course, is only a fraction of the story of the birthstone."

They were all terribly excited and they all wanted a stone.

In the end Mr Grainger said he would buy them all one, but it must be a very small one. He added that they must also make up their minds what they were going to do about Elizabeth, for whom they had come to buy a present.

Mollie suggested they put their money together and buy a beautiful necklace with her birthstone in it.

They were delighted at this.

Mr Grainger beamed at Mollie. "What a wonderful person you are, Miss Paget," he said softly.

She blushed and turned away to bring a tray of necklaces. She helped the children by picking up a delicately-patterned gold necklace inset with a ruby.

That was the one, they declared, they all loved it.

At that moment another customer came in and Mr Redgrave went to attend to her.

Mollie had never seen such excitement among young people and Mr Grainger calmed them down. He told them to go out to the carriages and wait for him. "I shall pay for your stones and the necklace." He stressed that they must all be quiet.

They beamed at Molly and thanked her quietly for all her help and she thanked them for their co-operation, and some of them promised her that they would soon be back for more presents.

Mollie found herself thinking what lovely children they all were. Mr Redgrave's customer had gone, and Mollie guessed that the woman had come in out of curiosity to find out who the two elegant carriages standing outside the windows belonged to.

Mr Grainger was settling up the bill and having a talk with Mr Redgrave. Mollie tidied away the trays and then came into the shop. The men were still talking. Then Mr Grainger came over to Mollie.

"I have so enjoyed my visit, Miss Paget. The children, I'm afraid, were a little boisterous."

"Not at all. You kept them under control. I am only pleased that they were all satisfied."

He raised his hat. "We shall be seeing you again."

"I'll looked forward to it, Mr Grainger."

Her heart was beating madly at the thought. But she must take care. He must know dozens of ladies. He was, after all, just being polite. But for a few moments she was lost in another world, a world of beautiful houses and clothes. Then she pulled herself up. They were not for her.

And there was Ritchie. She came down to earth with a bump.

More customers came in and only one walked out without buying anything. Mollie told Mr Redgrave that she could not understand why so many of them wanted to buy something.

"Because they think they will be looked up to as people who buy where a millionaire buys."

"It's crazy," she said.

"Crazy but true. I think that from now on there'll be more and more customers. That is, as long as the Graingers come."

"I'll keep my fingers crossed. I must tell Aunt Nell and Chantelle about them this evening."

"I only pray that Chantelle won't want to join our shop. By the way, Mollie, I'll give you a lift home this evening, but I won't come in. I don't want to upset Nell."

"You won't upset her. She'll be delighted."

They left promptly at seven o'clock and talked nearly all the way about the Grainger family.

"Their mother," Mr Redgrave said, "is a strange lady. Kind to the children but firm about their manners. She dresses very plainly and her husband refuses to take her out in her plain clothes. She always smiles in reply and

152

say that it's quite all right, she has no wish to talk a lot of nonsense with other people. She will be quite pleased to stay at home and read her books."

"What does she read?"

"No one knows, she keeps them locked up."

"Well, as long as she is happy."

"She seems to be. I only met her twice and she said that I must excuse her, she was not in the mood for talk. She was not unpleasant it was . . . well, I don't really know."

"Does she talk to the children?"

"Oh, yes, according to them she does. They all love Mama."

"How very strange."

He told Mollie other little snippets and the journey to the shop passed quickly.

While Mr Redgrave was refusing to come in and see Nell, she came to the door and asked him in.

He got down from the cab and said, "I didn't want to bother you, Nell."

"You are never a bother to me," she said softly. "You are always welcome. I hope you will stay and eat with us."

"Thank you, Nell, but no." He spoke firmly. "I have quite a lot of work to do."

"Another time then," she said brightly.

"Of course." This time he spoke softly.

When Mollie and Nell went into the shop, Chantelle moved away from the door and went into the kitchen.

"That wretched girl," Nell whispered. "Always spying on us."

Mollie, who was in a good mood, said, "It's just natural curiosity. We've had a marvellous day. I must tell you all about it."

As the meal was ready they sat down to it and Mollie told her story of the Grainger family. Chantelle interrupted when she heard about the birthstones and wanted to know about them.

"I'll tell you in a few minutes," Mollie answered.

When she had finished the tale, Nell said, "Well, I never, who would have believed it? You must have done very well out of it. I do wish that Philip had stayed. We've known each other for years and he never once mentioned birthstones."

"I don't suppose he would have known anything about them until he started his shop."

"Well, what are they?" Chantelle demanded.

Mollie suddenly remembered that Chantelle would not know about hers as she had no idea when she was born. They had decided to give her a birthday in the summer.

She explained this gently and Chantelle was quiet for some moments after Mollie had told her.

"It doesn't seem fair, does it? I miss out on going to the jewellery shop and I don't even know my own birthday." There was a hint of tears in her voice.

"You know the reason why you can't be in the shop, Chantelle. It just wouldn't work. There would be nothing for you to do. The only time women are in a jewellery shop is when a man and his wife work together, or perhaps a father and his daughter."

Mollie was not sure about this, she was only guessing.

"You and Mr Redgrave aren't even father and daughter."

"I don't want to talk about it any more."

"You get all the excitement," said Chantelle.

"It is my shop."

"Not yet, it isn't."

Nell said sharply, "Now don't start all that again." She got up and started clearing the plates away. "And don't you dare sulk, Chantelle, or you're out of here."

"Neither of you like me, do you?"

"Yes, we do, Chantelle. Do you think I would have brought you here if I hadn't, and do you think that Aunt Nell would have had you here, if she didn't like you. Of course not. Grow up."

"I'll try to." She spoke in a whisper. "I like being here and working with Aunt Nell."

"Well, then show it," Nell said, more kindly.

The three of them sat over the fire with their cups of tea and Mollie explained more fully about the birthstones.

"Not that I know all the stones of the months. I'm learning. It's very interesting but I don't really know whether it's all true or not."

Chantelle smiled. "Someday I shall buy every stone and the one that gives me a happy life I shall wear always."

Nell said, "It should have been a good time for you when Mollie brought you here. If she hadn't you would have been in a home for lost children and my heavens, you would have been miserable there. Be thankful for small mercies."

"Be thankful for small mercies," Chantelle nodded. "I must remember that." She was smiling again. "Tell us more, Mollie, about the Grainger family."

Mollie told them about Mrs Grainger and how kind she was to all the children, and by then Chantelle said she was ready for bed. She bade them a surprisingly gentle goodnight and went upstairs.

Nell said, when she was out of hearing, "I don't think I shall ever understand that girl. I only wish I knew when she was born. But I think that's an impossibility."

"Stranger things have happened," Mollie said. Then she told Nell how worried she was about Ritchie.

Nell smiled. "You need never worry about Ritchie. He's a young man who can take care of himself. But, if you're still worried when he comes home, ask him. It will probably be just a simple thing."

"I'll do that." Mollie stifled a yawn. "And I, too, am ready for my bed."

* * *

The following morning when Mollie arrived at the shop she thought that Mr Redgrave looked very tired and told him so.

"I do feel tired this morning, but I'm free this evening and I'll take you to your Aunt Nell's." He smiled. "That should rejuvenate me."

"I'll make some tea and that will help."

Mollie thought to herself she would have to tell her aunt Mr Redgrave's response. It would please her.

The morning was fairly busy but the afternoon was quiet. Mr Redgrave asked if Mollie would like him to go on with the birthstones.

"It's too tiring for you," she protested.

"No, that's not tiring, it was all the jewellery we sold."

"Well, I quite enjoy hearing about the birthstones."

"Right. I'll get my book."

He began. "'The first half of April is the tourmaline. In times past it was classed as a mineral magnet rather than as a gem. The reason for this is its unique electrical energies which cause it, when rubbed or heated, to produce in each of its crystals, a positive charge at one end and a negative at the other. It's a strange stone.

'People have called it colourless, but it has beautiful colours when it is moved around. It has pink, rose, blue, green and yellow shades.

'On account of its remarkable properties the gem is used as an amulet and is reputed to endow its wearer with perception and wisdom.

'It is a lovely stone and those who possess one, or those who have been given one, are exceptionally fortunate.'" Mr Redgrave looked up. "And that is the tourmaline. Would you like to go on to the last part of April?"

"Yes, if you are not too tired. I love hearing about them."

"Amber is the second half."

He turned the page. " 'This is the solidified and fossilised resin of trees that grew many thousands of years ago. Parts of plants and bodies of insects can be seen preserved in some pieces. Amber's colouring is rich at certain parts and can be a pale yellow in others. The best amber is a rich warm gold colour.

'It will soothe irritated throats as well as raising depressed spirits. But this stone's real power is in the curing of chest complaints, such as bronchitis, coughs, and asthma.

'Amber wearers are caring people and will do anything to help a neighbour or anyone sick.' "

Mr Redgrave got up. "That's all for today. Shall we have another cup of tea?"

Mollie said smiling, "Yes, sire, I'll make it."

He sat drinking it with his eyes shut. She found herself thinking about Ritchie and wondered if he had solved his problems. She hoped he had. It was so unlike him to be so flat. More customers came in and Mollie was glad when it was time to leave.

When she arrived at her aunt's shop she could hear Chantelle laughing. Well, at least she must have had a good day.

Her aunt was smiling too when she went into the kitchen.

Mollie said, "I take it that you've both had a good day."

Nell nodded, "It's been wonderful. I cut out three blouses, finished them at four o'clock and sold all three at half past six. And, what's more, had an order for a dozen."

"A dozen?" Mollie exclaimed. "You'll be working in your sleep."

"No, the woman is not in a hurry."

Chantelle giggled. "But she did say she hoped that Aunt Nell could let her have them by next Saturday."

Mollie said, "Wait until I tell Mr Redgrave about this. He'll be so pleased."

"I'm not so sure about that." Nell looked serious. "He'll be thinking that I will want a bigger shop and I don't. I really don't. I do want to marry him in a year's time."

"Then I shall stress that." Mollie was smiling again.

Then Chantelle said, in a teasing way, "No one asks me what I've done today?"

"Oh, Chantelle, I'm sorry. What have you done today?"

"I have made eight handkerchiefs and have not sold one!" She began to giggle then they were all giggling.

Mollie thought if their lives could always be like this what a heaven it would be.

The evening, however, was pleasant. After they had had their meal Nell and Mollie sorted out what material to use to make the dozen blouses. Nell cut out two blouses and while she was cutting out the second one, Mollie was stitching up the first one.

"I shall do this every evening," she said.

But Nell put her foot down. "You are working all day. You are not to tire yourself every night. And I mean it."

Mollie gave in.

They all went to bed that night at half past nine, but Mollie lay wide awake.

Her aunt was right. One job a day was all right if you relaxed in the evening. But if you came home to work it was all wrong. Her mind was full of gemstones and what styles to make the blouses.

It must have been three o'clock when her nerves were getting touchy and she threw the bedclothes back. But before she could put her legs to the floor, she thought she heard a sound downstairs. Perhaps her aunt was unable to sleep, too. Would it be wise to go down? They would start talking again. She lay back and pulled the bedclothes up. No doubt Nell would be wide awake owing to everything that had happened that day.

It would have been all right if she had had time to get settled down to the work. That would come later.

After a moment Mollie raised her head. What on earth was her aunt doing? It sounded as if she was in the shop and trying to turn a key.

The sound stopped and Mollie let her head fall back, telling herself she must have imagined it. She turned on her side and pulled the bedclothes over her head.

After a while she began to feel sleepy and she was in a semi-doze when she heard a second sound. She sat up then realised she could see a light from downstairs. She never closed her bedroom door. But, the light was moving . . . away. It was the light of a candle and if Nell was down there she should be coming up the stairs.

Mollie flung back the bedclothes and got up. She pulled on her dressing-gown, crept quietly out of the room and stopped at the head of the stairs. Although she could only see to the bottom of the stairs, she could see the light moving away in the direction of the shop. What on earth was Nell doing?

The next moment Mollie was aware of a smell . . . a smell of something burning. Oh, my God! She ran downstairs went through the kitchen and opened the door leading to the shop.

The light suddenly went out but not before she had seen a figure. Someone had gone out of the door and in the semi-darkness Mollie could see a figure running past the window.

She yelled "*Nell!*" at the top of her voice. She must light the lamp. No, she must find out who the person was.

She hurried to the door, looked out and saw a cloaked figure disappear around a corner. The smell of something burning was much nearer. When she turned she saw smoke rising. Whatever was burning burst into flame.

At that moment Nell and Chantelle ran into the kitchen shouting, "What's burning?"

159

Nell had a shawl on and she took it off to fight the flames. Chantelle picked up a cushion and joined in. Mollie, who had been standing frozen, ran into the kitchen, picked up a bucket of water and, rushing back into the shop, threw the water over the flames. It put the fire out. They stood staring at it, all three trembling. Mollie whispered, "I can't believe it. Not again."

Nell said, "Who do you think it was? Anne?"

"Who else could it be?" Chantelle ventured, her voice shaky.

Mollie was recovering. "I saw the person. It looked like a woman. She wore a cloak." She hesitated a moment then said, "Do you think it could be ... Anne?"

"Surely not. On the other hand, it might be. I just don't know."

A small piece of material began to smoulder and Mollie said, "I must go and get the tongs." She picked up the smouldering piece and carried it over the empty water bucket to the firegrate and threw it onto the dead ashes. She was still standing there staring at it when Nell and Chantelle came in.

Nell took the bucket from her and stood it on the hearth. "We ought to tell the police."

"They're over a mile away. What good would it do?"

"They'll have to be told. Do you realise we could all have been burned alive?"

Mollie shivered. "Don't mention it. It fills me with horror."

"If it was Anne, she should be stopped." This from Chantelle whose voice was still shaky.

Nell looked around her. "How did she get in?" She went into the shop and came back saying, "She had a key? Who on earth could have given her that? I'm the only person who has one. It's a mystery." She paused for a moment, then went on. "I do take the money from the till into my

160

bedroom at night, thank goodness. I did check it was there before I came downstairs."

Chantelle said, "Do you think that Anne will be at home?"

"I doubt it. Also, I think her mother would have an eye on her. But I will go to the police station in the morning and I'll try and find her house. I think it's round about here somewhere. I just don't know. But I will have to let Mr Redgrave know first what's happened."

Chapter Twelve

Mr Redgrave was shocked when Mollie told him what had happened.

"Good God!" he exclaimed. "You could all have been burnt to death. Have you any idea who was responsible for it?"

She told him about Anne and added, "After I've seen the police I'm going to find out where she lives. I want to get to the bottom of this."

"Well, be wary what you tell the police or they'll have one of you responsible. This happened to a friend of mine."

Mollie said she would be careful and left.

The police asked numerous questions, but Mollie was very cautious. No, she said, none of them had seen the person who had broken into the shop. They had caught the fire in time. Yes, there was only her aunt and Chantelle and herself in the shop. Yes, they lived above the shop.

At last they let her go and told her they would let her know if the person was found.

Mollie then decided to go back to the market and find out if any of the stallholders had asked for Nell's address. She questioned a number of people and was beginning to think she was on the wrong track when a man who owned a cake stall said, yes, a young lady had asked if he knew where Mollie's aunt's shop was. When Mollie asked what she was like he took off his cap and scratched his head.

"Now let's see. She was tall, had fair 'air and was a looker. A bit dressy and talked like a toff."

Mollie's heart began to thud. "Did she go in the direction of the shop?"

"Don't know, love. Had a few customers come up. And was kept busy. What's up?"

Mollie thanked him and left.

She was not far from her aunt's shop. She would go and see Nell and tell her about Anne then try and find out where she lived.

Nell was all oh's and ah's, but had no idea where Anne lived. Then Mollie suddenly remembered seeing a magazine that Anne brought to the shop and it had her home address on it. Oh, what was it? It had the name of the house on it too. Hustley House, Huster House. What was the address? Liversy Gardens? No, Lyvensy, that was it. Thank goodness. She would find the house she was sure if she went to the Gardens.

Mollie had to get a bus to find Lyvensy Gardens and recognised the house when she came to Hurtley House. She was certainly impressed by it. She had been told that Anne came from a good family but she had not been prepared for the size and quality of her home. She stood outside, looking up at the mullioned windows wondering if she dare contact them. Then she made up her mind. What had she to lose? Nothing. Squaring her shoulders, she walked to the door and rang the bell.

A girl in a white cap and apron opened it. Mollie said, "I would like to speak to the—" Oh, what was Anne's surname? She ended by saying, "to the lady of the house. Tell her it's about her daughter, Anne."

By then her heart was thumping. "Just a moment, Miss," the maid said, and disappeared on silent feet.

It seemed only seconds before she appeared again. "Would you come in, please."

Mollie pulled herself together and the maid led her to a room on the side of a lovely square hall, opened the door and ushered her in. She closed the door, leaving Mollie in a room full of beautiful furniture.

A tall, stately woman rose out of a chair and said in a very low voice, "I understand you know my daughter."

"Yes, is she here?"

"No, I'm afraid not. We haven't seen her for some time. Do sit down." Mollie moved automatically, feeling very disappointed that Anne was not here. She sat down on a chair opposite. Dare she mention why she had come? Then she thought, Anne was this woman's daughter. Her mother had probably no idea where she was.

Then her mother said gently, "We would be pleased if you could tell us where she is, Miss—"

"Paget," Mollie said, then added, "I'm afraid I don't know where she is either. We were robbed last night and we all thought that Anne might have had – well, something to—"

Oh, this was crazy.

"Something to do with it?" said Anne's mother.

Mollie got up. "I'm sorry, I should never have come."

"You had every right to come. My family have been nearly out of our minds with worry. Do sit down again, Miss Paget. If you can tell us something that might help to trace Anne, we would be very grateful. Please."

Mollie told her about her shop being burned down and then about the fire at her aunt's shop the night before. She paused, then added, "I could, of course, have been wrong about last night's fire. It was just that someone answering Anne's description had asked people at the market where my aunt's shop is. There is only the one shop in the whole market."

"Now I must tell you something, Miss Paget, that only my husband and myself and a few friends know about.. From being a child, Anne had one big fault. She was always wanting to burn things. She always had to be watched. The doctor told us that she would grow out

165

of it and this seemed to be the case. As she grew up she never mentioned anything at all about wanting to burn anything. But then she became seventeen and demanded that she should be allowed to earn her own living." Her mother was silent for a moment then went on.

"She was a likeable girl and we allowed her to become an assistant in a couturier's. It was what she longed to be. And, to our pleasure she seemed to do well. It was there she met a French girl named Chantelle. They seemed to get on very well together. Then she met a young man, whose parents are comfortably off. He wanted to take both girls to the music hall and although we were not pleased at them both going alone without a chaperone, his parents called and told us they would be in good hands. So we let her go. The rest you know. Your shop was burned down. A man was arrested for it and is still, I believe in gaol. But, Anne never returned home and we wondered if she was back in the days of her childhood."

"I'm so sorry," Mollie said, "I had no idea."

"Of course not."

"But what about the keys?" Mollie asked suddenly. "Where could she have got those from?"

"Simple, Miss Paget. This was something else belonging to her childhood. We never dreamed of course that she saved them for any other purpose than the way that children save books and toys. We never knew at the time that she must have used them. It all seemed so harmless."

"I would like to ask you something, Mrs—"

"Colledge."

"I hope you won't be offended, Mrs Colledge, but why, in your position, did you allow Anne to work in that class of shop? You would have been able to get her into one of the more prestigious shops like Hartnolls or Freemans?"

"We knew Mrs Brandford. She's a lovely person and I didn't think it would do Anne any harm to know the type of people who came into her shop."

Mollie said, "I rented the shop from Mrs Brandford. She is a lovely woman and stayed to help me over my first difficulties."

"I didn't know that, Miss Paget. You must have known my daughter for quite a while."

"Yes, and I liked her. I thought her most efficient."

Mrs Colledge sighed. "If only I could get in touch with her." She paused. "If you do by any chance get in touch with Anne, would you let me know, Miss Paget?"

"Of course I will," Mollie said softly, feeling so sorry for Mrs Colledge. She got up. "And now, I really must go. I have the shop to see to."

Mrs Colledge walked to the door with her. "I'm glad I've met you, Miss Paget. I would like to come to your shop sometime. There are always presents to be bought for friends and family." There was a hint of tears in her eyes.

"You will always be welcome, Mrs Colledge." Mollie felt near tears, too. It must be awful having a daughter and not knowing where she was. Nor knowing what kind of life she was leading.

When Mollie got back to the shop Mr Redgrave was busy.

"Thank goodness you're back," he said. "Would you serve that lady over there who's looking at rings?"

"Yes, of course. I have a lot to tell you when we have time."

They had no time to talk until lunchtime, when the customers drifted off. They brought out their sandwiches and ate them in the back room.

"Was it a satisfying morning?" Mr Redgrave asked.

"In one way, yes and in another way, no. I'll tell you about the reaction of the police and then what a stallholder told me. After that I'll tell you about going to meet Anne's mother."

When Mollie finished telling him he said, "It all seems so impossible."

"It made me wonder if it would ever be worthwhile getting married and having children."

"You'll get married, Mollie, and I hope you have children. I don't think that there'll be many children like Anne Colledge."

"I hope not. I feel sorry for the family. Mrs Colledge asked me to let her know if I heard anything of Anne. I feel at the moment that I don't want to know anything about her. We shall always have to be on our guard." Mollie told him about the keys she had collected.

"I wouldn't worry about that. I'll have special locks put on the door. An alarm bell will ring."

"Well, we'll hope for the best. You haven't had Mr Grainger and family in for more presents?"

Mr Redgrave laughed. "No, thank goodness! I don't think I would have been able to cope."

Mollie teased him. "You would have been able to cope if there had been fifty people in the shop."

"Thanks for the compliment. I would certainly have tried to handle them all."

"I know you would."

It turned out to be a very busy day. Mr Redgrave said when they were getting ready to leave, "I'll take you to Nell's this evening. It'll be in the carriage. I came in it this morning, but I will not be staying at Nell's for a chatter."

"I think you will when we arrive. There may be something I've forgotten to tell them and you can remind me."

"We'll see," he said.

They talked as they drove about all the customers, what they had bought and Mollie was pleased with the result. She said, "If it goes on like this I can see us getting another man in the shop."

"Chantelle wouldn't be pleased," he said.

"She can take it or leave it. Aunt Nell has warned her that if she behaved as she had been doing she would be out. Somehow I don't think she would dare make a complaint and she does like to work with Nell. They had an order for twelve blouses. They were both delighted with it. But whether they were able to get on with them today, I don't know."

Nell always seemed to be ready to see Mr Redgrave.

"I see you have the carriage this evening, so that means you can stay and have some dinner. I'm sure we'll have plenty to talk about. Come on in and take your coat off."

"I ought not to give in to your kindness," he said. Nell retorted, rubbish, what were friends for?

Over a tasty steak and kidney pie, Mollie told Chantelle and her aunt all the news she had and they all discussed it, feeling sorry for Mr and Mrs Colledge.

"The poor souls," said Nell. "How dreadful to have a daughter like that. You never know what's she going to do next."

Mr Redgrave nodded slowly. "But that's life, isn't it?"

Mollie asked her aunt and Chantelle if they had managed to get any sewing done and apparently her aunt had made four of the blouses and Chantelle had made six handkerchiefs.

"Splendid," Mollie declared. "Keep up the good work. We'll all be millionaires before long!"

"That'll be the day," laughed Nell. "I would hate to be rich."

Chantelle teased her. "Speak for yourself, Aunt Nell. I would enjoy being rich. Just think, no more work."

Mr Redgrave said, "Tell me honestly, Chantelle, would you really like to have nothing to do? You would be bored."

"Mr Grainger, his brothers and sisters and cousins are not bored."

"They are a big family."

"I would like to be part of a big family. Perhaps I was at one time." She sat staring into space and there was a puzzled look on her face.

They all sat watching her, then she said, "For a few moments I had a feeling I had a big family. Now that feeling is gone." She gave them all a lovely smile. "I shall be content to go on embroidering handkerchiefs."

"That's sensible," answered Nell. "We should all be glad that we're alive and can live a normal life. There are thousands of people starving every day. Now, who wants prunes and rice or bananas and custard?"

They all said what they would like and in spite of the upset of the day before it was quite a pleasant evening.

* * *

During the following week Mr Redgrave and Mollie had no time to themselves. It was not that they were madly busy, but the lock had been changed on the door, an alarm had been fixed and there were more customers, but not all bought something. It was, as they said, just to look around.

Then the following week, Ritchie was home and it seemed as if he haunted the place, wanting to know if the takings were good, how much had they made that day, and the next and eventually Mollie asked him coldly if he was hard up.

There was no one in the shop at the time. Mr Redgrave had gone out and Ritchie paused a moment or two before replying. "As a matter of fact, I am. I was wondering if I could borrow something from you for a while. I'll soon pay you back."

"I doubt it," Mollie replied. "What has happened to all your stock?"

"I bought too much, but it will sell eventually."

This Mollie did not believe. She knew that Ritchie was uneasy. He had hardly listened when she told him about the fire in the shop. She guessed the reason and now faced him with it.

"You're gambling, aren't you?"

"No, what made you think that?" He was tense and seemed unable to look at her.

"I'm not a fool, Ritchie. You were hardly listening when I told you about the fire. Normally you would have been terribly concerned."

His shoulders went slack and he gave a sigh. "You're right. I have gambled. And now regret it."

"In heaven's name, why gamble? You had loads of money. More than you need."

"I know, I know. We all learn by our mistakes. I'll never gamble again as long as I live."

"And I've heard that plenty of times. You know the old saying, once a gambler, always a gambler."

"I got carried away. It seemed fun to me at first. I couldn't do a thing wrong." He paused. "Then, of course, my luck changed and I went quickly downhill."

Mollie knew that if it had not been for Ritchie's generosity she would not have been in the position she was now. She hesitated. She had lost nothing; gained a great deal in fact.

"How much do you need?"

There was only a slight hesitation. "A thousand."

She stared at him. "*Pounds*?"

He nodded.

"God Almighty! You must have been round the bend. I haven't got that much money."

"You have stock."

She felt she could have smacked him across the face.

"If I gave you a thousand out of stock, what am I supposed to do? I would hardly have anything left. I did sign a paper that the stock was mine and I would pay you back in instalments."

"I know, but this is an emergency."

She felt bitter. "I had the first business ruined and no, I am not going to lose this one."

"Then I'll go to jail."

"What are you talking about?"

"The people I borrowed from want their money back. If they don't get it, they'll take me to court."

"Oh, Lord." Mollie sank into a chair and closed her eyes. She could hardly believe that Ritchie, the happy-go-lucky man-about-town, could be such a fool.

"I did back you in the first business," he said, "and in this second one."

She opened her eyes and said through clenched teeth, "And don't I know it. What sort of men are demanding this money? A rough and tumble lot, I suppose?"

"No, they all come from wealthy backgrounds. They might accept a thousand, and if I could work for you for nothing they—"

"So, who feeds you?" she demanded.

"Aunt Nell would give me something."

"I don't know how you dare suggest such a thing! A woman who has been struggling to exist for years on a pittance."

"You've got it all wrong, Mollie. Aunt Nell has money stashed away. It's money she won't touch. She wants us to have it between us when she dies."

Mollie was staring at him again. "I don't believe you."

"It's true, but she wouldn't admit it to you if you were to ask her."

A sudden coldness seized Mollie as a thought came to her. Was it Ritchie who had tried to set fire to the shop last night? He could have been disguised with a cape. If it was true about the money, she and her aunt could have

172

been burned to death, and Ritchie would have got it all. She began to shiver.

Ritchie was immediately concerned. "Mollie, you're ill." He came nearer and went to put his arms around her.

She got up and moved away shouting, "Don't touch me!" She wanted to shout 'Murderer', but the word refused to come.

Mr Redgrave appeared at that moment and wanted to know what was wrong with Mollie.

She was suddenly normal again. "I'm all right now," she said. "If I can just sit quietly for a few minutes."

Mr Redgrave said, "I'll make a pot of tea." He filled the kettle and put it on the stove, then a customer came in and he went to attend to them.

Mollie was no longer afraid of Ritchie. She knew now that for all his faults, he was not involved in that way. He was too big to behave like a woman. And the figure last night in the cape *had* been a woman.

When the kettle boiled, Ritchie made the tea and kept glancing at her. Then, standing well away from her he said, "I'm sorry I upset you, Mollie. I'll take my punishment and go to jail."

"No." She spoke sharply. "We'll think of something."

Mr Redgrave came in, "Feeling a little better, Mollie?"

"Yes, much better, thanks. I want the three of us to have a talk later. That is, if you two men are willing?"

They both agreed and as they drank their tea, Mr Redgrave talked about stocks getting low; they would have to replenish soon. Ritchie looked uncomfortable. He left when customers came in and promised to return in an hour.

When he reappeared there were no customers in and Mollie said they should start their talk while they had the chance.

She began by saying that Ritchie was heavily in debt because of gambling, and needed help. She said that he had to find a thousand pounds to satisfy his creditors and added that he would have to go to court if it was not paid.

Mr Redgrave gave a low whistle. "Phew, that's an amount that will take some finding. We need stock in the shop. Can't exist without it."

"We could employ Ritchie, and he would be paid a wage. I had said only the other day that we needed another man in the shop and I do think that Ritchie would fit in."

"But Mollie, there's no way we could pay out a thousand pounds."

"I know we can't pay it, but it did occur to me if I worked for you, and we told them that we would pay the money in instalments, they might accept it."

"I very much doubt it. Men who come from wealthy families are not always rich."

"I know, but if we told them that the son of a millionaire always brought the family to us to buy presents, what then? We could also tell them that other wealthy people are beginning to come in for jewellery."

Ritchie already looked brighter. Mr Redgrave rubbed his chin.

"It might work. We could suggest it. But, I must say here and now if we don't have enough money to buy stock, we may as well close down now."

Ritchie protested at this. "No, I would rather go to prison. I mean it."

"Nothing's won by shirking the issue," Mollie said. "Suggest it to them and see what happens."

Mr Redgrave gave in and Ritchie said he knew where he could contact one man now. He would go and talk to him.

After he had gone, Mr Redgrave said, "I think we're making a mistake. If Ritchie goes on gambling, we'll never build up the business. It gets in the blood."

"I'm not sure, but I feel that Ritchie will stop gambling. If he doesn't then we'll have to change our plans."

"What plans *can* we change?"

Mollie sighed and said she didn't know. But suddenly an idea came to her mind. It might work, or it might not. She would have to wait and see how Ritchie behaved.

Ritchie did not return for two hours but, it was obvious that he was happier than he had been earlier.

"I've talked to all the men involved," he said, "and they've agreed to your proposal, Mollie. They're strict about it and if I don't meet the payments, they will take me to court right away. I can assure you both," he added, in grim tones now, "that I won't let you down."

It was not until then that Mollie realised how nervous she had been. She said, "You would be a bigger fool than I thought if you did let us down. I think it would be wise if you let Aunt Nell know the position."

His jaw dropped. "Is it necessary?"

"It's very necessary."

"I don't want Chantelle to know."

Mollie was hurt that Ritchie had thought it necessary to bring Chantelle into the equation, but said, "I'll agree to it." Mr Redgrave had nothing to say.

Customers began to come in. Ritchie said he would leave and promised to see Mollie at Nell's shop that evening. There was no mention of picking her up and she wondered if he had any means of transport now. He had probably sold his wagon.

When she arrived at her aunt's shop, Nell came in smiling. "Oh, it's you, Mollie. Ritchie is here. He was telling me that he's going to work in your shop. He says he wants to get some experience with jewellery. I wouldn't have thought he had time to take that on, too. But there, he knows best."

They went into the kitchen and Chantelle was giggling at a drawing that Ritchie had obviously done. He took it from her and tearing it up, threw the pieces in the fire.

Chantelle jumped up and tried to save them, but they had already caught fire.

"Why did you throw it away?" she complained. "It was good."

When she started to explain what the drawing was about Nell interrupted, "It wasn't all that good. The meal's ready. Come and sit down at the table. It's lamb's liver and onions."

"One of my favourites," Ritchie declared.

Mollie sensed he had been filling in time, no doubt waiting for her to arrive to tell Nell what was about to take place.

According to Chantelle, they had not got as much work done as previously. It was difficult to get started when you had other things on your mind. She turned to ask Ritchie how long he would be here this time.

He dismissed it with, "I don't know yet," and changed the subject. "It's warmer abroad. Quite sunny and no rain." He cut a piece of liver and chewed it. "Mmm, this is lovely, so tender, Nell. What's for pudding?"

"Apple tart and custard."

"Oh, splendid. Another one of my favourites!" He began to talk about Dutch food and remarked that he ate a lot of fish when he was there. "It's so fresh it seems as if it had just been caught."

He went on about foreign food and Mollie was just beginning to to worry Nell and Chantelle would think he was making something up when Nell said, "Oh, Chantelle, I wonder if you would take a book to Mrs Earle this evening? I forget all about it and I know she loves reading."

"Yes, of course I will."

At last the meal was over. Chantelle went off with the book and Nell turned to Ritchie. "So, what was all that talk about. What's wrong?"

Ritchie looked at Mollie. "Do you want to tell Nell?"

She raised her shoulders. "I may as well." So she told

her aunt about the mess Ritchie had got himself into and how she thought they might work it out.

"Gambling, *you*?" she exclaimed to Ritchie. "I can't believe it! *Why*? You were all right for money. I never thought of you as being greedy."

He explained it wasn't greed; he thought it would be fun.

"*Fun*? I think you've been most unfair to Mollie. Offering her money to get another shop, then wanting the money back."

Mollie stepped in quickly. "I must remember that Ritchie not only lent me money to open one shop, but the jewellery business too. Mr Redgrave and I felt we needed another man in the shop, and thought of Ritchie. I think it might work out. If it doesn't, then I'll join you, Nell, in making blouses."

Chapter Thirteen

There was one thing about Ritchie. He took a keen interest in all the stock and made no effort to try and serve until he had mastered the quality and prices of all the items for sale. Mr Redgrave was very patient and Ritchie was quick to learn. Before long Mr Redgrave announced that he was ready to face customers.

Ritchie said smiling, "Thank heavens I have one decent suit. I'll put it on tomorrow."

*　*　*

Mollie was impressed when he arrived the following morning. He looked more handsome than ever in a dark grey suit. It was certainly top quality. Mollie had expected Ritchie would want to stay with Nell, but it was Mr Redgrave who offered to put him up. The two men got on splendidly together and Mollie was pleased about it.

She had definitely not wanted Ritchie to stay with Nell. It would not have been wise with Chantelle so besotted with him. The evenings he did go and have a meal with them she would sit gazing at him, oblivious to everyone else.

One thing did please Mollie. Ritchie noticed this fault in her and had told her last night if she didn't stop staring at him, he would refuse to come any more. That seemed to work, but Mollie did wonder how long it would last.

The conversation on the last two occasions Ritchie had visited, was mostly about jewellery, and Mr Redgrave said he had never known anyone pick up so much knowledge in such a short space of time.

Ritchie replied that it was because he had found it all so fascinating. "Take rings," he said. "There's some lovely looking rings for five pounds, and yet another ring with a smaller stone sells for fifty pounds."

"It's the stone that sets the price," Mr Redgrave said. "It's the same with a diamond. You could pay a reasonably low price or a high one. Some people drive about in beautiful carriages while others tramp to work on a cold, wet morning and remain in wet clothes all day. It's life, isn't it?"

Nell smiled fondly at him. "Yes, you are right, but let's change the subject. We should be talking about the spring to come when everything is turning green and primroses and violets and daffodils are blooming."

Ritchie teased her, "We could also talk about the summer and very hot days when people find it hard to work with sweat rolling off them and they can't even get a drink of water. Or you could talk about the winter, when the snow comes and children play with snowballs. Poor children as well as rich."

Nell laughed. "You always have an answer, Ritchie."

"One has to."

Mr Redgrave said solemnly, "Ritchie is a very clever man when he puts his mind to it." He got up. "And I'm afraid we must be going; I have some businessmen coming in this evening. Thank you for a lovely evening, Nell. And may I ask you all to a meal at my house?"

Nell smiled at him. "And who is going to cook it?"

"Oh, one of the women I know. There's about ten or more."

"Liar," Nell said, laughing. "I'll find someone. Just let me know the date."

After they had gone, Nell said a little dreamily, "Sometimes I wonder if I can wait a year to get married."

"Why wait? Anything can happen in the future."

"But it's my customers. I can't let then down. They depend on me. Always have done."

"It's up to you, Aunt Nell. It wouldn't make any difference to your customers. You'll still be in the district. They can call and see you."

She shook her head. "It wouldn't be the same. They feel cosy in the shop. They wouldn't be able to let their hair down in Philip's house. No, I'll stay here a while longer anyway."

Mollie said no more. Chantelle came in from the shop and said she felt like going to bed.

"You go ahead," Nell said. "We'll be following soon."

She lingered, tidying a few things away and Mollie told her to leave them.

Chantelle stood hesitant for a moment then said, "Why is it that Ritchie should work in Mollie's shop and you both keep me out?"

Nell gave a heavy sigh. "We've told you told you over and over and we definitely will not tell you again. It needs another man in the shop, a man with brains, not a young helpless girl."

"I'm not helpless." There was anger in her voice.

Mollie said wearily, "Chantelle, just go to bed will you."

"I'll go." Her voice had changed, "I love you both. I love Ritchie and I love Mr Redgrave, but in a different way. I think of him as a father."

"Oh, Chantelle." Molllie got up and put her arms around her. "Why are you always behaving in this way? We love you, but you go into such tantrums. Accept things as they are."

"I'll try to," she said, near to tears and Mollie couldn't help thinking that Chantelle had said it so many times.

Mollie kissed her cheek. "Now, off you go."

She went upstairs, head bowed and Mollie said to Nell

when she was out of sight, "Why do I always feel so mean when I've scolded her. She deserves it."

Nell sighed, "I know. I feel the same. Let's talk about something else. Do you think that Ritchie will be successful in your shop? Philip seems to be very pleased with him."

"Yes, he is. I think he's astonished that Ritchie has been so quick in mastering all the prices."

"If only he can keep off gambling."

"I imagine he will. Mr Redgrave said he was a clever man and only a weak character would be unable to stop it." Nell paused, "Mollie, why don't you call Philip by his Christian name?" She smiled. "He is supposed to be your uncle."

"I know, but I don't think I could. I think I would feel disrespectful."

"Of course you wouldn't. You could easily call him 'Uncle'. I think he would be pleased about it. I'll mention it to him."

"I'm not sure that you should. Chantelle would want to do the same and I feel she might take advantage of it."

"I'll mention it and leave it to him."

Although Mollie felt she had to say something else against it, she rather liked the idea of having an 'Uncle'. She had hardly known her father and had not even known if there had been any other uncles in her young life.

Three nights later Mr Redgrave brought Mollie to her aunt's shop again and before he left he told her, smiling, that he would be very pleased to be 'Uncle' to her.

She smiled, too. "I might forget at first. You've been Mr Redgrave to me for some time, but I will try to remember."

Nell said, "Philip is also 'Uncle' to Chantelle. She's over the moon. I felt I had to make you both alike."

"I'm glad. It'll make her feel she belongs to a family."

* * *

182

The following day the Grainger family arrived: Mr Grainger, three of his brothers, a sister and three older cousins. Mollie felt a twinge of excitement inside her.

"Here we are again!" he greeted her. "How nice to see you Miss Paget, and looking as lovely as ever."

Mollie ignored the compliment, guessing he would say the same to every female he met.

"Nice of you to say so, Mr Grainger. Which one of the family are you shopping for this morning?"

"Which one do you think it is?" he teased her.

Mollie kept smiling as she looked at the line of faces. All but one were trying to be solemn. She reached out a hand to one of the youngest boys, who she guessed to be seven or eight years old.

There was a burst of laughter and cries of, "How did you guess?"

She decided not to tell them. "It's because I work in this shop. It's a great source of education in getting to know people."

One of the girls asked Mollie, eyes wide, if she told fortunes?

"Oh, no. I should imagine that any assistant in a shop would be the same."

"I know they are not," declared Mr Grainger. "This is the nicest one I've been in. Mr Redgrave is just so charming, too. It's a natural charm. Most people simper and I can't stand it."

"Neither can we," came a chorus from the younger ones. One of the boys brought Mr Redgrave forward without saying a word and Mr Redgrave showed no embarrassment.

"My niece and I are very pleased to be of service to you all. May I ask what the present is to be this time?"

Mr Grainger beamed at him and then turned to Mollie, "My youngest cousin wants to buy a present for his father

183

and would like to buy the present on his own. The others are willing to put their money together to buy something different. What do you suggest, Mr Redgrave?"

He gave a slight bow, "My niece has always been successful in her choice. May I ask what she would suggest?"

It was difficult at the best of times to make a choice when the price was limited. She said, "Would you all care to look around while I think about it?"

"Of course," said Mr Grainger. "And don't hurry. We have all the time in the world."

Mollie could hear the children talking excitedly and Mr Grainger telling them they must be quiet. She said in a whisper to Mr Redgrave, "What can I suggest?"

"I don't know. It's the price you're up against. Have a look around."

She went into the back room. Everything was there watches, rings, brooches, cravat pins. Mollie stopped suddenly. What about those new sports pieces which had just come in that morning? She brought a box of them out of the cupboard. Every one had to do with men's sports: tennis, cricket, fishing . . . They could be pinned to a hat or a lapel. She liked the one for fishing: it was chased silver in the form of a fish, and was intended to be worn on a hat.

The small boy picked that one straight away. He was excited. His papa went fishing. He was sure he would like having one for his hat.

Mr Grainger beaming, said to him, "There now, Jeremy, didn't I tell you that Miss Paget would know exactly what your Papa would be pleased with?"

"Thank you, Miss Paget," Jeremy said shyly. "It's so kind of you to find me something that I just know Papa will like."

"I'm so glad I was able to help."

"Now then," said Mr Grainger, "is there anyone else needing to buy a present at this moment?"

Mollie hoped there would be.

The three older girls all said that they would like to buy presents while they were here. Then Ritchie came in.

Mollie gave a quick glance at Mr Redgrave and Ritchie then said, "I'm sure that my – uncle and Mr Ritchie would be pleased to help. They are very good at recommending certain goods."

They were accepted and the next half hour was a pleasure for Mollie. Nearly everyone who had come decided that they, too would like to buy a present. Birthdays were not too far away; and it was fun, all of them added, to have such helpful assistants.

Mollie was delighted, of course, at the success of the morning. Ritchie was very popular with the girls and Mr Redgrave was popular with the boys in offering advice. The new sports pins became an instant favourite with most.

While orders were taken and money paid, Mr Grainger took Mollie aside and said in a low tone, "Miss Paget, I must thank you again for your kindness. May I ask if you would come out to dinner with me one evening?"

She felt shocked. "I'm sorry, Mr Grainger, but I couldn't. It would be impossible."

"Why?"

"Well, it's ... We belong to a different class of people."

"What has that to do with it?"

"Everything. I should think your parents would not be pleased. You lead a different life."

He chuckled. "It might interest you to know that my great-grandparents came from farming stock and at times were half-starved."

Mollie found herself interested. "Then how did your parents get so much money?"

"Ah," he smiled. "I shall tell you if you promise to have dinner with me."

Mollie took the plunge. "Yes, I will, but only on one condition. That you take me to a small, quiet restaurant."

"You will deny me the pleasure of showing you off."

"Mr Grainger, I am just an ordinary person and want to be treated as such."

He sighed. "I think you are very stubborn, Miss Paget, but I also know I have to agree. When? Tonight?"

Mollie, who had been wondering what dress to wear said, "Tomorrow would be more suitable, Mr Grainger."

"Shall I call for you here, Miss Paget, or—"

"Here, would be fine. Say half past seven?"

"Splendid, I shall look forward to it. Thank you so much, Miss Paget." He bowed low over her hand, "I feel I'm a very lucky man."

When they had all gone, Ritchie said, "What's all this about having dinner with Mr Grainger?"

"Why shouldn't I?" she asked. "Do you think I'm not good enough to go out with him?"

She saw he was trying to control his anger. "Of course you're good enough, but I would have thought it wasn't done for a lady to go out with a wealthy customer."

"I see no reason why I shouldn't go out with him. I'm not intending to spend all night with him. It's just a meal. I found him interesting to talk to. I want to know the history of his life."

Ritchie said, "As long as you are satisfied. I really have no right to interfere."

"No, you haven't," she replied and walked away.

That evening Mollie had a lift in Mr Redgrave's carriage to her aunt's shop. Ritchie was with them and both men talked about the way Mr Grainger and his family and cousins spent so much in the shop. "All very welcome of course," declared Mr Redgrave. "What

Mollie and I are hoping for is older people coming to buy."

"I should imagine they will in time," Ritchie said. "What do you think, Mollie?"

"Yes, I think they will. It takes time for people to change their shopping area. I am only pleased that having Mr Grainger and the children does bring other people in."

The talk continued until they arrived at her aunt's and Mollie was disappoined that the men were not stopping. There was a meeting that evening at Mr Redgrave's.

"Apologise for us to Nell," Mr Redgrave said. "Give her our love and tell her we shall see her next week at my house."

Nell came to the shop door. "Was that Philip and Ritchie?"

Mollie repeated the message and Nell said, "I haven't made any arrangements to go to Philip's house next week. What's he talking about? I have enough to do here!"

"He's a busy man; probably thought he had arranged it."

"Well, he should have done," her aunt said, but not with any anger; more in a matter-of-fact way. She asked Mollie what sort of day she had had, but before Mollie had a chance to answer, said, "Chantelle and I have had an exceptional day! Together we've made six blouses and sold two of them to customers."

They were in the shop and walking towards the kitchen. "That's very good indeed," Mollie said, "but shouldn't you have kept them for your order?"

Abruptly, the kitchen door was flung wide and Chantelle looked beyond them. "Where are the men? I heard you talking."

Mollie explained why they had not come in and Chantelle said peevishly, "They ought not to bring you here then not come in."

Neither Nell nor Mollie answered. Mollie took her coat off and hung it up.

Nell said, "Oh, Mollie, I didn't give you a chance to say how you had done today?"

"Splendidly! Mr Grainger came with some of his brothers and sisters and cousins and they all had a good spend." She hesitated a second, then told her about being asked out to dinner by Mr Grainger. "For tomorrow night," she added.

"Oh, have we romance in the air?" Nell asked, laughing.

"No romance on my part," Mollie announced firmly. "But I do like the man. He's interesting and we are not going to a well known hotel; just a small place."

Chantelle said, spitefully, "He shouldn't treat you like that. It's an insult. He should have taken you where there were his own class of people."

"That was where he wanted to take me," Mollie said quietly. "I insisted on a small place."

After they had finished the evening meal, Mollie offered to help work on the blouses. Nell accepted, and they all had a busy night.

After Chantelle had gone to bed, Mollie told her aunt about Ritchie and how annoyed he had been that she was going to have dinner with Mr Grainger. "He was really angry," she said.

"Because he's jealous, of course."

"I'm not sure of that."

"You should be sure. He'd got into the habit of thinking that he owned you, because he had lent you money for rent and the sale of the jewellery. You were his woman. It shocked him that you were interested in someone else."

"I never thought of myself as belonging to Ritchie. I like him, always will, because he has been good to me. But I certainly don't want to be possessed by him."

"You couldn't possibly be, not when he's getting money

back from you in order to pay his debts. He's been a fool. To be honest, I would never have imagined him as a gambler. I only hope he can keep off the gambling."

"So do I. I think he's in good hands with Mr Redgrave looking after him."

"Yes. They get on so well together and Ritchie does fit in with his lifestyle. Mr Redgrave has nothing but good to say of him, and I only hope it will last."

Chapter Fourteen

The next morning Mollie took her dark green velvet dress with her to the shop so she could change into it that evening. She hoped it would be dressy enough. She felt it needed some decoration and wondered if she should borrow a necklace. Then she thought, no, she was the one who had asked to go to a simple place.

Both Mr Redgrave and Ritchie greeted her, wanting to know if she was looking forward to the evening, Mr Redgrave in a natural, friendly way, Ritchie with a wry smile.

"Of course," she said. "Mr Grainger is an intelligent man."

"Be careful," Ritchie said. "I should imagine he takes dozens of young ladies out to dinner."

"Together or one at a time?" Mollie asked with a smile. "It doesn't worry me how many young ladies he takes out. I am being taken out and I shall enjoy it."

Mr Redgrave asked quietly, "Do you think that we should do the May list of stones this morning, or wait to see how many customers come in?"

Mollie said, "I do have my dusting, and I think it would be wise to get it done first."

Both men agreed. When no one had come in they sat down at the table. Ritchie's wry manner had disappeared and he was the business man again.

Mr Redgrave opened his book. "The stone for the first half of May is jet."

'This intensely black stone began its existence about one hundred and eighty million years ago, when branches and trunks of trees broke and fell into pools of stagnant water or were carried out to sea by the currents.

'The waterlogged wood then sank to the seabed where it was covered with mineral-rich mud which caused chemical changes.

'Sufferers from sinus problems, the common cold and breathing difficulties are sometimes encouraged to inhale burning essence of jet. In ancient times the stone was used against toothache, headache, epilepsy, loose teeth and swollen feet.

'In the very early days it was neglected as a stone to bring good luck, but throughout the Bronze Age it was considered one of the most magical of all amulets and talismans.

'Wearers of jet are strong and always ready to tackle any job that seems impossible. They usually win in the end.'"

Mr Redgrave laid down his book. "And that is the end of the first half of May. There are still no customers. Shall we go on to the second half?"

Both Mollie and Ritchie were keen to keep learning so Mr Redgrave picked up his book again.

"'This deals with the diamond which is the hardest of all stones. There are ancient legends telling of magnificent diamonds that brought ill luck to their owners. But the diamond is also symbolic of purity, innocence and of strength.

'How then can these different influences be explained? It's simple. The evil influence of the gem is derived from the evil wrought by men in securing it.

'In Roman days the gem was bound to the left arm of the warrior to endow him with courage and fortitude. People in medieval England wore a diamond to protect them from pestilence.

'Between lovers or a married couple the stone promoted constancy.'"

Mr Redgrave closed the book. "I think that all diamonds should go to the State."

Mollie protested. "I don't agree, I would like a diamond. They're just so beautiful, so brilliant."

"And can be terribly harmful."

The doorbell pinged and they all got up laughing. Ritchie said, "Let's see if we can sell one."

Two customers came and browsed around, but Mollie had a feeling they had come with the intention of seeing if any particular wealthy people were looking around. They left without buying anything.

They continued to be busy for the rest of the day. In fact, when the shop was due to close Mollie had not had any tea. Ritchie said at once that he would make some for her but she said no, she would wait and see how much time she had.

Neither man seemed to be in a hurry to leave and she wondered if they wanted to see long it took to get her to get ready. Well, they would know in a few minutes.

There was a small washroom off the back room and she washed her face and changed her dress. She then brushed her hair and stood studying it in the mirror. She had worn it pinned up since she had worked in the other shop. She felt it made her look a little older. Her hair had a natural curl and she drew the curls up to the top of her head and encircled them with a piece of ribbon, pleased with the result.

She was still uncertain whether to borrow a necklace. When she came out of the back room to look into a full-length mirror in the shop, both men whistled.

"You look great," Ritchie said. Mr Redgrave agreed.

"Why don't you both go home?" she asked. "You're spoiling my evening!"

They both got up and apologised. They hadn't wanted her to feel they had left her on her own.

"I'm sorry if I seemed rude, but I felt you were watching me and I was a little flustered."

They put on their hats and coats, but before they left asked if she was sure she would be all right. She still had over half an hour to wait. Mollie had not realised that she had so long to wait. She told them she would be all right and the two men left wishing her a happy evening.

She went into the back room again and sank into a chair. They had treated her as if she were a child. No, that was unkind. They hadn't wanted her to wait alone. She glanced at the clock. There were fifteen minutes to wait. It would soon pass.

She kept smoothing her hair. She had a flimsy scarf to put over her hair. No lady wore a hat when going out to dinner. After all, she would step straight out of the carriage into the restaurant.

She kept glancing at the big clock in the shop. The minutes went by slowly. She went to the door, hoping to see a carriage. There was plenty of traffic on the main road but Mollie felt somehow lost.

She realised she ought to have made the date earlier. But did women make the date? It usually came from the man. She prayed he had not booked at an expensive restaurant. He had said he wouldn't but he might have changed his mind.

She had never known time go so slowly. Twice she thought a carriage was stopping at the shop, then discovered it was only that a carriage was held up by traffic. She went into the back room again. What if Mr Grainger was not a good time keeper? Oh, Lord, why did she have to go through all this for a night out?

Then he was there, knocking on the door. Her heart began a wild beating as she called, "Coming!"

She left only one light on, locked the door, and stepped outside. There stood a smart carriage in shiny dark brown with a crest on the door.

"You look lovely, Miss Paget," he said softly as he helped her into the carriage. It had beautiful upholstery and was very comfortable. What luxury.

"Have you had a busy day?" he asked.

"Yes, but I like to be busy."

"The family all send their good wishes to you."

"Thank you. It was very kind of them."

"The children think the world of you." He added softly, "And so do I."

Mollie knew she had to put a stop to such things if she was to enjoy the evening. She half turned to him. "Mr Grainger, you musn't say such things."

"Because we are from different classes?" He was smiling.

"Exactly."

"It's all wrong."

"Mr Grainger, I must ask you to stop. If you don't, then I shall have to ask you to take me home."

"Oh, no, please. I've been looking forward since yesterday to spending an evening with you. I promise not to say another word of praise about you." He was half smiling as he said it but Mollie decided to accept it.

"I'm glad you have given your word. I was looking forward to the evening too."

"Good. Now, I feel I've chosen the right place to dine. It's small, but families hold parties there and quite a lot of older people like it too. Oh, yes, and there are usually several young couples."

Molly smiled. "It sounds just right."

The restaurant was lit up with candles. It was a lovely scene, with a family toasting a young girl, whose birthday it appeared to be.

One waiter took their coats and another bowed them to a quiet table. He handed them each a menu and asked if they would like something to drink. Mr Grainger started to discuss the various wines with her, but Mollie said she would leave it to him. He chose a French red and she made up her mind to be careful not drink too much.

She studied the menu while this was going on and was pleased to see that there was nothing French. All the food was English. Thank goodness.

The wine was poured, Mr Grainger tasted it and the waiter withdrew discreetly.

Mr Grainger raised his glass. "To many more good days."

Mollie raised her glass too. "Thank you, and to your good health."

She asked after the children and he said, "Oh, they're fine. They're good little souls. Two of the older girls are going through a romantic period at the moment. Both are becoming engaged in a month's time. I am hoping that their fiancés will buy the rings from your shop."

"I hope so too," Mollie said, but was doubtful. They would no doubt be marrying wealthy men.

They ordered soup for the first course and made small talk in between. Then when it was finished and they were waiting for the next course Mollie said, "When we last met you said that your great-grandparents came from farming stock?"

"That's right. They worked very hard in those days. Then, one day, my great-grandfather had a find when he was out ploughing and dug up a bag full of Roman coins."

"That was lucky."

"Yes, but he knew that he was not likely to be able to keep them. There are rules. He had to prove that the land was his. He was a self-taught man. He read numerous books and found out that the land went back generations. It did belong to his family. But it had to be proved.

"He spent hours every night studying the books and apparently the judge who dealt with the case appreciated having a self-taught man to deal with. Although all the big men were afraid of losing the money they had no choice but to let my great-grandfather have it. And that was the start of our wealth."

"How amazing," Mollie said. "Thank goodness your great-grandfather persevered."

"Yes, but do you know, we could never find out how this came about. We don't even know where the books came from. A page had been taken from the front in each one. No doubt the names had been on them. They were good books in their day."

Mollie asked him if he had read them all and he said yes, but he could not say that he understood all of them. They were totally different to the present day ones. Rather dull reading, as a matter of fact.

The waiter brought the next course, roast turkey with four vegetables and roast potatoes. A sauce was served with it and Mollie had never tasted anything so delicious. How nice it must be, she thought, to be able to eat a meal like this every day. But she had never been starved and must appreciate what they did eat.

After that course Mr Grainger talked again about the children, saying how different they all were in temperament. He added, "It's the same with every family. I have numerous cousins and they're all different, so different one would think they belonged to another family. The two youngest boys in our family are like chalk and cheese. Hammond, who is seven is, on the surface, a gentle boy, but if he quarrels with Carlton, who is eight, he goes wild, shouts for his rights." Mr Grainger laughed. "Then, when it's all over, they are the best of friends again and Hammond can't do enough for Carlton."

"And how does Carlton behave?"

"He is more inclined to be aggressive, but it bothers him when Hammond gets angry. The girls are the same too. Contrary in their ways. I would like to have a big family when I marry. There's never a dull moment in our house. My mother, who appears not to take any notice, does take notice. She has them all at a word and they love her. I would like you to meet her. She would be pleased to meet you."

"I'm – afraid not, Mr Grainger."

"Why not? She knows you through the children and there's no obligation. I swear it. To her you are just a kindly shop assistant. You could bring Mr Redgrave with you, I wouldn't mind at all."

Mollie smiled and said she would think about it.

They had trifle to follow the main meal and after that cheese and biscuits and Mollie realised later that Mr Grainger had drawn her out about her own life. She did not regret it, she felt that he should know what sort of a family she came from. She had never really known her father, he had died when she was barely walking. Then her mother had been in and out of hospital and it was really her Aunt Nell, who had more or less mothered her.

Mollie was glad afterwards that Mr Grainger had not said he was sorry for her. What he did say was, "I've always thought that it takes all sorts to make a world. Everyone has a part in it." She also hoped that he would not put his arm around her in the carriage going home. He took her to her door, shook her by the hand and thanked her for a most enjoyable evening and added, he hoped they could do it again.

"His manners were impeccable." She told her aunt what they had talked about and how he had invited her to his home to meet his mother.

"He sounds a wonderful person," Nell said. "I hope he asks you to marry him."

"I don't want to be married to him. I want to run my business and make a success of it."

Nell was silent for a moment. "Do you know what I

198

think, Mollie? We are two of a kind. We want to have our cake and eat it. I want to marry Philip but I don't want to give up my shop. And you could have a very sensible and caring husband, but at the same time you want to make a success of your business." She paused. "Could it be that you're in love with Ritchie but you're waiting to see if he gives up his gambling?"

"No," she said strongly and meant it, but later began to wonder if her aunt was right. She did hope that Ritchie would stop his gambling, but she was not sure about wanting to marry him. She didn't want to marry anyone, but she admitted to herself that she would like to meet Mr Grainger's mother, who sounded an unusual woman. She would think about that and perhaps by the next time the Grainger family came she would know what to say.

* * *

During the next few days they were busy in the shop, so busy there was no time for studying. There were some quite big sales, and Mollie began to watch Ritchie, who was unusually jubilant and she began to wonder if he was taking anything from the till. She felt mean that she was unable to trust him but decided she would mention it to Mr Redgrave when she had an opportunity.

Her chance came one lunchtime when there was a lull and Ritchie asked if he could slip out for fifteen minutes or so to see a friend. As soon as he had gone Mollie asked Mr Redgrave about the till.

Mr Redgrave said at once, "No, everything is in order." He showed her a list he had in his pocket. "I also check the stock. It all tallies."

Mollie heaved a sigh of relief. "I'm so glad, I couldn't have borne it if he was still gambling."

"I think he's over it. I certainly hope so. I know how you felt about it."

Ritchie was back in less than fifteen minutes and looked very pleased with himself. Did he have a lady-friend? She tried to dismiss it, but the feeling persisted. She knew she did not want him to have a lady-friend. Not because she herself was love with him, but she thought it possible that he might be taking a gift to someone – not necessarily a woman. A 'gift' to be sold. But then, why take it at lunchtime? It would have been wiser to take it in the evening. Was it possible that Mr Redgrave had been wrong in his assessment of Ritchie? Oh, Lord, was she always going to have this constant worry? By the end of the day she knew she would have to discuss it with Mr Redgrave. But when? The men always left together.

When Mollie got home that evening her aunt told her that she had had a short note from Mr Redgrave inviting them all to his house on the following Sunday for lunch.

"Are we going?" Mollie asked.

Nell gave her a dreamy smile. "I ought not to, because I have so much to do, but I think we must, don't you?"

"Yes, I do. We can do some work when we come back. What did Chantelle say about it?"

"Oh, she's excited about it. I believe she thinks that all this has been arranged by Ritchie. Philip does not get any thanks for it. But who cares? We are eating out and that is a treat. What shall I wear, I wonder?"

"You'll have to decide before then!"

It was not until later that evening, when Chantelle had gone to bed, that Nell remembered that there was a letter for Mollie.

"So sorry, I forgot all about it."

Mollie wondered who it could be from. A letter was a rare thing. She slit open the envelope.

The next moment she looked up smiling. "It's from Cook. And guess what? She's married!"

"Who to?"

"The police sergeant who used to come to Beverley House every morning for his breakfast. They're living in a little cottage."

Mollie read some more. "She says it's lovely to be married, that the sergeant is such a lovely, warm and caring man."

"Ah," said her Aunt Nell. "That's nice. What else does she say?"

"She's pleased that I like doing shop work and hopes that one of these days she might be able to come and see me." Mollie laid the letter down. "I doubt that she'll ever be able to visit me, but it's nice of her to say so." Mollie paused. "A lot of water has flown under the bridge since then."

"Does she ask after Chantelle?"

Mollie looked up. "No, she doesn't. That's strange, isn't it?"

Nell chuckled. "If she's just married that's all that matters to her."

"Yes, but what do I tell Chantelle? She'll be hurt that Cook hasn't mentioned her. Heaven knows, she has few friends."

"You can say she mentioned her."

"She'll want to see the letter."

"It's your letter. Tell her it's private."

Although Mollie had felt sorry for Chantelle at times it was the very first time that she really understood how Chantelle must feel and knew how hurt she would be that Cook had not even mentioned her.

She looked at the letter. It was written in pencil and the words were a bit higgeldy piggeldy. She said, "I think I could copy this writing. I'll send a little message to her."

"I would just forget it."

"No, it's the least I can do."

Mollie got a pencil from her bag. "If I make a mess of it then I'll have to destroy the letter."

"Do what you think is best."

Mollie wrote carefully. Where Cook had said, "Good wishes to you," Mollie followed it with, "and very good wishes to Chantelle. Hope she is happy with you."

"There, that's not bad, is it?"

"I don't know whether Chantelle deserves it. She leads us a dance at times."

"Wouldn't we be the same if we had nobody close to us? I was lucky that I had you to care for me, Aunt Nell. I don't know what I would have done if I had had no one to love me."

"Oh, Mollie—" Her aunt got up and put her arms around her. "You've always been like my own."

There were tears in her eyes and Mollie felt touched. Nell drew away. "Come on, it's past our bed time."

* * *

The next morning Mollie told Chantelle about the letter and said she could read it if she liked.

Chantelle pressed it to her heart. "Just think, Cook sends her good wishes to me. Isn't that kind of her? Oh, I'll really treasure that."

Although Mollie would have liked to have kept her one and only letter she told Chantelle she could keep it if she liked.

Chantelle said, "May I keep it for one night? I'll give it back to you tomorrow."

Mollie felt a little choked and made up her mind she would write that week to Cook and thank her for the letter.

Chapter Fifteen

During the next two days Ritchie paid Mollie a lot of attention. He joked with her and she wondered why he was so pleasant towards her. Was it possible that he was jealous of her going out with Mr Grainger?

On the second evening Mr Redgrave said that they would take her to her aunt's but that they would not stay. He told her that Nell had written to say they would be pleased to come to lunch on Sunday.

Nell came to the shop door when the carriage arrived to ask them if they would not come in for a few moments, but Mr Redgrave said, he was sorry, but they had an important meeting later.

Nell was peeved. "He's acting like a stranger. I don't know whether we'll go to his house on Sunday."

Mollie scolded her. "You're behaving like a spoilt child. That's not like you, Aunt Nell."

Nell gave a rueful smile. "No, it isn't. I must stop it."

Mollie suddenly felt that her life was in a rut. Every evening was the same. Having a meal, then sitting round the fire and doing sewing and talking. About what? Nothing really. She could turn out to be a spinster with a jeweller's shop.

Well, wasn't that what she wanted?

Oh, Lord, she must stop getting into this depressed state. She had been invited to Mr Grainger's home and she would go. Why not?

* * *

Business was surprisingly slow the next day and Mr Redgrave suggested that they could at least start the next birthstone and see what happened. Both Mollie and Ritchie agreed.

Mr Redgrave brought out his book and opened it.

" 'The first half of June is the aquamarine. Every energy has its colour and the life force is sky blue, like the aquamarine. If this radiating energy is steady then all is well.

'Aquamarine once bore the title, 'All Life'. The Romans valued its six-sided form and wore aquamarine earrings, a favoured decoration, with their crystals uncut, not understanding that a stone can be cut or even powdered and still retain its original properties.

'Apart from the virtues attributed to it in the past, practitioners found that this stone improves eyesight, calms itchy eyes, is a healing balm for swollen feet and a fine soother of jangled emotions and nerves.

'A woman has less trouble than a man with all of these complaints, but a wife will always look after her husband.' "

Mr Redgrave looked up. "There are still no customers. Shall we go on?" He turned over another page.

"The next is topaz. 'This is found in several colours, of which the pink, yellow and white are the most prized. It is symbolic of faithfulness.

'It's an excellent touchstone or pocket companion. It helps those people very much who have faith. Topaz of all colours will help those who suffer from coughs and colds and insomnia. It also helps nerve disorders and stomach troubles.

'Topaz has been used as a medicine for the ailments of women, trouble at birth, especially when twins are born. But these children and the mother will grow up strong after having used the topaz.

'If husband and wife use the stone, they and their children will be strong and happy.' "

The door bell pinged. Mr Redgrave stopped abruptly. "Ah, a customer . . . No – customers!"

* * *

On Saturday evening Mr Redgrave reminded Mollie, smiling, that she and Nell and Chantelle would be having lunch at his house the next day.

"We hadn't forgotten," Mollie assured him. "We're looking forward to it."

"Ritchie will collect you all in the carriage. I think it's going to be a lovely day. The sky is red. You know what they say, 'Red sky at night, sailors delight. Red sky in morning, sailors take warning.'"

Mollie said, "I don't know why it should only be sailors delight. Everyone will be delighted to have a good day after all the poor ones we've been having."

"You're right, Mollie." This was from Ritchie. "I'll call for you all, promptly at half past eleven."

"We'll be ready."

Mollie walked to the corner to get the omnibus, wishing she could have had a lift this evening. She hated Saturday evenings. The omnibus was always very crowded. There was one thing she was not going to do that evening and that was stitch up blouses. She felt weary. It had been a very busy day.

"Have you been doing a lot of sewing?" she asked Nell when she got home.

"Yes, but we're not going to do a thing this evening. We're just going to sit over the fire and talk."

"Good, that's all I want to do too. I'm going to have a lazy day tomorrow. I need a rest."

"That's all right," Nell said. She added to Chantelle, "And it's all right if you want to rest too."

"No, I shall work. I like it. Mollie has had a very hard week."

Mollie knew she should feel a little mean for not doing anything but she accepted her role of a hard working woman.

* * *

On Sunday morning, however, she felt fit again and asked Nell if there was anything she could do to help. "I'll cut out if you like."

"Oh, splendid. Could you cut out two, while I'm stitching this one up?"

"Yes, of course."

Nell brought the rolls and Mollie managed to cut out four. She also did some sewing while Nell did some buttonholing.

At eleven o'clock they stopped to get ready. Ritchie arrived at exactly half past eleven in the carriage to collect them. He teased them, "I wasn't sure whether you would all be up."

"Up?" Mollie laughed. "We were up at seven o'clock and working like demons until now."

"Working, on the Sabbath?" Ritchie eyed them solemnly. "You'd better not tell the vicar."

"What vicar?"

"The one who's been invited to lunch with us."

Nell, who had her foot on the step of the carriage stopped.

"Well, I'll be one less. I gave up going to church when my husband died."

Ritchie grinned. "I was only teasing. There are only the five of us."

"Oh, you!" Nell got in the carriage.

It was a lovely day. The air was mild and the sun shone.

Mr Redgrave met them at the gate and helped each one out, saying, "I'm so glad it's a pleasant day."

Ritchie led the way into the house and showed them into a cloakroom where they left their hats and coats. Then they followed him into the lounge. Mollie looked around her. It was well furnished and there was a low fire in the grate. Mr Redgrave came in. "How about a drink? My cook tells me that lunch will be ready at twelve o'clock."

"And are we to meet her?" Nell asked.

"Of course. Why not come and meet her now?" They followed him down a long passage and into the kitchen. Mollie was aware of a delicious smell of cooking.

Mr Regrave made straight for a big blackleaded oven and looking over his shoulder said, smiling, "This is my cook."

There was a silence, then Nell laughed, "You sly thing! You are doing the cooking."

"And it's ready. I want you all to go into the dining room and I shall bring it in. My young helper will put the dishes out."

A girl of about fourteen came in, took some soup bowls from a table and hurried along the passage.

Nell said, "Philip, do you really mean that you have done all the cooking?"

"I do." He smiled. "Go along into the dining room. I'll bring the bird."

Soup was already in the bowls.

Nell whispered to Mollie, "I still can't believe that Philip did all the cooking. Isn't he amazing?"

Ritchie offered wine. Mollie took a little, just to be sociable. The girl came with dishes of vegetables.

Philip carved the bird with a flourish. Where had he learned to cook? It really was a wonderful meal, and there was still the sweet to come and Mollie guessed it would be followed by cheese and biscuits.

The sweet was served in tall, slender glasses and had

layers of vanilla, strawberry cream, chocolate and, Mollie guessed, two different kinds of wine. Mollie was sure she could not eat anything more but she tackled the cheese and biscuits, and then gave a sigh.

Philip smiled. "You must make room for your coffee."

Impossible, they all said, but they all went into the lounge to have it.

The weather had suddenly changed and had gotten colder. The fire had been built up and glowed red. There was a low rattle of thunder, followed by another.

"Well, what a change," Ritchie said.

"Not much 'sailor's delight' in this," declared Nell. She and Philip sat down together on a big settee and Chantelle sat on Philip's other side. Ritchie pulled Mollie down beside him onto a smaller settee and put an arm around her shoulders. She wanted to draw away but Ritchie gripped her shoulder and whispered, "Sit still."

A vivid flash of lightning made them all jump. And at once the heaviest rattle of thunder yet crashed overhead.

Mollie moved unconsciously to Ritchie. "I hate thunder and lightning."

"It'll soon be over."

"I wouldn't count on it," said Philip. "It's started to rain."

As Mollie looked past the other settee to look out of the window she saw an expression of hatred on Chantelle's face as she stared at her.

Oh, Lord, she thought she must have taken it that she was trying to steal Ritchie from her. She made to get up again but Ritchie tightened his arm around her.

"Stay still," he said. "Lightning can be dangerous."

Mollie felt sad that the Chantelle's jealousy had spoiled a truly enjoyable day.

Chapter Sixteen

Mollie was all set, when they got back to her aunt's shop, to tackle Chantelle about the horrible look she gave her when Ritchie had his arm around her shoulder.

Instead it was Chantelle who tackled her, in a gentle way.

"I'm sorry, Mollie," she said. "When I looked at you so hatefully when we were at Uncle Philip's house this afternoon, I realised that I had no need to be angry with you. Ritchie is not in love with you. He loves me."

Mollie stared at her. Was this possible? Could Chantelle be so smug? Should she let it go? No, not without saying something. She said, "Chantelle, you'll never be able to keep a man if you possess him the way you are doing. Don't you realise that that was why Ritchie gave me a hug? He wanted to prove to you that he likes other women as well as you. I like him, but I'm not in love with him, nor is he in love with you."

"He is, he is!"

Nell, who had gone upstairs, was now coming down. Mollie, not wanting her aunt to know what was going on, said quietly, "Has he ever told you he's in love with you?"

"He doesn't need to!"

"Oh yes, he does. Think about it."

Chantelle turned away and snatched up some embroidery as Nell came into the kitchen.

"Good heavens! You're not thinking of doing sewing

after our lovely day?" Chantelle mumbled something but Nell, not having heard, went on, "Do you know, I don't think I will ever believe that Philip did all that cooking. I'm going to be the lucky one, not having any cooking to do."

Mollie managed to chuckle. "Philip told me that that was the only time he was going to do it."

"Oh, no. He can't do that to me."

"I don't know why you're grumbling, Aunt Nell. You're a good cook."

Chantelle turned her head. "Yes, you are, Aunt Nell. Uncle Philip wants you to cook for him. He's looking forward to it."

"He is?" Nell brightened. "Oh, that's good. I shall have to take some lessons from him. I could do, couldn't I, in the next few months?"

Mollie suddenly smiled to herself. "I thought you were going to wait a year before you married Uncle Philip?"

Nell grinned. "A woman can change her mind, can't she?"

Although it was just turned seven o'clock, Nell started to clear the grate and light a fire. It was a wild night, rain was deluging down and when the fire burst into flame they were all glad to sit around it.

They talked mostly about Philip's house and although Chantelle wanted to know about his wife, Nell simply said, "She died and I don't think we should talk about her."

*   *   *

The next morning it was still raining, although not so heavily as the night before. It was cold, however, and Mollie put on scarf, mackintosh and sou'wester and ran nearly all the way to where the omnibus stopped.

As she went into the shop she called, boldly, "Good morning, Uncle Philip."

He came out of the back room smiling. "I'm glad you

210

remembered. I wondered if you would. What a dreadful day. Let me help you off with your mackintosh. Oh, here's Ritchie."

Ritchie had been running too to get out of the rain. "Lord, what weather. I doubt we'll have many customers on a day like this."

"Well, we've always got the birthstones to do," declared Philip. "It's something to do. We'll have a cup of tea first."

While they were waiting for the kettle to boil, Mollie told Philip about Nell who had shortened their engagement to months. Philip was all smiles. He said, "I thought that the cooking might make a difference."

Mollie chuckled. "Oh, it did, she's hoping to have cooking lessons from you."

"No! I don't believe it."

"Don't worry," said Mollie, "we all praise her cooking and she will see to that part of the housekeeping."

They were still drinking their tea when Philip brought out his book. He opened it and turned a page. "We finished with the topaz and now start July with the red coral. 'This beautiful, much loved pink or red coral comes from the seabed of the Mediterranean. The name comes from a Greek word that means 'Nymph of the Sea.' Legend has it that delicate twigs and branches of coral that grew along the seashore were taken by sea maidens to their caves along the ocean floor. There they tended them until they lost their sickly look and grew well and strong.

'They not only grew strong but developed a tendency to heal people who suffered disorders. They could banish nightmares and ward off demons of darkness. They could also cure a dreadful breathlessness, toothache and skin eruptions.

'In many countries coral is hung round the necks of children to protect them. Coral calms the nerves and creates harmony of a gentle kind. Men and women who wear coral will quarrel at times but it's never for long. Most live long

211

and happy years.' That is the end of the coral."

He looked out of the window. "What a day. It's pouring down. There won't be many people out shopping. Should we consider going on with the gemstones? I'm willing. It would help to pass the time."

Both Mollie and Ritchie agreed.

"This time it's the zircon," Philip said. "Not one of the most popular of birthstones, but certainly an interesting one. I have always liked it and I think that both of you will enjoy it too.

'This many-coloured, transparent gem should not be underestimated, either as a jewel or as a means of healing. It was said by the ancient Greeks that the zircon brought strength to the mind and joy to the heart. The zircon took precedence over all other gemstones because of its lustre and its glory of light, often rivalling the faceted diamond.'"

Philip looked up. "I would agree with that. 'The zircon holds within itself the essence of the Sun and Jupiter, which carry the energy of existence. Its vitality, which acts with the effectiveness of a laserbeam, will cure brain damage, venereal diseases and acute skin disorders. It disperses fluid in the lungs and cures inertia and ailments of the spleen.

'It also prevents sleeplessness, stomach ulcers, acute back-ache, strengthens weak ankles and will prevent bleeding in any part of the body. What other birthstone does so much?

'On the spiritual plane it furthers self-development and the extension of the higher mind, an effect especially noticeable when the heat-treated variety of blue is used.' I think it's a wonderful stone."

"I do too," Mollie said. "Just think of all the ailments it can cure. Amazing."

Ritchie nodded. "I'll go along with that."

Philip looked out of the window. "Good Lord, is this rain never going to end? Can you both stomach another gemstone?"

They both said yes and Philip, with a small sigh, turned over yet another page.

"August begins with the chrysolite. It's a short one and was known by the ancients as the 'Golden Stone'."

"With a title like that it seems promising to me," Ritchie said.

"'It's a greenish-yellow in hue, although varieties are found with an olive green or a bright green colour, which are known as oliveen or peridot, as the case may be.

'The chrysolite was worn at night to banish devils and to be sure of a good night's sleep. There were no aches and pains if the chrysolite was worn. During the day it brought literary or poetical inspiration. 'A tenderness developed in both men and women and if they married their marriages were exceptional. Children benefited too by wearing a piece of chrysolite in a bracelet.'"

Ritchie said eagerly, "I saw a bracelet with a piece of chrysolite in another jeweller's shop the other day and wondered if we should buy some."

"I don't think we should at the moment," Mollie said. "We have ordered quite a lot of jewellery and this chrysolite has not been asked for. Shall I make some tea?"

The men agreed and Mollie put the kettle on, hoping that she had not upset Ritchie. They had had to cut the order to pay off Ritchie's debt. But he certainly did not look upset and chatted about this and that. And, a few minutes after they had finished their tea some customers came in.

It was not a busy day, but it kept them going reasonably. Every customer who did come in complained about the weather and Mollie hoped it would be fine the following day. She also hoped that Mr Grainger would call. She was anxious to meet his mother. It depended, of course, whether his mother still wanted to meet her . . .

* * *

213

It was cold the following day and the rain had eased to a drizzle. Mollie arrived at the shop to find Philip and Ritchie already having a cup of tea. Ritchie grinned and said he would pour her a cup.

Mollie took off her mackintosh and Philip took it from her and hung it up. "Pray heaven it won't be as slow as yesterday."

"I hope not." She took a sip of hot tea. "This is welcome."

Philip said, "You'll never guess who we saw last night at a friend's house. Mr Grainger. He was leaving as we arrived. He seemed so pleased to meet us. Said he would be calling today. He wanted you to go with him and meet his mother. He's a nice chap, I like him."

Mollie's heart was thumping and she glanced at Ritchie. He seemed unconcerned.

She said, "I hope he brings some of the family to buy presents."

"Not today. He's coming just to see you. He stressed that. That's right, Ritchie, isn't it?"

Ritchie glanced up. "Did he? I wasn't listening."

Mollie felt annoyed. Of course he was listening. He would want to know every little thing Mr Grainger said and did. He was jealous of him.

Mollie got up and, taking her tea with her, said she would be getting on with the dusting.

As Philip unlocked the shop door Mr Grainger came in and swept off his hat.

"Good morning to you all." He turned to Mollie and gave her a huge grin. "I came to ask you if you would come to our house this evening and meet my mother."

"I'm not sure, Mr Grainger. I must ask my uncle." Her heart was beating madly.

Philip said, half smiling, "You have my permission, Mollie."

"Would it be possible, Mr Redgrave, for your niece to leave the shop a little earlier than usual? All the children are very fond of her and want to see her. Say, six o'clock?"

"That would be quite all right, if it suits you, Mollie?"

"Yes, oh, yes."

"Then I will leave you and get on with my other business. Good day to you all." He half bowed and left, after throwing a smiling glance at Mollie.

Her legs were shaky. She sat down. When he was out of view she said, "I don't know if I'm doing the right thing."

"Of course you are," Philip said smiling. "We can do with a few more millionaires. What do you say, Ritchie?"

"The more the merrier." His tone was bitter.

It was those words that decided Mollie to go to the Graingers. She had no need to be beholden to Ritchie.

Several customers came in and she was glad that they took her mind off the Graingers for a while. She thought of going back to her aunt's house at lunch time to get another dress, then changed her mind. She would go in the one she was wearing. The Graingers were used to seeing her in the black dress. She did have a white lace collar she could wear.

They were reasonably busy until after lunch, when there was a lull. Philip asked if they were interested in doing another birthstone and although Mollie was not in the mood, she agreed.

Philip sat down with the book. "We have the cornelian for late August. We are getting through them. That only leaves four months."

Mollie was surprised at how close they were to the end. Philip turned a page. "'The cornelian,'" he said, "'is actually carnelian, from the Latin word for flesh. Its colours are a pinkish yellow tinged with red. It does,

215

however, change colour at times, especially in sunlight and can become a mixture of red, brown and yellow. As both the cornelian and the amethyst have iron as a colouring agent, they can be used together to benefit the bloodstream, combat depression and help the owner shake off sluggishness and become vigorous and alert.

'From ancient times cornelians have been used in amulets and talismans to ward off the baleful evil eye, and to preserve the body from the dangers of fevers, pestilence and lightning.'"

Philip looked up at this stage. "It's surprising to learn how many thousands of people were killed by lightning in the very early days." He went back to his book.

"'The stone, in powdered form, was used to check bleeding and if the powder was used with water it could ease very painful stomach pains.

'Cornelian people suffered a lot of pain if they did not wear the stone. They had backache, painful knees, cramp in their hands, severe headaches, lung trouble, had sleepless nights and knew a terror of the evil eye.

'If a man and woman married and both had faith in the stone they would be a very contented couple. But if either did not, they would be constantly quarrelling.'"

Philip looked up at the clock. "That is the cornelian ended. We could go on to September. What do you think?"

Ritchie and Mollie both agreed.

He began. "September starts with the garnet, a rather strange stone." Then he paused and looked up.

"I don't mean by strange that it's not a likeable one. It's very likeable but not many people seem to think so. Possibly because it's a very gentle one and most people want a powerful stone."

He looked again at the book. "'Idealism is what garnet people strive for: a desire that all things should work

216

smoothly and that no jarring note should be introduced into the harmony of life. Selfishness and intolerance are quite foreign to them. Wealth, for its own sake, means little, but would be appreciated if it helped other people.

'Sometimes their excessive idealism is taken by others to mean superiority and they want nothing more to do with them. These Garnet people should learn to recognise true friendship and to develop and make use of their brain power as a means of bringing material success.

'Husbands and wives are usually loving and faithful. Not always, however. There can be friction. But they do take care that their offspring are brought up very sensibly. In many cases a loving and faithful couple will produce a happy and joyful family.'"

Philip closed his book. "That is the garnet dealt with. And we shall make that the last for the day. I think that Mollie will want to keep her mind open for this evening."

"No," she said, "I shall take it like any other evening. I do want to meet Mrs Grainger, but I have no idea if she will be pleased to meet me or not. I'm prepared for either."

"That's sensible," declared Ritchie. "If you feel she doesn't want you in the family, you simply walk out."

Mollie smiled to herself, knowing that Ritchie would be hoping for that. She said, "I don't think I could be quite so rude. I do want to keep the Graingers as customers."

"Oh, of course."

Philip chuckled. "Ritchie and I will be on tenterhooks. We are both hoping for another big order."

Mollie squared her shoulders. "So am I, Ritchie, so am I. I'm going to take a look out of the front door and see if I can see any prospective customers coming this way."

In the next few minutes customers kept coming in and buying as though they had been allowing the three of them to have their daily study session uninterrupted.

The lunch break was quiet but the afternoon was busy

again and Mollie had a bit of a rush in the end to be ready by six o'clock when Mr Grainger would call for her.

She had curled her hair around her fingers and caught it all up on the top of her head so that the soft curls fell over her ears and the back of her head.

She was pleased with the white lace collar on her simple black dress and when she came into the shop both Ritchie and Philip gave a whistle and said she looked really beautiful.

Colour rushed into her cheeks. She picked up a flimsy scarf to put over her hair but didn't get the chance to put it on before Mr Grainger arrived, a few minutes before six.

He gave her a broad smile and said softly, "I feel I'm a very lucky man, Miss Paget."

"You are," declared Ritchie boldly, but Mr Grainger took it in good part. "Thank you." He held out his arm to Mollie and she put her hand through it and said to Philip, "Tell Aunt Nell that I shall not be late back."

Mr Grainger whispered as he led her outside, "I hope we will be late."

Her heart gave a little lurch and she hoped that he would not linger on the way home.

He had come in the beautiful brown carriage and Mollie felt very pleased indeed that so many people noticed it. Then she clasped her hands and prayed to God to let her enjoy the evening.

Mr Grainger talked mostly about the children and said how much they were looking forward to her visit.

When they arrived at the house Mollie noticed that every room had candlelit chandeliers. How beautiful it looked.

Mr Grainger helped her down from the carriage and said softly, "I know my mother will like you."

The door was opened before they got up the steps and when Mollie went in she was aware of a well furnished hall with armour-plated figures placed all the way around it. A manservant took their coat and hats.

Mollie began to feel nervous. Mr Grainger put his hand under her elbow and walked her to a door on the left. He knocked and the door was opened by a maid. Mollie saw a tall, beautifully poised elderly lady rise from an armchair.

It was not until she approached that Mollie realised that Mrs Grainger's mother was a little shabbily dressed.

Mr Grainger introduced Mollie and Mrs Grainger held her hand in a surprisingly hard clasp and said in a sharp voice, "I'm pleased to meet you, Miss Paget. Do, please, sit down."

Mollie swallowed hard and sat in the chair offered.

Mrs Grainger said, "The children are looking forward to meeting you." Then she smiled and and seemed to change completely to a warm-hearted woman.

Mollie, now completely at ease, said, "I've had a lot of pleasure from the children, Mrs Grainger. They were so grateful to be helped to choose a present."

"And don't I know it," she said, still smiling. "We'll have a drink, then we'll have them in. It will soon be the younger children's bedtime."

She looked to her son. "Will you pour, dear boy?"

He got up at once and asked what wine Mollie would like.

Mollie had to refuse. She was not used to alcohol and did not want to make a fool of herself. "Not for me, thank you," she said.

"A cup of coffee? Tea?" Mrs Grainger asked.

"A cup of tea would be nice, thank you," she said.

A maid was summoned and it seemed she was back in two minutes, with a tray containing cup and saucer, cream, a teapot and some cakes.

Mrs Grainger said they would let the tea stand a few minutes and asked Mollie about her family. She told her that she lived with her aunt but made no mention of having the shop. Then she realised that Mrs Grainger obviously wanted to know about her life and was wondering if she was suitable to marry her son. It was strange how cleverly she had done it.

Mrs Grainger and her son sat drinking wine, with Mr Grainger looking very pleased with himself. Oh, heavens, what was she to do?

There was a knock at the door and a middle-aged lady came in to say that the children wanted to see Miss Paget. Could she bring them in?

Mollie drank her tea, and her mouth was still dry. When Mrs Grainger asked if it was all right to bring them in, she said, "Yes, of course, Mrs Grainger."

The woman left and within two minutes there was not only the Grainger children but their cousins and friends too.

The youngest ones came rushing up to Mollie and flung their arms around her ... and the next moment were scolded by Mrs Grainger and also their nurse. They stepped back and apologised but stood looking at Mollie with shining eyes.

Mrs Grainger waved the nurse aside. "I shall allow them to talk to Miss Paget for a few moments then they must go to bed."

The children told Mollie what other presents they wanted and then Mrs Grainger told them they must now all go up to their nurseries. One small boy moved closer to Mollie and was ordered by his grandmother in a firm voice to do as he was told. He hurried away, but kept looking back and smiling.

After they had gone the older children were allowed to come over and so many were speaking at once Mollie lost the gist of the conversation. After they had all told her they would be coming again to buy more presents only some of the older ones were allowed to stay a little longer. The two young ladies who Mr Grainger had said were going to be engaged whispered to Mollie that they would send the two men to Mollie's shop.

"Oh, don't," she whispered back. "Please don't." But they simply smiled.

When they were told it was time to leave they tripped out, waving to Mollie.

Mrs Grainger gave a sigh of relief. "The family gets larger every year." Then she asked her son if he would leave. She wanted to have a talk to Mollie.

He left, all smiles, as though he knew that a wedding was going to be arranged.

When he had gone Mrs Grainger turned to Mollie. "Now, Miss Paget, we have some talking to do. I like you, I like you very much indeed, and I wish I could agree to you marrying my son, but it is impossible."

Mollie felt that a load had been lifted from her.

"Thank goodness for that, Mrs Grainger."

"Wh – what?" She stared at Mollie. "I thought that—"

"No mention of marriage has been made to me by your son, Mrs Grainger. This is the first I've heard of it."

"Oh, dear, he led me to believe that he had asked you and that you had agreed."

"Mr Grainger has never said a word about marriage. I like him very much but I'm not in love with him. In fact, I'm in love with another man."

"Thank goodness for that. His father would have been very annoyed. In spite of the fact that our grandparents had known hardship and that we now have plenty of money, he wanted more to come into the family. I must admit, Miss Paget, that you have relieved my mind."

"I'm glad, and I'm sure that your son will accept in time that I couldn't possibly have married him."

"Thank you, my dear, and I only hope that he will still want to bring the children to your shop to buy presents."

Mollie thought that this would be very awkward, and

yet they needed the money – and the prestige. It brought other people into the shop. Oh, heavens, why were there always problems?

Mrs Grainger said, "I shall have to ask Nicholas to come in. It's not a pleasant task that I have to perform."

She seemed uncomfortable and shrugged a fine silk shawl from her shoulders. It was then that Mollie noticed how old her dress must be. There were stains on it. Then she remembered Mr Grainger telling her how his father would not take his mother out because she would not dress up. It was strange, very strange.

Mrs Grainger summoned a maid to ask her son to come in.

He came in, a broad smile on his face. "Well?" he said, "and is it settled?"

"No, darling it isn't," replied his mother sternly. "You let me think that Miss Paget had agreed to marry you and she tells me that she knew nothing about it."

He looked quickly at Mollie. "But I thought that—"

"Miss Paget is already promised to another young man."

Mr Grainger looked as if all the life had been taken from him. He sank on to a chair.

Mollie said gently, "I'm sorry this has happened, Mr Grainger."

"I was at fault for taking you for granted. I thought—"

His mother said, "I hope that you have not led the children to believe you were going to marry Miss Paget?"

"No, not at all."

Mollie got up. "I must go." Then, thinking about the shop, she said gently. "I do hope you will bring the children to the shop. They so enjoyed their visits."

"Oh, yes, I wouldn't want to spoil their pleasure." He paused. "Would you prefer someone else to take you home?"

"No, of course not. I hope we can still be friends."

222

He brightened. "You are so kind, Miss Paget. Thank you."

Mrs Grainger gripped her shoulders and said in a low voice, "I'm so sorry I can't have you as my daughter-in-law. Come and see me again sometime."

Mollie promised she would and they left.

When they were in the carriage she said, "Do you think we could drive around for a while? I don't want my – my uncle to think I'm home too soon."

"Of course." He hit his palm on his forehead. "What a fool I've been, taking you for granted. I'll never forgive myself."

"Think no more about it. I've already forgotten it."

"What a dear person you are. I'm so very glad that I can come back to the shop with the children. Dare I ask if I can take you for a meal to make up for my terrible *faux pas*?"

Mollie, who had not had anything to eat since her sandwiches at midday, was glad to agree. She had not wanted to return home less than half an hour after she had left. This would solve the problem of having to explain what had actually happened.

It was ten o'clock before they left the small restaurant and Mr Grainger had been so easy and talked so beautifully about his family that Mollie wondered if she was not a little in love with him, after all.

Chapter Seventeen

The following morning Mollie felt unhappy, without exactly knowing why. The night before she had been sure she had been in love with Mr Grainger, but was she? Wasn't it simply because he had been so kind, so nice to her? She began to wish she had never gone to meet his mother.

Within a few minutes of arriving at the shop Philip asked her if she was not feeling well, and the next minute Ritchie asked the same thing.

Knowing she would have to pull herself together, she forced a smile. "I think it's just this dreadful weather. It's so cold and wet."

Philip said, "The kettle's on, we'll have a cup of tea and cheer ourselves up. How did you get on with Mr Grainger's mother last night?"

Mollie was aware of Ritchie watching her closely. "Oh, splendid. She's a lovely woman, so warm and caring. And the children, well, I've never had so many caresses."

Ritchie said, a dry note in his voice, "So, are you thinking of getting married?"

"We didn't discuss it, but the Grainger family will be coming to the shop to buy presents, which is very satisfying." She brought the subject back to the weather. "This dreadful rain. I hope it eases off soon."

They were drinking their tea when a customer came in. Philip got up saying softly, "I hope this is the first of many."

When he had gone into the shop Mollie said, "If no

one else comes in I don't want to do any birthstones this morning. Any spare time I have I want to think of last night. It's a beautiful house." She described the hall and the drawing-room, then added, forcing a smile, "Sorry, I got a little carried away."

Ritchie leant back in the chair. "Would you really like to live like that?"

"I'm not sure. A cottage would probably suit me better."

"I doubt whether a cottage would be acceptable for the wife of a millionaire's son." His tone was still dry. Philip returned to the back room.

"One silver watch sold. A few more wouldn't come amiss."

In fact, they had quite a few customers and whether Ritchie had told Philip that Mollie was not in the mood for birthstones or not, they were never mentioned that morning.

It was late in the afternoon when there was a lull and Philip mentioned looking at the next two gemstones, which were lapis lazuli and jacinth. Ritchie and Mollie agreed.

Philip brought his book from the shelf and flipped through the pages until he found the one he wanted. He began without any preamble.

"'Lapis lazuli is a deep blue or bluish-green mineral whose name derives from Latin and Arabic words, which refer to the colouration. When polished it displays sparkling metallic flecks that are due to the particles of iron ore within its matrix. It was used by the ancients for the decoration of buildings and also to make brooches and other ornaments. In later years it was used in other countries.

'In the Middle Ages the mineral was crushed to make a powder and pills were made from the powder to ease pain. Lapis lazuli worn next to the skin would ease many pains. It cured an aching back, eased pains in legs, shoulders and was especially good for neuralgia. Water in which the mineral had been standing was used as an eye-wash to allay inflamation.

'The stone has been employed as a talisman. It was customary to thread a few pieces of lapis on a gold or silver wire to put round the wrists of children to keep them from harm.

'The sparkles of the iron pyrates in the deep blue of lapis lazuli were compared to the twinkling of the stars in the heavens and the mineral was called the 'Heavenly Stone'."

"Well," Philip said, "That's the end of September. Shall we do October, which starts with the jacinth?"

Philip began, " 'This stone is known also as the hyacinth after the Greek youth whose blood was changed into the flower bearing its name. Hyacinth was killed by a quoit thrown by Apollo which Zephyr blew against the youth's head. It is a variety of the zircon and is orange or cinnamon red in colour.

'Medicinally the jacinth was used to prevent or cure disorders of the stomach and to strengthen the action of the heart.

'As a talisman jacinth was said to bring happiness to its wearer and to protect him from fevers and poisoning.' "

Philip looked up from the book. "That is the end of Jacinth." Then, "No, there is a little more."

" 'Jacinth people were good and were always willing to help people in trouble. Unfortunately this was taken as interfering and it was some time before people appreciated their kindness.' And that is the end."

Mollie was pleased when the day ended and she was able to go home.

When she opened the shop door she was aware of a soft buzz of chatter. Nell, who had been talking to a few customers, left them at the counter and came hurrying over to her.

"Oh, Mollie, I've got some exciting news for you.

You'll never guess what's happened. Chantelle's father is here!"

Mollie stared at her. "Chantelle's . . . *father?*"

"Yes, he's been searching for her since she left Paris and he's only found her now. Come along, you must meet him. She's just too excited. She's been laughing and crying together. I can't believe it. I think I'll close the shop." Nell hurried the women out and locked the door.

"Oh, dear, I don't know whether I'm on my head or my heels." She opened the door that led to the kitchen and Mollie followed her in a dream.

A well dressed man got up out of the chair and Chantelle said, "Papa, this is dear Mollie who saved me from the workhouse, and brought me here to her aunt. She saved my life."

He bowed to Mollie and with tears in his eyes said, "I can never thank you enough, Miss Paget."

Mollie was surprised that he spoke perfect English.

Nell said, "Mr Sellick is English, his wife is French. They searched for her in Paris, but had no luck until he spoke to a woman he knew."

Mr Sellick took over the story, telling it in a low voice.

"Chantelle had been in an accident and had lost her memory. I called one morning to see how she was and was told that she had left the hospital with a woman."

"Did you know this woman?" Mollie asked.

He nodded slowly and there was a bitter expression on his face. "Oh, yes, I know her, but it was not until recently that I would have killed her had I not been stopped. She told me she had taken her to a big house in Kettering in England. I went straight away in search of my darling but the people denied knowing anything about her. I was walking away after another failure when a servant came running after me. She told me where Chantelle was but she was terrified and told me not to tell anyone that she had told me."

228

"It was little Bess," Chantelle said, tears in her eyes again. "She was terrified of everyone in the kitchen except you, Mollie, and Cook. And Cook has left now, as you know."

Chantelle continued softly, "Poor Papa. I told her that if anyone in the house was angry with her, she must write and tell him and he would see she got a job in his own house."

Mr Sellick sighed, "That's the whole dreadful story."

He wanted to take Chantelle away there and then, but Nell begged him to let her stay until the following morning. Chantelle too begged to be allowed to stay, saying she had so many friends she had to say goodbye to.

Her father smiled and gave in.

Nell asked him to stay for supper but he said he must go back to his friends. They had no idea where he would be. He would be back the following morning to collect Chantelle.

When he had gone Chantelle said, "I just can't believe it! I can't believe that I could forget all about my home. I have a lovely mother and brothers and sisters." She paused a moment. "The woman who brought me to England was Papa's former mistress. She wanted to have her revenge because he had finished with her."

Mollie and Nell exchanged horrified glances but made no remark.

That evening, Philip and Ritchie called at the shop to be greeted with the exciting news.

Chantelle flung her arms around Ritchie. Wasn't it all wonderful? Her dear Papa was here. Ritchie could come to Paris with them. They could get married.

Ritchie removed her arms. "That is impossible, Chantelle. I don't love you."

"You do, you do!"

"I don't. Nor have I ever told you that I loved you."

"But you do love me, I know it."

"Chantelle." There was a sharpness in Ritchie's voice. "I shall tell your father that I have never, in any way, suggested that I love you. Loving me was all in your mind. You will have the choice of numerous young men when you get home.

A dreamy look came into her eyes. She nodded. "Yes, I will, won't I?" She smiled. "It will be very intriguing. I shall write and tell you all about it."

A tiny sigh escaped Ritchie's lips but she seemed unaware of it. Chantelle too gave a small sigh. She was lost in a dream land. She had it all mapped out. They would all come to Paris for a holiday. What a wonderful time they would have. Her mama loved entertaining.

Nell said she would be unable to come – she had a lot of orders for sewing.

This did register with Chantelle and she said, "Oh, Nell, I forgot all about the blouses. You will have to come and live in Paris. In the meantime Mollie will help out. She's a very quick worker when she sets her mind to it."

Mollie glanced at Nell with a despairing look, and Nell said, "Oh, yes, Mollie is a worker, a very hard worker indeed."

Mollie got the message and thought thank heavens Chantelle would be leaving.

Chantelle never stopped talking and by half past nine was ready for bed.

"I must go to bed," she said, "otherwise I will be sleeping on the train and Papa would not like that." She turned to Philip and Ritchie and asked them if they would be sure to come and say goodbye in the morning.

They both promised they would.

Chantelle trudged upstairs.

Nell said, "Poor girl, she's her own worst enemy. I know that she thinks that she's going to have a wonderful time at home, but from the look of her father I know she won't have all her own way. He's a strong man."

"It's what she needs." Ritchie said.

Mollie felt a little annoyed He had told her himself that he had made love to Chantelle. It might not, of course, have been making love as she had thought of it.

Well, she was certainly not going to worry about it.

Philip got up saying they must be going. He said it must have been a strain on Nell and Mollie, not having expected Chantelle's father to find her.

They would, however, be back to say goodbye to Chantelle in the morning.

"Yes, of course," Nell said. Chantelle would be upset if they didn't call.

After the men had gone Nell and Mollie talked over Chantelle's life with them.

Nell said, "I know we cursed her at times when she went into a temper, but she helped me a lot with the sewing and doing the embroidery on the handkerchiefs and the screens. And don't think I expect you to help me with the blouses. I shall give them up when I marry Philip."

"I think it would be wise. You'll have a lot of house-keeping to do."

"What will you do, Mollie, when Philip and I marry?"

"Live over the shop, perhaps. All I need is a bed, a table and a chair."

"I won't have you living like that. You can live with Philip and me."

"No, you've been together for such a short time. You'll be on your own, as you should be when you marry." Nell hesitated. "You do know that Ritchie is in love with you, Mollie?"

"He isn't."

"He told me weeks ago that he had been in love with you since the day he met you. The trouble is that he can't tell you because you might think he's after your money."

"Which he is, of course, or he wouldn't have told you. He knew you would pass it on."

"He made me promise not to. I swore I wouldn't tell you but I thought it was a shame that you should live apart when you do love each other."

"I'm not in love with him, nor could I ever be after the way he treated me. Asking me point blank for the return of the money he had lent me. I would rather marry Mr Grainger." Mollie got up. "Sorry, but I must go to bed too."

Mollie was annoyed with herself for getting angry with her Aunt Nell. She tossed and turned then made up her mind she would apologise to her in the morning.

It was not a good night, but she did get some sleep and was up earlier than usual the next morning.

Philip and Ritchie soon arrived and Ritchie kept telling Chantelle about all the wonderful men she would meet in Paris and before they parted Chantelle was dreamy-eyed and smiling.

Both Philip and Ritchie kissed and hugged her and she made them promise that they would both write.

Mollie told Philip that she would come to the shop after Chantelle and her father had left.

With the men gone Chantelle kept running upstairs to fill an old suitcase of Nell's with her clothes.

When her father arrived and she put the suitcase at his feet he told her they would not be taking it, he would buy her new clothes in London before they left.

Mollie, aware of Chantelle's distress, said brightly, "New clothes! Aren't you lucky?"

Chantelle smiled. "Yes, I am lucky aren't I?" She was cheerful after that and no more tears were shed because, she said, they would all be soon together in Paris.

Mollie and Nell saw them off and waved them out of sight and then the tears came, not knowing whether they would ever see Chantelle again.

Chapter Eighteen

Mollie felt no more cheerful the following morning. What was she going to do? She couldn't marry Nicholas, even if she had wanted to. His father had chosen a bride for him. And she did not want to marry Ritchie. She would turn out to be a spinster shop owner. Well, things could be worse. There would be the Grainger children calling this morning to choose a present for one of the members of the family. Mrs Grainger had promised to let them come but what if she changed her mind and would not let them come any more? Life would be unbearable.

She could, of course, marry Ritchie but knew she would never do that, not after the way he had treated her. She had been a fool to go and meet Mr Grainger's mother. It was a big mistake. She would be sure to stop her son from bringing the children and it would be a big loss to the shop. They would be bound to lose the customers who only came because they had a millionaire buying from them . . .

By the time Mollie got to the shop she had cheered up a little. Philip and Ritchie were drinking tea. Philip got up to pour Mollie a cup and asked her how she was.

"I'm fine," she said.

"No engagement ring yet?" Ritchie asked sarcastically.

"No, of course not. I have too much to do to think about getting married!"

"Such as?"

"Looking after the shop."

"You won't need it, not when you're married to the son of a millionaire."

She felt tears rising. Ritchie must have seen them. He said softly, "Don't, Mollie love, I can't bear to see you crying."

He went to put his arms around her and she shouted, "Don't touch me! All you want is my money."

"That's not true, Mollie." This from Philip. "Ritchie had lent two friends money in his gambling days, and they returned it to him yesterday. He gave it to me last night. It's reduced the amount considerably."

"I'm sorry," she mumbled to Ritchie. The tears were still there.

Philip apologised, "I'm at fault for forgetting to tell you. Come and sit down and have another cup of tea."

"No, I'll do some dusting."

"Do it later. *Please.*"

She gave in, knowing that Philip was upset for forgetting to tell her. She wondered as Philip poured the tea if Mrs Grainger would stop Nicholas from bringing the children to the shop. If so, it would make a big difference to the takings. Stop it, she told herself. Mrs Grainger had told her she would allow the children to come. It was no use adding misery to misery.

The doorbell pinged and a cheery voice called, "Good morning to you all!" It was Mr Grainger. Mollie dried her eyes and went into the shop.

"Good morning, Mollie. I was in the district and just had to call and see how you were."

"Oh, I'm fine, thank you. No children this morning?"

"They'll be here tomorrow. They are sorting out who it is they have to buy for. I must be going. I'll tell them that you were asking after them." He whispered to her, "I still love you, Mollie, but Papa has a young lady he wants me to marry. I have no choice but to agree. I'll see you tomorrow."

236

He was at the door and called out to the men, "Goodbye to you both. I'll see you tomorrow."

They both came in to the shop and apologised; they had not heard him come in. "It's this wretched rain," Philip said. "I hope it soon clears up."

"I think it will by tomorrow," Nicholas said. "I'm bringing some of the children tomorrow, I'll see you all then. 'Bye for now."

He left and Philip said, "Thank goodness we'll be seeing him with the children. We need them."

Mollie was glad when it was time to go home. Philip was unable to take her home that evening and she had to go by bus. It was packed, but a young man gave her his seat. She thanked him and and sank down. When she arrived at the crossroads she got off. It was raining heavily and she ran all the way to the shop.

Nell said, "Oh, dear, this awful weather. Give me your hat and coat and I'll hang them up. Go and sit by the fire and I'll bring you a cup of tea."

Nell brought two cups and sat down beside her, "I haven't done any sewing today. I missed Chantelle. What was your day like?"

"Awful. I hope it's better weather tomorrow."

"Philip and Ritchie didn't come this evening?"

"No, Philip had a meeting this evening. And I think that Ritchie was glad to get a lift home."

"I take it that you didn't get any more friendly with Ritchie?"

"No, and I don't want to be any more friendly."

"That's a pity. You'll be on your own when Philip and I are married."

"I'll be all right. I've always wanted a shop."

"Why don't you take mine over?"

"No, I don't want to do any more sewing."

"But you'll only have the men. Oh, why don't you marry Ritchie? He's definitely in love with you."

"No, I don't want him, *ever*. Please don't mention it any more, Aunt Nell. I'll be content with the jewellery, and Mr Grainger is bringing some of the children tomorrow. He called first thing this morning to tell me that his father had chosen a bride for him."

"How did he feel about that?"

"He seemed satisfied. She is an attractive young lady it seems, and she adores children as he does."

"So no marriage there for you?"

"No. A while ago I thought I could have married him, but now I know I couldn't. I'll be all right. I'll be a spinster with a shop!" She laughed. "It was what I wanted."

"It was what you *thought* you wanted."

"That's true."

"Mollie, wouldn't you consider marrying Ritchie? He's in love with you."

Mollie jumped up. "No, no, *no*. Please, *please*. Don't mention it again!"

"I won't, I promise. But I'll tell you this: I won't leave you on your own. I won't marry Philip until you are settled."

"That's not fair!"

"It is to me. You are like my own daughter, always have been. I'll just go on with the blouses. I'll get into the rhythm of them again and I'll still have all my customers."

"And make Philip unhappy?" Mollie demanded.

"No, he won't be. He's been alone for so long. He won't mind, I know it."

Mollie knew differently and only hoped she could persuade her aunt not to keep him waiting any longer . . .

* * *

When Mollie went to the shop the following morning, Philip had nothing to say. When Mollie asked him what was wrong, he said, "Nell seems to have changed her mind

238

about marrying me. She's crazy about her shop. I don't think she will ever give it up."

"That's not the reason. She asked me if I would live with you both and I told her, no. Then she said she would not marry you, unless I agreed, and I wouldn't do that. You should both be on your own. You've waited long enough."

"I have an answer for that," Ritchie appeared at her side. "Why don't you marry me? That would solve the problem."

"You are the *last* man I would marry," Mollie snapped.

"We needn't live together; not at first, anyway. But you would want to later because you *are* in love with me and you won't admit it."

"I am not in love with you and never have been. So the problem is not solved."

"Would you allow Nell and Philip to live apart because you simply refuse to admit that you are in love with me?"

"I am not, and never shall be in love with you. So you can forget that."

"Couldn't you just pretend?"

"Why should I?"

"Because they are a lovely couple who have longed to be together for such a long time. It wouldn't hurt you to live apart from me for a time. I promise not to make any demands on you."

"You have a nerve to even suggest such a thing! What would people say? 'She marries a man, and doesn't even sleep with him'."

"Who's going to tell them? You won't, and I have no need to."

"Oh, Ritchie, forget this farce, because that is all it is. I've put it right from my mind and I expect you to do the same."

"How can you put it from your mind? Everyone in the community knows that you love me."

239

"Who told them – *you?*"

"Of course not. They keep asking me when I am going to marry you."

"I don't believe it."

"You should believe it," Philip said. "Dozens of people have asked me, and I know that you've loved Ritchie for a very long time."

"But I haven't! I don't love him. Never have done."

"Oh, yes, you have, Mollie, you've forgotten."

"Tell me! Tell me, when I ever told you that I was in love with Ritchie."

"I remember one night when Chantelle had been teasing him, saying she would love him always; you were furious and told her she would never take him from you."

"I'm sure I would never say such a thing."

"But you did, Mollie, you said it when I was there. I had never seen you in a temper before, but my goodness you were in a terrible temper that night."

Mollie did have a vague recollection of the evening, but refused to admit it. "You are imagining it all, Philip," she said.

"Well, I won't fight you about it," he replied. "It's not an easy thing to admit."

She did, however, think about it that night and knew then how much she had once been in love with Ritchie. But he had not been gambling then, nor had he spoken to her in such a way; wanting his money back from her. It was the way he had asked for it that had made her so furious. Demanding it; that was what it was. Then, later, finding out how much the gambling debt was. The nerve of him, the cheek! No, she had been very generous to him and he was trying to say that everyone in the village knew she was in love with him. It was a whole lot of rubbish. She would never marry him and that was that.

All the same, there was one nagging worry which stayed

with her. A time would come when the debt would be paid and he could then go and live somewhere else. But would he want to? He got on well with Philip. But surely Philip would go and live with her Aunt Nell, eventually? What if he didn't push to live with her? Then she would be blamed for driving him away. Oh, Lord. It looked as if she would have to live with Ritchie. She would have to insist though, that there would be no sex. Would he agree to that? He would have to agree . . .

* * *

The following morning, there was a letter for Mollie from Chantelle; a heartbroken, pleading letter asking if she could come back to London to live with Nell and Mollie. Her father wanted her to marry a man who was about sixty. A kindly, warm-hearted man, but she could not marry him. She had refused to listen. She would pay for her keep by helping to make blouses. Would Nell and Mollie agree? Please say yes, she pleaded. Mollie handed over the letter.

Nell read it, and returned it, saying, "I would never come between father and daughter. In fact, I wonder now if Chantelle ran away from home the last time in search of adventure."

"Oh, Nell we can't turn her away. We are not French, so we don't understand her parents' ways."

"You can please yourself, Mollie, but I am not going to be involved. The girl is nothing to us."

"I just feel so sorry for her."

Suddenly, there was a knock on the shop door and Nell got up to see who it could be at this time in the morning. She came in, followed by a sobbing Chantelle who flung herself into Mollie's arms. "Please don't send me back," she pleaded. "Mr Bellamy is a nice man but he's nearly sixty! I want a young man to love."

241

Nell poured her a cup of tea and made her sit down. "We'll discuss this, Chantelle, but we can't keep you against your father's wishes."

"I want to marry Ritchie, we love one another!" she wailed.

"No, Chantelle, you loved Ritchie but he didn't love you."

"He did, I know he did. Where is he? I want him here!"

"You can't have him, Chantelle." This was from Nell. "You'll have to go back to your father."

"No, never! I want a young man to love."

"Well you can't have Ritchie," Nell said, "so what are you going to do?"

"I certainly won't go back until I've seen Ritchie."

Mollie suddenly wondered if Ritchie would give in to Chantelle. She would rather marry him herself than see that happen . . .

At eleven o'clock that evening Mr Sellick arrived, saying he guessed where Chantelle would be. He ordered her to put her hat and coat on. He was taking her home. But Chantelle refused to move until she had seen Ritchie.

Nell said, "Well, that can't be until tomorrow. I'll give each of you a bed for tonight, but tomorrow you must both leave." Mr Sellick thanked Nell for her kindness and understanding.

Mollie knew that she must go and see Ritchie and tell him the position. When Chantelle and her father had gone to their beds, she left and tramped to Philip's house.

Fortunately the two men were still up and when Mollie had told them the story, Ritchie said to Mollie, "Now you *must* marry me. I refuse to have anything to do with Chantelle!"

"And you must keep to your word that we live separately."

He agreed to this, and Mollie prepared to leave. Philip said he would get the carriage out and take her home.

* * *

Ritchie and Philip called early the next morning. Chantelle, who was up, flung her arms around him and said she wanted to marry him. He removed her arms and told her that it was impossible and that he and Mollie were getting married in a month's time. There were floods of tears, of course, and when her father came down for his breakfast, he told her to stop behaving like a spoilt child. This did stem the tears, but she accused Ritchie of leading her to expect to marry him. He swore he had never led her to expect any such thing and her father accepted this.

"Don't worry," he told Ritchie. "We are going back home today and she will be married to a respectable elderly man who will make her a good husband."

"Old enough to be my *grandfather!*" Chantelle cried.

"That is enough," her father replied.

Mollie felt upset, and taking Mr Sellick aside, she begged him to let Chantelle marry a younger man. He told her it was impossible; the family needed the money, and Mr Bellamy was very wealthy. Mollie gave up. She knew nothing of French culture. But Chantelle must have known the reality of her situation from birth. She must stop herself from feeling sorry for the girl.

Ritchie was furious with Chantelle for jeopardising his future with Mollie, but calmed down later when Chantelle had left.

"You are still marrying me?" he said to Mollie.

"Yes," she said, "and I know now that I truly want to be your wife. Chantelle made me realise the truth. I love you, Ritchie."

"My darling love. We shall be married in four weeks' time."

This pleased Mollie. "That is no problem."

*   *   *

Nell ordered the wedding breakfast, which was to take place in the market square and was open to anyone who wanted to come.

Nearly everyone in the community turned up. Jack Jones played his violin and and Eddie Williams played the accordion. The people danced and sang, and as everyone said afterwards, it could not have been bettered. Later, Mollie and Ritchie left to spend their wedding night in Philip's house. He had moved out and was spending the night with friends.

When Mollie was in bed, Ritchie came in and whispered, "I want to make love to you, darling Mollie. I love you, adore you."

She whispered back, "Ritchie, I don't know what married couples do."

"I'll teach you all I know about lovemaking," he said.

He was tender and gentle with her at first, but later she responded with equal fervour and Ritchie found unexpected passion in her embraces.

"You are truly wonderful," he said, then added, "I want to have children with you."

"So do I," she whispered.

Four months later, Mollie knew she was pregnant. Ritchie was over the moon; so was she.

Chantelle married Mr Bellamy at her parents' home a few weeks later. All the family were pleased with the thousands of pounds he provided as a wedding gift.

Nell said, "I know he will keep her wealthy for as long as she lives. Or should I say, as long as Mr Bellamy lives." Mollie, having known true love, felt sorry for her.

Nell and Philip, who had married not long after Ritchie and Mollie, could hardly wait to become grandparents. Mollie felt on top of the world, and made up her mind she would go on having babies as long as she could.

One evening Mollie's thoughts went back to the time when she was working in the big house at Kettering. No. She decided not to think of the past. That was gone. She must think of the present. Then unexpectedly she had a visitor. It was Mrs Colledge, Anne's mother with sad news. She said, "Anne was found drowned in the river today."

"Oh, Mrs Colledge, I'm so sorry."

"Don't be," she said. "I'm glad. Glad that she won't have any more excuses to burn things. God has been good to her."

Mollie said, "I never thought of it in that way, but you are right. She must be very peaceful now."

"I think so."

Mrs Colledge left with a promise from Mollie that she would come and see her after the baby was born. She apologised for calling at such a time.

Mollie said, "I'm glad I know. It's put a part of my life in order at last."

Chapter Nineteen

Many months later, Mr Grainger came into the shop with about ten children. A strange young lady was also with them. Was it his bride-to-be Mollie wondered? She was attractive, and had a gentle face. Nicholas introduced her as Lady Emily Dashley. Mollie said, "I'm pleased to meet you, your Ladyship."

She said softly, "No, please, just Emily. I'm so pleased to meet you, Miss Paget. All the children worship you. Coming to the shop is a dream for them."

Nicholas had them all lined up. "The important ones today are Frederick and Percy, who want to buy a present for an uncle. He's very difficult to buy for. Do you think he would like a ring with a gemstone in it? It would mean all of you putting your money together to get an expensive one, like you did for your Papa." After some chatter, they all agreed with this and Mollie brought a tray out.

His birthstone was a tourmaline. Strangely enough they all liked the same one, and turned a ring over and over in their hands. Nicholas liked it, and suggested getting his own father a tiepin and ring. They all agreed with this and Emily helped them to choose one. Then, realising this was Mollie's choice, she apologised.

"No, no," Mollie said. "You will be mother to them soon and will be most helpful to them."

One of the small boys said, "But you, Miss Paget, have always chosen the right thing that we wanted to buy."

"Very well," she said. "I like this tiepin," and everyone

was pleased with the choice. Nicholas kept close to her all the time, "I'll love you always," he whispered once.

Mollie said, "No, you must not do this."

He drew away from her.

"You will have a lovely wife who will give you many children. Enjoy her youth. Be as happy as I am."

"I have been thinking about it," he said, softly. "She is a most lovely person. Thank you for all your kindness, Mollie." He kissed her gently on the cheek.

After the first baby was born, a beautiful little girl, Mollie had a further five children. Then all too soon she knew that her own children were growing up and ready for marriage. What a wonderful life she and Ritchie had had. It could not have been bettered.

She now had her own jewellery shop, a loving husband and some beautiful children. History would certainly know her as one of Fortune's Daughters.